PARK

A Regency ... ...stairs

Survival of the fittest ...
one on top...but the ...
is about ...

The Montagues have found .... at the centre of the
ton's rumour mill, with lords and ladies alike claiming the
family is not what it used to be.

The mysterious death of the heir to the Dukedom, and the
arrival of an unknown woman claiming he fathered her son,
is only the tip of the iceberg in a family where scandal
upstairs *and* downstairs threatens the very foundations
of their once powerful and revered dynasty...

Montague Family Tree

Hannah Stratton
Housekeeper
b.1766

Duchess of Rothermere
b.1767
d.1800

Duke of Rothermere
b.1758

Charles
b.1761
d.1797

Claire
b.178[?]

Adam
b.1784

Jamie
b.1786

Giles
b.1788

Henry
(Harry)
b.1791

Kate
b.1792

Edward
b.1796
d.1815

Phaedra
b.1796

Ross
b.1787

Araminta
b.1795

KEY:

↔ Legal Marriage

| Child

┄ Suspected illegitimate child

── Sibling

━━ Half sibling

Phaedra,

My darling and determined daughter. Your wild free spirit is infectious and I wouldn't want to change you for the world, but I am not getting any younger and having a tomboy for a daughter is proving somewhat tiresome. On more than one occasion I have had to ask you to change out of your breeches and remove straw from your hair when I have guests visiting Castonbury, and I am sorry to say this can't go on for ever.

I know I cannot forbid you to ride your beloved horses and seeing how much joy they give you makes me a happy man, but please—for me—try and spend a little less time in the stables and a little more time in the drawing room…!

Your weary father

First published in Great Britain 2012
Mills & Boon, an imprint of Harlequin (UK) Limited,
Eton House, 18-24 Paradise Road, Richmond, Surrey TW9 1SR

© Nikki Poppen 2012

ISBN: 978 0 263 90190 0

52-0113

Harlequin (UK) policy is to use papers that are natural, renewable and recyclable products and made from wood grown in sustainable forests. The logging and manufacturing processes conform to the legal environmental regulations of the country of origin.

Printed and bound
by CPI Group (UK) Ltd, Croydon, CR0 4YY

Unbefitting
a Lady

 BRONWYN SCOTT

For Catie and Lady, and all your horses that have come before and the ones that will come after. Keep your heels down, always sight your next jump, get deep in the corners and, above all, don't squeeze that horse unless you want the big girl to run. Love, Mom.

Chapter One

Buxton, Derbyshire, March 1817

He was magnificent. Lean-flanked through the hips, well-muscled through the thighs of his long legs, his face framed aristocratically with the darkest, glossiest of hair that was perhaps a bit too long for convention, giving way to the strength of his broad chest. There was no doubt he was a male specimen beyond compare. Only the fire in his dark eyes belied his perfection. But Phaedra Montague liked a little temper.

She could ride that body all day long. Already her own body was anticipating the feel of him between her legs, her thighs tightening around him, urging him on. He turned her direction, eyes locking on her in the crowd. His infamous temper *was* rising. She could see it in the way he held himself, tense and alert as if his strength might be required of him at any moment. That temper had led him to the auction block and it would lead him to her. Today, she would bid on him and she would win.

She already thought of him as hers.

Her colt. Warbourne. She would have him and no other.

Impatiently, Phaedra shifted on her feet beside her brother Giles in the auction tent, the smells of beasts and men evidence to the mounting excitement as the horses were led in. Warbourne was fourth. He stamped and snorted from his place in line, tossing his glossy black mane as if in protest of being made to suffer the indignities of an auction.

The first three horses went quietly and respectably at middling prices. Then it was Warbourne's turn. He pranced elegantly on the end of his handler's lead rope, preening for the excited crowd. Phaedra tensed and nudged Giles. 'Are you ready?'

Giles laughed gently at her nerves. 'Yes, my dear.' She elbowed him harder this time in sisterly frustration and affection. He knew very well it was killing her to stand there and let him handle the business when she wanted to bid for herself.

'I see no reason why a woman can't raise a paddle as well as a man.' Phaedra fumed. But she knew very well even if women could bid, Giles wouldn't allow it on her behalf. She was the daughter of the Duke of Rothermere and it simply wasn't *comme il faut*. The family dignity must be preserved, especially since that dignity had been somewhat under attack recently.

Giles chuckled at her pique. 'Women are too emotional.'

'Kate would lay you out for that,' Phaedra scolded good-naturedly. 'So would Lily for that matter.' Their sister, Kate, was an avid activist for equal rights and Giles's betrothed, Lily, considered herself the match of any man.

'Yes, my dear, but they're not here.' He gave her a wide grin but they both sobered immediately when the auctioneer introduced the next horse.

Warbourne.

Phaedra hardly needed to listen. She knew his pedigree by heart: sired by Noble Bourne, who'd won several races at Newmarket in his day and distinguished himself at stud since, his foals going on to prodigious careers, and Warrioress, the dam, equally famous for her ability to produce plate winners. But Warbourne had broken the mould. He'd not gone on to success like the others. He'd thrown every rider at the start and then some. That was why he was here so close to racing season, unrideable, untrainable, an outcast. Of course, the auctioneer didn't mention *that*. But Phaedra knew. She knew every inch of his three-year history and that of his line. It gave her reason to hope where others had despaired.

'We will start the bidding at one hundred pounds!' the auctioneer cried. Half a room of paddles went up. Phaedra counselled herself to remain calm. At one hundred pounds, Warbourne was a bargain. It was natural anyone who could would bid on him, she reasoned to keep her nerves in check.

By the time the price hit two hundred fifty, the bidders had thinned out. Phaedra tried to look calm. After all, he was an excellent horse and she'd known they'd have to do more than simply raise their paddle and claim him.

The bid hit three hundred. Giles reluctantly raised his paddle. Phaedra scanned the room. At this price, the field had been narrowed to three bidders. She would have thought the battle for Warbourne nearly over at that point if one of the remaining bidders hadn't been Sir Nathan Samuelson, a neighbour but no friend of the Montagues. He'd outbid Giles just for spite if he could.

'Three hundred and fifty!' the auctioneer called with vigour, well aware he had a bidding war on his hands. The third bidder dropped out. Now it was a duel between Giles and Samuelson. Phaedra sucked in her breath. Giles's paddle went up slowly one more time. That it had gone up at all was a testament of brotherly love. Finances were finally stabilising for the Rothermere coffers thanks to Giles's efforts over the past year but that didn't mean there was money to burn on an untried colt with temper issues, no matter how much her brother loved her.

There was hope still. If Rothermere had been hit by post-war economic issues, Sir Nathan Samuelson had been hit too, and he'd not had the advantage of a ducal coffer to start with. Five hundred pounds would finish him, close him out of the bidding. What had Giles said just yesterday? That Samuelson had been forced to sell off his bottom land to pay the bills? Nonetheless, bottom land notwithstanding, Samuelson's paddle went up. He glared across the room at Giles. The man was bidding on malice now.

'Do I hear four hundred?' The room held its collective breath. Phaedra fingered the pearl pendant at her throat.

Both paddles went up rapidly.

'Four-fifty.'

Samuelson's paddle went up.

Giles remained motionless. Phaedra stared at him in disbelief. 'Giles!' she whispered urgently as if he'd merely had a lapse of attention and needed to be jarred back to reality. But Giles remained stoically impassive.

'Giles!' Phaedra whispered louder, really it qualified as a low hiss. People were starting to look.

'Going once!'

'Giles, please!' Panic edged her voice. Her dream was slipping away.

'Phae, I can't.' Giles shook his head ever so slightly.

'Going twice!'

Across the room Samuelson was gloating in pre-victory triumph.

'Since when have Montagues given way to the likes of Samuelson?' Phaedra argued hotly.

'Things are different now, Phae. I'm sorry. I gave it my best shot. It has to be enough.'

The past three years of struggle and loss flashed through her mind: her brother Edward dead at Waterloo, her father retreating from the world and a host of other calamities that had plagued them.

'No,' Phaedra said in not so quiet tones, startling Giles.

'Phae?'

'No. No, it's not enough.' Phaedra flashed Giles

a smile. There would be hell to pay for this. She might as well start buttering him up for forgiveness now.

'Going three times!'

Phaedra seized the paddle from Giles's lax grip and raised it high. 'Five hundred!' she called out, effectively drawing all eyes her direction. A stunned silence claimed the tent. She lifted her chin in a defiant tilt, daring Samuelson, knowing full well to go higher would beggar him.

The silence seemed to last an eternity. She saw and felt everything in those moments. Giles drew himself up beside her, widening his stance, feet shoulder-width apart, his military training conspicuously evident. Only a fool would gainsay him. It would almost be worth it for Samuelson to try, Phaedra thought, just to see Giles plant the man a well-deserved facer.

'Sir?' The auctioneer turned to Samuelson. 'The bid is at five hundred. Will you raise?'

Samuelson shook his head in slow defeat. The battle was over. The auctioneer pointed the gavel at Giles. 'Five hundred, sir, is that correct?'

'Five hundred, it is,' Giles affirmed unflinchingly, letting the whole tent hear his confirmation of her bid and subsequently of her. She understood. He was publicly supporting her. He would scold her in private for this latest wilful act but in public he would not tolerate anyone's disparagement of his sister or the family.

'Sold! For five hundred pounds.' The gavel banged. Congratulatory applause broke out. The colt was hers! A rush of joy swept through her but Phaedra tamped it down. She could not celebrate yet.

Giles led her aside away from the eyes of the crowd. 'You've got your colt, Phae. How do you propose we pay for him? I thought we'd agreed only three hundred or three-fifty at the very most.'

'With these.' Phaedra tugged without hesitation at her earbobs. 'They will bring the difference.' She lifted her hair from the back of her neck and turned. 'Help me with the clasp.' She didn't want to think too hard about what she was doing, what she was offering. She couldn't lose her courage now.

'These were Mother's.' Giles offered a modest protest, working the clasp of her pendant.

'And Warbourne's my dream.' A dream she believed in so thoroughly she would trade her mother's legacy for it. Phaedra turned back to face him, meeting his grey eyes while her fingers nimbly worked the clasp of her bracelet. 'I know what I am doing.' She knew in her bones Warbourne was made for her. She could save him and, in turn, he could save her.

She dropped the bracelet in Giles's hand. Giles favoured her with a half-smile. 'Your colt had better be the most plated horse in racing history.'

Phaedra smiled and closed his fingers over the jewellery. 'He will be. Now, go settle the account like a good brother. I'll wait outside. Considering the circumstances, I think that would be best.' Besides, she didn't want to lose her nerve, didn't want to watch Giles hand over the pearls, one of the only tangible reminders she had of a mother she could barely remember.

She was magnificent! Bram Basingstoke followed the honey-haired woman with his eyes, watching her exit the auction pavilion and, in his opinion, taking most of the excitement with her. How anyone could bid on the remaining horses after her claiming of Warbourne was beyond him.

Of course it was a fool's claiming. Anyone who knew anything about Warbourne knew the colt was a failure. Nonetheless, her bravado in the face of certain defeat was to be admired along with much else about her person. It would be an understatement to say she was pretty. She was a beauty of rare comparison, all honey and cream with her dark gold hair, rich and thick where it brushed her shoulders beneath her hat, and the ivory of her skin. Truth be told, he'd been watching her from the start long before the bidding war had begun.

He'd been drawn by her poise, the elegant set of her head and the intensity of her gaze when she looked at that horse. Men would slay armies to garner such a look. There was no question she was a lady. It was there in her stance, her well-tailored clothes, her very attitude, even in her chagrin that someone would challenge her over the horse. She *expected* to win, as if it were her right. She wasn't spoiled. She was confident. There was a difference.

The larger question was whether or not he could expect to admire her at closer range. That depended on who the woman's escort was. Brother? Husband? Betrothed? Bram hoped not the latter. It boded ill for the marriage if fiancés allowed their intendeds to yank auction paddles out of their hands. Husbands too, because then it was too late to rethink one's matrimonial position. Bram pitied the poor bastard if he'd married such a haughty virago. But Bram didn't think that was the case. The image of being a henpecked husband didn't fit with the man's commanding, military presence. Not a husband, Bram decided, or a fiancé.

He could admire her up close, then, not that husbands had ever stopped him before, at least not until recently. Mrs Fenton's husband hadn't taken kindly to Bram's expression of 'admiration' for his wife. Now, Bram was here in the middle of Derbyshire on a repairing lease for the lengthy duration of the Season—a Season, which he was none too pleased to note, hadn't even started and wouldn't start for another two months. That meant six months of exile in Derbyshire.

What did one do in Derbyshire for a week, let alone six months? He would be bored to tears, bored unto *death*; it was to be a miserable existence. Which was precisely what his father had intended. But his father hadn't counted on *her*. Bram grinned to no one in particular; a madcap scheme was starting to shape. If she wanted to tame the colt, she was going to need help. Fortunately he knew just the man for the job.

Bram whistled a little tune as he removed his jacket of blue superfine, his waistcoat of paisley silk and rolled up his shirtsleeves, cuff links deposited ignominiously in a pocket. He'd go find her chaperone and get his plan under way. He felt better than he had all week.

Things were improving in Derbyshire.

Chapter Two

Coming outside was *not* much of an improvement. It meant waiting in a closed carriage. Waiting was not something Phaedra did well even though she knew Giles would be as quick about business as he could. The drive between Buxton and home would take the better part of their afternoon and Giles would want to be back in time for supper. They'd spent the night at an inn last evening but Giles would not tolerate another night on the road especially with Warbourne in tow and Lily waiting for him at journey's end.

A loud whinny drew her attention outside the carriage window. A handsome chestnut stallion was giving trouble, rearing up and jerking on the handler's rope. No wonder. There was motion all around him, horses and people and loud voices.

Quite a cacophony for the senses if one wasn't used to it.

Phaedra recognised the handler as Captain Hugh Webster, one of Samuelson's cronies. Webster tugged hard on the lead rope but that only served to make the stallion angrier. He reared higher, his hooves now a dangerous weapon, his eyes rolling.

Phaedra's anger rose. Couldn't Webster see his methods only infuriated the horse? The rope slipped from his hands and for a moment Phaedra thought the animal would succeed in breaking free. She held her breath. That would be calamitous for both the crowd and the horse. A high-strung stallion could step on a dragging lead rope and trip, doing permanent damage to his legs, to say nothing of the hazards associated with a panicked horse running through a panicked crowd. Webster regained the rope and struck the horse with the knotted end which only served to infuriate the horse more.

That did it.

Phaedra threw open the carriage door and jumped down, striding towards the scene of the melee purposefully. 'Lady Phaedra!' John Coachman called out from atop the box, but she didn't stop. She would put an end to this barbarism.

Before the horse could rear again, she stepped

in front of the rough handler and seized the rope, effectively shoving him out of the way. 'Easy now,' she said in firm tones loud enough to be heard. Slowly, she gathered in the rope, making it more difficult for the horse to rise up, talking to him all the while, looking him in the eye. When she was close enough, Phaedra drew an apple slice from the pocket of her jacket and held it out to the horse. He was quivering, still unsure, but definitely quieter than he'd been minutes before. He took the apple and Phaedra reached up to pat his neck, breathing in the scent of him.

'Good boy, you're a good boy,' she crooned, feeling him settle beneath her hand. He was a good boy too; he'd merely been startled by something in his surroundings and Webster's response had only aggravated him more. She'd have a few words for the captain in a moment.

'Well, if it isn't Lady Phaedra Montague.' She didn't have to look up from the stallion. The snide voice was all too familiar. 'I should have known if there was any commotion you'd be at the heart of it.'

Sir Nathan Samuelson strode forward, a sneer of contempt on his face.

Phaedra kept her hand on the horse's neck, her gaze meeting Sir Nathan's unwaveringly. She would not be cowed by him. 'And I should have known if a horse was being mistreated, it would have been yours. The captain is doing a poor job of introducing this animal to his new life.' Might made right in Sir Nathan's view of the world, a philosophy he exercised quite regularly in his stables and Phaedra suspected in his personal life as well. He was unmarried, but not for a lack of trying. Last year he'd tried a suit with her sister, Kate, and even more recently with Aunt Claire. Both had refused him on grounds of moral and philosophical differences, to put it politely.

'Step away, Lady Phaedra. I have miles to go and an order to pick up from my tailor in town before I can be under way.' He made an impatient gesture with his hand and then paused with a smirk. 'That is, unless you have more pearls to sell?' He made the remark sound nasty and a few of the men gathered around to watch the scene laughed. He came towards her, intentionally dwarfing her, crowding her with his size and breadth. She had a little height of her own but Sir Nathan was of hearty country stock. 'All your pearls are gone except one.' His voice was a low sneer. 'The one right between your legs. Who knows, for a good rub, I might give you the horse, show all of you

Montagues you're not too good for the likes of me. We're fellow peers of realm, after all.'

Phaedra stiffened, wanting to get away but having no exit. She was trapped between Sir Nathan and the horse. 'Having a title doesn't make you a peer of the Montagues. You aren't fit to wipe our boots.'

'You little bitch.'

Sir Nathan lunged but his body never reached her. A strong hand at his neck dragged him backwards and spun him around. 'Didn't your mother teach you how to talk to a lady?'

No sooner had Sir Nathan faced the newcomer, than the newcomer's fist landed squarely against Sir Nathan's jaw, sending him staggering into the assembled crowd. Phaedra had only a quick glimpse of her sudden protector in the intervening moments, a dark-haired devil in a billowing white shirt and the face of an avenging angel, handsome and yet raw with power. She would not soon forget that face.

Her avenger turned towards her, a gallant cavalier from a storybook, his eyes alight with blue fire when he looked at her. 'Are you all right, miss?'

'I'm fine. Thank you.' Phaedra managed to find her voice, a most unusual occurrence to have lost it in the first place. But it wasn't every day a handsome stranger leapt to her defence.

'Shall I punch him again for you?' the stranger drawled, watching Sir Nathan right himself with the help of friends.

There was no chance to answer. Giles materialised, parting the crowd with his broad shoulders. 'That will do, I think. Get along with all of you. There's nothing more to see here.' The crowd began to dissolve at the voice of authority. One didn't have to know he was the son of a duke to decide obedience was the best option. Giles motioned for someone to take the chestnut stallion and the throng around them thinned. But her hero remained.

'This wasn't the introduction I'd planned,' Giles began. 'But I see the two of you have already met. Bram, this is my sister, Lady Phaedra Montague. She's the one I was telling you about. She's been overseeing the stables since old Anderson got hurt. Phaedra, this is Bram Basingstoke. He'll take over Tom Anderson's duties until the man recovers.'

Her hero was the new head groom? Phaedra mentally revoked his hero status and squelched her disappointment. She'd hoped Giles had forgotten all about the need to hire a replacement. She'd been having far too much fun taking care of the stables over the winter. 'I'm sure that's not necessary,' she said in her best haughty but polite tones. 'The poor man will hardly get settled, Giles, and Anderson will be up and about. Until then, I can manage. I don't mind.' She did not want any help, no matter how handsome the face that came with it. The stables were her domain, the one place where she had some autonomy. She wasn't about to let a stranger take that away.

Giles gave her a thin warning smile that said he was not to be crossed on this. 'Phaedra, you'll be busy with the colt now.' What he really meant was that she owed him. He'd backed her on her ridiculous bid, now it was time to do things his way.

Phaedra swallowed. 'You're right, of course. Warbourne will take much of my time if he's to be ready to race in May.' It was a gutsy gambit, based on the hope that Giles would not contradict her in front of the newcomer. They'd not discussed racing Warbourne this year with any specificity and certainly not in May. But only three-year-olds could race the Epsom Derby. This was his year if she meant to do it.

Giles looked at her sharply. 'That remains for another discussion.' He flipped open his pocket watch, an effective conversation closer, and checked the time. 'Let's get home and get

Warbourne settled before we plan his racing career.'

The ride was accomplished without mishap. Their home, Castonbury, was two hours from Buxton, and Warbourne travelled the distance well with a few rests. Phaedra travelled the distance well too. She was thankful Giles didn't take advantage of the carriage's privacy to berate her for her behaviour at the fair. She was thankful, too, for the myriad thoughts crowding her mind, all of which made the time pass quickly. There was Warbourne to consider, which stall he should have, how she should begin his training, and then there was the stranger riding up on the box next to John Coachman. He took up a fair share of those thoughts.

Only he wasn't really a stranger now that Giles had hired him on. He had a name and a position and he posed a threat to her autonomy. She would need to get the rules of their association established early. They were *her* stables and they were going to stay that way from now on. She was twenty and plenty old enough for some responsibility of her own.

The carriage turned into the Castonbury parklands, passing through the wrought-iron gates of the entrance, and began the slow, grand, winding drive to the house. They travelled past the boathouses and over the bridge that spanned the river and up to the mansion. Phaedra smiled quietly to herself as she looked out of the window. Castonbury's majesty never failed to impress even her and she'd grown up here her whole life. Bram Basingstoke was probably sitting atop the carriage, his mouth agape at the wonders of Castonbury Park and thanking his lucky stars her brother had hired him on. It wasn't every day a man got to be head groom at a ducal estate, even temporarily.

The big house came into view but they passed by and headed west where the stable block lay behind the main house. Phaedra looked across at Giles, whose eyes had opened when the carriage halted. 'We're home.' She placed a hand over his. 'Thank you for everything.'

'You're welcome.' Giles hesitated before asking, 'Could I leave you to give our new head groom a tour?'

He wanted to ride down to the vicarage and see Lily, Phaedra guessed. She smiled. 'It's the least I can do.' A tour would be just the thing to set the right tone, just the right way to assert herself.

But Bram had other ideas. The moment the carriage halted, he'd jumped down and taken charge of getting Warbourne untied before Phaedra had barely set her feet on the ground. Warbourne responded to him without any fuss and she had to admit that on first impression he had a good way with horses and with men. The other stable hands leapt to do his bidding. She hastened her pace to catch up and walk beside him, wanting at least to give the impression he needed her.

His sense of authority was unnerving, actually. It was almost lordly in its demeanour, not a quality one found in the average groom or stable master. And then there was the issue of his boots. She noticed they were awfully fine. Aunt Wilhelmina was fond of saying a girl could always tell a gentleman by his shoes. Based on those polished, high boots he wore with only a touch of the day's dust about them, one might almost mistake him for a gentleman—except that he wasn't.

His dark hair was too long to be fashionably tolerated and his wardrobe lacked certain necessities. A gentleman wore a waistcoat and a coat in the presence of a lady. A gentleman didn't walk around with his shirtsleeves rolled up and a gentleman most certainly didn't engage in fisticuffs at a horse fair. No, Bram Basingstoke was clearly not a gentleman no matter how fine his boots or lordly his demeanour. Some men were just born to command. He was one of them, something she'd do well to remember when dealing with him.

Phaedra pointed out the stall she'd decided on for Warbourne. She slipped a slice of apple to the colt for good behaviour while fresh straw was laid down. Satisfied the colt was well settled, she turned to Bram. 'Warbourne has had his tour, now it's time for yours. I'm sure you're anxious to get your bearings.'

The hint of a smile played about his lips. 'I have my bearings quite well, but I'll accept your offer of a tour.' Humour danced in his eyes.

Phaedra's mouth went dry. Giles's new groom was a flirt. Her stomach fluttered a bit as it had at the fair. He was the handsome man again, the daring hero. But that would not do for a Montague servant. In the stables or in the house, the Montague staff were impeccably trained and impeccably mannered, except maybe the errand boy, Charlie. The staff certainly did not *flirt* with the ducal family. Except for Monsieur André, the head chef. He'd wooed and won Aunt Claire. All right, there were apparently *some* exceptions. But that did not excuse *him*.

Bram allowed Phaedra to sweep ahead of him. 'The stable block is divided up into sections,' she explained, pride evident as she continued. 'This section is dedicated to the saddle horses. We keep twenty horses for riding purposes. This is Giles's favourite hunter, Genghis, rescued him off the battlefield.' She kept up the introductions, stroking the muzzle of each horse they passed until she'd shown him all of the animals and given him an overwhelming history of each.

It was clear she wanted him overwhelmed. She wanted him to be in awe of his surroundings and he was. Castonbury had one of the finest stables in the north. Bram had seen several stables owned by men who considered themselves fine breeders of the thoroughbred, and Castonbury was impressive. He'd noted the elevated iron hay racks in each of the stalls, eliminating the need to keep a large feed trough running the length of the aisles and taking up space. He'd noted, too, that Castonbury had converted the traditional three-sided stall to the modern-styled loose box stall. The horses looked healthy and strong, no doubt a result of their excellent housing.

Phaedra finished with the riding wing and moved to the centre section. 'This is the carriage house. We have six carriage bays. As you can see, most of the bays are currently occupied. There's the ducal travelling coach, there's the landau for spring outings, the gig for trips to the village and so on. It will be important to familiarise yourself with them. On occasion they will need some light maintenance.' She seemed willing to move through this section far more quickly than she had the prior. He saw why and it more than provoked his curiosity.

Bram put a light hand on her arm. 'What's that?' He pointed towards what appeared to be a large full-sided wagon complete with windows and a roof in the last bay.

'It's a horse trailer,' Phaedra said tersely, determined to move on with her tour. But Bram was intrigued. He strolled over to the contraption, compelling Phaedra to follow him. He circled the perimeter, bending low to take in the undercarriage.

'It's for horses,' Phaedra said finally, giving him the distinct impression she didn't want to talk about it.

Bram stood back from the vehicle and gave her an encouraging look. 'Transporting horses when they could just as easily walk?' That loosened her tongue a bit. It appeared Phaedra Montague couldn't stand stupidity in any form.

'It's for racehorses, so they don't *have* to walk,' she replied sharply. The offering was enough. The pieces fell into place rapidly after that.

Bram nodded with approval, studying Phaedra with a new excitement that had a little less to do with the sway of her skirt. 'To take a northern horse south, perhaps?'

He could see the ingenuity of this. Most racing was regional, confined to a district because of issues with distance.

In the north, racing was done in Yorkshire and at Doncaster, while in the south of England, the great tracks were at Newmarket and Epsom. Racehorses couldn't walk to far locales and be in top shape for racing after a lengthy journey. It was one of the reasons racing magnates congregated in Newmarket with their strings—to avoid the travel and risk of injury to the horse.

'Precisely.' Phaedra smiled a bit in reply, starting to warm to the subject.

'It's ingenious.' Bram took another tour around the wagon. He didn't have to ask for whom the wagon was intended. It was for Warbourne and wherever she meant to take him. 'You were pretty certain you'd win the bid today.' Lady Phaedra had invested quite a lot in that horse before he'd even been bought. The wagon couldn't have been cheap. In itself, the purchase had been a risk. 'What if you had lost?' Bram held her eyes, watching her expression carefully.

'I am not accustomed to losing, Mr Basingstoke. Shall we continue the tour?'

After that, she showed him the last bay where the carriage horses were kept—matched greys for the ducal coach and a set of Cleveland bays for the landau. Then they were off outdoors to see the facilities—the oval training track put in by her great-grandfather at the height of the racing craze in the previous century, and the riding house, also a legacy of her great-grandfather.

'It's an amazing facility,' Bram said at last when they finished walking through the indoor riding house with its viewing gallery of the arena below.

She fixed him with a stern stare. 'Yes, it is.'

'That's what you wanted me to say, isn't it?' He grinned. 'You've been trying to overwhelm me since we started.' Bram held out his hands, palms up in surrender. 'You have succeeded admirably.' He *was* impressed with the facility and with her. Warbourne had not been a spontaneous purchase driven by the whims of a pretty, impetuous young lady.

'Yes,' Phaedra admitted. 'You've landed yourself a plum. You should be thankful for a job when so many people are out of work. This is more than simply a job. It's a very *good* job at a very fine stable. It's not quite on par with Chatsworth just yet, but any horseman would be grateful for it.'

Bram chuckled outright at the mention of the great northern stable. To compare one's self to Chatsworth was brave indeed for fear of coming off wanting. But Castonbury was in no risk of that. 'We're not too proud are we, princess?'

'Not proud. Honest,' Phaedra countered with a confident tilt of her head. 'Let me show you your quarters and introduce you to Anderson.'

'I'll want to talk about an exercise schedule for Warbourne too, so I can get started with the horses right away,' Bram asserted as they began the walk back to the stable block. The assignment he'd taken on was becoming more intriguing by the moment, largely due to the woman beside him. She had wanted Warbourne. She saw something in him others had not. After seeing the stables, Bram was starting to think there might be something to that. He was itching to get his hands on that colt.

Phaedra faced him squarely. 'Let's get one thing straight, Mr Basingstoke. You're here to help Anderson. Warbourne is mine. *I* don't need your help.'

Bram tossed her a smile. 'Of course you don't.'

He'd not expected her to say otherwise. But that didn't mean it was true. She would need him before they were through in one way or another.

Chapter Three

Lady Phaedra Montague was a haughty minx, but that was part of her charm. His intuition about women was seldom wrong and his first impressions from the auction had been correct. Bram was still chuckling as he stowed his things in the small room he'd been given over the stable block. Regardless of the hauteur she cultivated so successfully, she was all fire. He must tread carefully.

Bram folded a shirt and put it in the three-drawer chest in the corner. She was a duke's daughter. He hadn't expected that. He *had* expected her to be nicely situated country gentry and gently born, but not quite so *high*born. One simply didn't open affairs with such lofty creatures. The penalties were too high. One might tolerate facing pistols at dawn over the Mrs Fentons of the world but there would be no scandalous pistols over Phaedra Montague.

There would only be a ring and marriage, two very permanent reminders of one's momentary lapse in judgement. It was probably for the best. Giles Montague was no doubt a deadly shot when it came to his sister's honour.

It was too late to back out now. He'd taken this gamble on scant knowledge, lured to it by Phaedra's spirit and the challenge of the colt to offset the looming boredom of six months in Derbyshire. He'd never imagined she'd be Rothermere's daughter. He didn't know the duke personally, but the peerage was not so large that a duke could escape notice. Bram knew *of* Rothermere but no more.

Still, he could leave whenever he chose if he didn't like how things progressed. He wasn't reliant on the position for a wage or a reference. He could vanish in the night and no one would be the wiser. As long as he dressed the part...

Bram studied the items in the drawer—three linen shirts and two waistcoats from London's finest tailors. They simply wouldn't do for stable work. He'd have to go down to the village and look for ready-made work clothes. He'd also have to see about making arrangements to discreetly retrieve his trunk from the inn in Buxton too. It was unmistakably a gentleman's travelling trunk and would have raised too many questions. There'd been only time to stop by the inn on the way out of town and pack a quick valise. Even that had been tricky since the inn had been in close proximity to the luxurious Crescent area of Buxton, expensive quarters for a man looking for work.

Bram shut the drawer. What did he care if he was caught? The scandal would serve his father right. There was an irony to it. He'd been sent away to avoid further scandal, not to foment it. His father would die a thousand social deaths if it became known his son had taken employment as a groom in a duke's household and lived above the stables with the other grooms and male workers. He didn't want to get caught too soon though, not before he had a chance to see if the colt could be tamed—or Phaedra Montague for that matter.

A heavy footfall at the door caused him to straighten. He had company. He half expected it to be Phaedra. 'So, you're the one who has come to replace me.' The voice was thick with the broad sounds of Derbyshire, the sounds of a man who'd grown up here all his life and wandered very little, a man who would see assistance as an intrusion.

'Not to replace you, to *help* you. For a while,' Bram said in friendly tones. He strode forward, his hand outstretched. 'You must be Anderson.' The man looked sixty at least, with a shock of white hair and weathered face. But he was sturdy in build with the stocky frame of a Yorkshire man.

He shifted his cane to his left side and shook hands. 'Tom Anderson I am.'

'I'm Bram Basingstoke. Have a seat. I'd like to talk to you about the horses.' Bram belatedly glanced around the tiny room to realise the only place to sit was the bed.

'Why don't you come down to my rooms once you're settled. We'll talk more comfortably there.'

'I'm ready now. I didn't have much to unpack.' Bram gestured towards the door. 'I am hoping you can recommend a place in the village I can get work clothes,' he said as they made the short trip towards Anderson's rooms on the first floor.

Anderson waved his cane. 'Don't bother. I've got a trunk of shirts and trousers left over from the last fellow who was here. He was tall like you, they should fit well enough.'

Anderson's rooms were slightly larger as befitted his status as the stable manager, and furnished comfortably with well-worn pieces. A fire was going in the hearth, a definite improvement over Bram's cold chamber.

'The last fellow?' Bram enquired, taking a seat near the fire.

Anderson chuckled. 'You don't think you're the

first man Lord Giles has hired to help out, do you?' He pulled out a jug of whisky and poured two pewter cups.

'I hadn't thought either way on it,' Bram said honestly. He'd been too busy thinking about Phaedra and the colt to contemplate the nuances of his position.

'You're about the fourth in as many months.' Anderson passed him a cup. 'Winter hasn't been kind to this old man. I've been down with one thing or another since November and now my hip is giving me trouble. I can't work the horses with a bad hip.' Anderson paused and raised his cup in a toast. 'Here's hoping you'll last longer than the rest.'

Bram studied Anderson over the rim of his cup. Bram could see the age around Anderson's eyes, his face tanned and wrinkled from a life lived outdoors. Anderson reminded him of the old groom at his family home. His father still hadn't found a way to pension him off without hurting his pride. 'The stables are well-kept and the quarters are decent. What drove them off?'

It was Anderson's turn to eye him over a swallow of whiskey. 'It wasn't a "what". It was a "who". Some men don't like taking orders from a lady.'

Ah. Phaedra Montague. He should have guessed.

She'd been far from pleased with her brother's announcement at the fair. 'She makes life difficult?' Bram asked. Did she plant frogs in their beds? He couldn't envisage her stooping to such juvenile levels.

Anderson wiped his mouth with his hand. 'Nah. She doesn't do it on purpose. It's not her fault she knows more about horses than they do. She doesn't mean to drive them away.'

The first thing that struck Bram was that he doubted it. She probably did *hope* they would move along. She had not hidden her disapproval at the horse fair. The second was that she had the old groom wrapped around her finger. He was clearly defending her.

'She's that good?' Bram took another swallow, trying to cultivate an attitude of nonchalance while he probed for information. It was always best to know one's quarry before one began the hunt.

'She's that good. Lord Giles is a bruising rider but she holds equal to him. It's not just the riding though. It's everything else. It's like she can look in their souls, that she can reach them on a level no one else can.' Anderson poured himself a second drink. 'I'll tell you something crazy if you want to hear it and if it won't send you packing.'

Bram was all ears. This part of the country was

known for its superstitions and ghost tales and Anderson had the makings of a fine storyteller.

'Two years ago last June we had a white stallion named Troubadour. He belonged to her brother Edward. Edward was off fighting Napoleon but Troubadour had been left home. One night around the fourteenth, he started acting all crazy-like in his stall, kicking, stomping. He wouldn't eat. No one could get near him except Miss Phaedra. She sat with him for hours getting him to calm down. Mind you, there was no one here. All four of the boys were at war. It was just Lady Phaedra and Lady Kate and the duke, of course. When Lady Kate came out to see her, Lady Phaedra was crying something fierce. She told Lady Kate Troubadour was dying and that she feared young Lord Edward was dead. Before sunrise, Troubadour lay down in his stall and refused to get up. A month later, word reached us that Lord Edward had fallen at Waterloo, the very night Troubadour died.' Anderson tapped his head with his finger. 'She knows them, knows what's in their heads.'

Bram nodded. He'd heard stories about horses that could sense their masters' distress. He'd never heard of anything quite as drastic as Anderson's tale. So, Lady Phaedra talked to horses and read their minds. Well, he'd see about that for himself, but it was clear Tom Anderson believed it in full.

They passed a companionable evening discussing the horses and their workout needs. There was the spirited mare the eldest daughter, Kate, had left behind when she'd gone to America not long ago. There were the general horses kept for guests, not that there'd been many guests outside of family in recent months. There was Giles Montague's black beast of a stallion, Genghis, nearly as dark as Warbourne. And there was the elegant chestnut thoroughbred, Merlin, Lord Jamie's horse.

'Lord Jamie?' He quirked his eyebrow in question. Yet another younger brother, perhaps? How big was this family? Bram was beginning to wonder.

'Lord Jamie is the eldest. But he went to war too, and didn't come home. Only Lord Giles and Lord Harry returned.' Anderson shook his head. 'It's been a bad business all around for the family. Lord Giles wanted to be a career military man. He never wanted to be the heir, never was jealous of Lord Jamie. But it wasn't to be.'

'He died too?' Bram asked quietly. He knew several families in London who'd lost loved ones thanks to Napoleon. Families both rich and poor alike had lost sons.

Anderson shrugged, a light twinkling in his old blue eyes. 'Don't know. That's a whole other kettle of fish brewing up at the house these days. Lord Giles is pretty closemouthed about it, as he should be. But there was no body ever recovered and then last fall this woman shows up with a little 'un just about the right age claiming she's Lord Jamie's wife. She's living at the Dower House. The family is trying to do right by her, although the whole thing seems off to me.'

'Why?'

Anderson jerked his head the general direction of the horse stalls. 'Merlin's still alive. He and Lord Jamie were as close as a horse and human can be, just like Edward and Troubadour,' Tom Anderson answered matter-of-factly, as if everyone bought into folklore without question.

Bram refrained from comment. He supposed stranger things had happened. When he'd driven through the gates of Castonbury today, it had looked normal enough—the manicured grounds, the outbuildings in decent repair, the stables immaculate. It had looked *better* than normal. From the outside, one would never guess the turmoil that simmered beneath the surface. What exactly had he let himself in for? Whatever it was, it certainly wasn't 'boring.' All fears of ennui had been effectively banished.

Phaedra rose early and dressed quickly in breeches and a loose shirt. Rising early was imperative if she wanted to escape the eagle eye of Aunt Wilhelmina. She did not approve of Phaedra roaming the estate in breeches nor did the redoubtable lady approve of rising before ten in the morning. Neither of which was surprising. Aunt Wilhelmina spent most of her life disapproving. Still, Phaedra preferred not to be on the receiving end of her aunt's disapproval and there seemed to be a lot more of it headed her direction since Kate had left after Christmas with her new husband.

In the breakfast room, Giles was already present with his coffee and newspapers. He looked up as she entered and uttered a brief good-morning. She nodded. This had become their ritual. Both of them enjoyed rising early but early rising was not synonymous with a desire to engage in conversation. They wanted to eat first, let their minds sift through the agenda of their days.

Phaedra piled her plate with eggs and hot toast. Chances were she wouldn't be back to the house for luncheon. Her mind was already sorting through the things that needed doing at the stables: check on the gelding with the sore leg, make sure the hay delivery had arrived from the home farm, do a general walk-through to check on the stalls and horses. There was Warbourne to see to and horses to exercise.

The activity would fill her day until sunset. The busyness was a blessed relief from the empty house. She'd grown up in a large family, used to being surrounded by brothers and a sister, but war and the passing of years had brought an end to that. The boys had gone to battle. Only Giles had come home and then only because duty demanded it. Harry had come home and left again. Kate had married. Really, Kate's marriage was the last blow, the last desertion. The two of them had lived here together during the years the boys were at war. It had brought them close in spite of the difference in their ages. Now Kate was gone, choosing Virgil and a new life in Boston over Castonbury and the familiar. And her.

Now it was just her and Giles, the oldest and the youngest, nine years separating them. She hoped it wasn't disloyal to Jamie to think of Giles as the oldest. But Jamie was dead now, whether there was a body or not, and Giles had done his best to pick up the reins of duty in the wake of great tragedy.

Phaedra sighed and bit into her toast. Since Kate

had left, mornings were hardest of all, the time when she was most acutely aware she'd been left behind. The once merry and heavily populated breakfast room was empty. Giles was here but he had Lily and in the summer they would marry. They would fill Castonbury with a new generation of Montagues. Time would move on. Would she? What would happen to her? What would *become* of her? Anything could happen. She told herself she had Warbourne now. He was her chance.

Phaedra pushed back from the table, her appetite overruled by the need to see Warbourne, to get to the stables where worries and thoughts wouldn't plague her.

'Leaving so soon?' Giles looked up from his paper. 'Anxious to see your colt?'

'Yes.'

'I don't suppose we'll see you before dinner?' Giles arched a dark brow in query.

'There's a lot to be done. I was gone for two days,' Phaedra said.

'That's what Basingstoke is for. Let him do the job he's been hired for.' Giles gave her a patient, brotherly smile. 'You need time to be yourself, to do things you enjoy, Phae. You've been working too hard. Don't think I haven't noticed.' Giles folded the newspaper and set it aside.

'I've been meaning to talk to you about this spring, Phae. I know now isn't the best time, but perhaps after dinner tonight?' It was a token of how much Giles had softened this year that he was asking at all. Last year Giles would simply have issued his edict and considered it done.

'Perhaps,' Phaedra offered noncommittally. Giles could talk all he wanted. She wasn't going to London for a Season. She had the Derby to think about. She couldn't be spending her days on Bond Street trying on dresses to impress men she wasn't going to marry, not when Warbourne needed her here. Phaedra grabbed up an apple from a bowl on the sideboard and made a hasty retreat before Giles decided to have the discussion right then.

Unlike the quiet house, the stables were a hive of activity. Horses and grooms rose early. Phaedra went straight to an old, unused tack room she'd converted into an office during the winter and began going through paperwork that had arrived while she was gone. There wasn't much of it, but the ritual was soothing and it centred her thoughts. Here, sitting at the scarred desk she'd found in the stable storage loft, she felt at home. This was her place. A rough desk, a rough chair, the worn breeding ledgers lined on a shelf that detailed every foal born at Castonbury—all of it defined her world.

Phaedra pulled down a book that catalogued the horses at Castonbury. She flipped through until she found a blank page towards the back. She reached for the quill and inkstand on her desk and carefully wrote *Warbourne*, followed by his lineage, the price paid and date of purchase. She blew on the ink to dry it and surveyed the entry with a deep sense of pride. It was time to see the colt.

Phaedra strode through the stable, stopping every so often to stroke a head poking out of its stall. She was nearly to Warbourne's stall when she sensed it. Something was wrong. No, not wrong, merely different, out of the usual. Phaedra backtracked two stalls and halted. Merlin's stall was empty.

Jamie! Phaedra tamped down a wave of uncertain emotion, part fear and part wild hope tinged by memories of Troubadour and Edward, who had not been parted, not even in death. Phaedra strode through the stables at a half-run looking for Tom Anderson. 'Tom!' she called out, finding him cleaning a saddle. 'Tom, where's Merlin?'

'Now settle yourself, missy. There's nothing wrong,' Tom said in calm tones. 'Bram's got him out in the round pen for a little work. You know how he's been giving the boys trouble. No one's been on him for quite a while and the longer he goes without discipline, the harder it will be to instil any in him.'

Phaedra's emotions settled into neutral agitation. A stranger had taken out Jamie's horse. It was true, Merlin needed work. But it still felt odd. 'The round pen, you said?' She would go and have a look, and if anything was amiss, it would be the last time Bram Basingstoke helped himself to Jamie's horse.

Phaedra pulled her hacking jacket closer against the cold as she made her way towards the round pen. The day was overcast and grey, the sky full of clouds. In short, a typical Derbyshire March day. There would be twenty-seven more of them, probably all of them save the variance in rainfall. Derbyshire wasn't known for 'early springs.'

In the offing, she could see the chestnut blur of Merlin as he cantered the perimeter of the pen. *Cantered?* That was promising. Phaedra quickened her pace. Lately, Merlin usually *galloped* heedlessly in the round pen, not minding any of the commands from the exercise boys. This morning, he was collected, running in a circle at a controlled pace.

As she neared, Phaedra made out the dark form of a man in the centre, long whip raised for instruction in one arm, the other arm stretched out in front of him holding the lunge line. But that wasn't what held her attention. It was the fact that the man in question was doing all this shirtless. This time, Phaedra's shiver had nothing at all to do with the weather.

Chapter Four

Bram Basingstoke stood in the round pen stripped to the waist and gleaming indecently with sweat. Phaedra was torn between continuing forward—which would result in him putting his shirt on, or standing back to discreetly watch him work, which would result in the shirt staying off a bit longer—a very enticing proposition, especially when one was as well made as he and she'd had very few opportunities to see such a finely honed man. It wasn't nearly the same as seeing one's brother *en déshabillé*.

Phaedra opted for the latter and stayed back by the hay shed. No girl with an iota of curiosity about the male physique would discard the chance to see such a display of manhood. *Déshabillé* was hardly an apt description. *Déshabillé* implied casually or partially dressed. She supposed breeches and boots counted as partially dressed, technically. But the point remained, he was closer to 'half naked' than partially dressed and gloriously so.

The muscles of his arm were taut with exertion from holding the lunge line, showing developed upper arms and well-formed shoulders. There had been considerable power behind the fist that had floored Sir Nathan the day before. Broad shoulders gave way to a well-defined torso, a veritable atlas of ridges and muscle leading to a tapered waist. With that kind of strength on display it was no wonder Merlin was cantering dutifully through his exercises.

Bram brought Merlin to a halt. She should probably make her presence known. She couldn't stand here all day ogling the help. Aunt Wilhelmina would have an apoplexy if she knew or if she saw… Phaedra stifled a laugh at the thought of Aunt Wilhelmina seeing Bram like this. She doubted Aunt Wilhelmina had ever tolerated a naked man in her presence. More the pity for her. Phaedra squared her shoulders and prepared to pretend she hadn't been watching him work.

Bram saw her crossing the field from the hay shed and smiled. He'd felt her even before that.

Bram reeled in the big stallion length by length. It *had* been her. She'd been watching him. The little minx had finally decided to make her presence known. He would be interested to see what she would do now that she had to do more than admire him from a distance. Chances were she wasn't in the habit of viewing men's bare chests on a daily basis.

'Good morning!' he called out cheerfully, waving an arm her direction. He should put on his shirt, but what would the fun be in that? Still, propriety demanded it. Bram reached half-heartedly for the garment but his hand stalled at a closer view of her. Good Lord, the woman was wearing riding breeches—and wearing them well. Bram left his shirt where it hung on a post.

'That's Jamie's horse,' Phaedra said without preamble. She propped a booted leg up on a rail, calling far too much attention to the shapely thigh encased in buckskin. In skirts, one wasn't aware of just how long her legs were. In breeches, there was no avoiding the fact. Bram adjusted his gaze to her face, trying to dispel hot thoughts of those long legs wrapped about him, the curve of her derriere neatly nestled in his hands. The effort succeeded only marginally.

'I know whose horse it is. The stable lads mentioned he hadn't had a proper exercise in a while on account of his unruly nature,' Bram answered coolly, keenly aware Miss Phaedra Montague was a pretty handful of trouble herself. Was she?

Did she have any idea what those legs in breeches did to a man, to say nothing of the white shirt falling loosely over her breasts. He'd always been rather partial to a woman in a man's shirt. There was something undeniably sexy about it, especially if that was all she wore. Although Bram thought Phaedra Montague was doing a fine job just as it was.

Phaedra tossed her long braid over her shoulder and gave a shrug. 'He seems to respond to you.' Her posture was nonchalant but her gaze wasn't. She was having a hard time looking at him. Bram stifled a grin.

'He needs a strong hand or he'll forget you're the master.' Bram reached out a hand to stroke Merlin's long face.

'Are you going to put on your shirt?' Phaedra's eyes flicked to the post where his shirt hung.

'Did you want me to?' It was an audacious thing to say to a lady but he wanted her to be honest with herself. He'd never held with the notion of missishness when it came to the opposite sex. He liked a woman who knew her own appetites.

She blushed but didn't look away. 'And you thought Sir Nathan didn't know how to talk to a lady.' Her eyes flashed with something Bram couldn't pinpoint—disapproval, or maybe something more electric. Bram's temper rose at the comparison.

'I will not be confused with the likes of him. He called you a bitch, I only called you out.'

'That is a most indecent suggestion!'

They were nearly nose to nose now, the breasts beneath her white shirt almost brushing his chest. He could see the flecks of blue in her grey eyes, could smell the sweet tang of apple about her—a horsey smell and a womanly smell all at once. 'Be honest, Phaedra, you were watching me. There's no sin in admitting it.' He smiled and released her, reaching for his shirt. 'There's no sin in liking it either, only in lying.'

Phaedra's chin tilted in defiance. 'I think—'

Bram cut her off with a chuckle. 'Oh, I know what you think, Phaedra Montague.' He pulled his shirt over his head, remembering at the last it was a work shirt and lacked front fastenings, not his usual Bond Street affair. He shoved his arms through and tucked it into his waistband. 'Now that's settled. This old boy could use a ride.' Lady

Phaedra could take the last remark any way she liked.

He patted Merlin's neck. 'Why don't you come along? You can show me the bridle paths.' It would give him a chance to talk to her about the colt and a chance to see whether Tom Anderson's admiration was misplaced.

It wasn't. While he saddled Merlin, Phaedra led out a strong bay mare with a striking white blaze and tacked her with considerable speed. They were out of the stable fifteen minutes later, both horses eager for their head in the cold March morning. The ground was flat and they let the horses run until the house and the stables faded behind them. They slowed the horses, turning them towards the stand of trees lining the perimeter of the Castonbury forest. The forest itself marked the border of the vast parklands.

The grandeur of Castonbury was not lost on Bram. Even the park acreage that extended beyond the cultivated lawns and gardens commanded breathtaking views, unadulterated with follies and man-made vignettes. In the distance, the Peaks made a striking granite backdrop to the forest on his left and the lake waters on his right. In the summer, those Peaks were probably reflected there. Today, though, the waters were grey and choppy.

'It's prettier in the spring,' Phaedra commented, following his gaze to the lake. 'The heather blooms and there are wildflowers. By summer, it's a paradise.'

'I like it this way.' Bram turned in his saddle to look at her. 'It's dark and hard, more masculine, I think.'

'Of course you do,' Phaedra replied. 'It's not wearing anything. The countryside is naked in winter.'

Bram hooted with laughter so loud Merlin sidestepped. 'Do you always say the first thing that comes to mind?' He hoped so. It was an absurdly refreshing departure from the cleverly spiked repartee of the London ladies he knew.

'Oh, hush up, will you? You'll scare the horses.'

Phaedra shot him a scolding look, pursed lips and all. It only made him laugh louder. Phaedra's mare swung in a tight circle, looking for the source of the noise.

'Now you've done it.' Phaedra quieted the mare long enough to slide off her back. 'We'll have to walk them until they settle down.'

They led the horses down to the lake and let them drink. Absolute silence surrounded them.

Bronwyn Scott

Bram could hear the horses' lips lapping the water. He could feel the wind that rustled the tall pines. He could not recall the last time he'd actually heard such individual noises. London was one big cacophony of sound. The city had a single volume—loud—which was useful for drowning one's thoughts but not much else.

'Your mare is beautiful. She has good conformation, a strong chest. I bet she's a great jumper. Isolde, right?'

Phaedra looked up from watching her horse drink, a soft smile on her face, a smile he hadn't seen yet. She was pleased he'd remembered. 'Isolde's the best jumper in the county.'

The haughtiness, the hardness, was gone, her defences unguarded in that moment. This was Phaedra Montague revealed. She was utterly lovely when she smiled like that. The man in him went rock-hard at the age-old paradox of wanting to protect that loveliness while wanting to claim it for his own. Such a treasure spoke to the primal nature that lived at the core of a man.

Bram held her gaze intentionally, watching the pink tip of her tongue flick ever so slightly across her lips, watching her eyes flit away and then back. She was unsure and yet excited about the emotional undercurrent rising between them.

She blinked first. 'You wanted to talk about the colt.' She stared out over the lake, breaking the spell.

'Yes, what are your plans for him? Are you going to make a hunter out of him?' Warbourne would be passably good in that capacity, although Bram thought him a bit on the slim side to truly match the broad-chested strength of Isolde.

Phaedra's gaze swivelled towards him, her authority returning. 'I mean to race him on the flat. Have you forgotten already or do you think, as my brother does, that it can't be done?' She was defensive over the colt, protective. She had her armour on now.

Bram gave a considering nod. He'd not forgotten. She'd said as much to Giles in Buxton and the implication had been clear when she'd shown him the wagon. Bram ran over the colt's features in his mind; the long, thin cannon bones in the colt's legs and the lean hindquarters bespoke the potential for speed—if that speed could be channelled. If Warbourne was anything, he was a racer.

That was the great 'if' with Warbourne. Then there was his age to consider. As a racer, Warbourne was running short on time. 'He'll be four soon. Most colts race earlier. That could be a problem.'

'I'm not waiting until next year,' Phaedra said resolutely. 'I'm racing him in the Derby. It's only open to three-year-olds.'

Bram shot her an incredulous look. 'The Derby? The Derby at Epsom? That's in May, less than three months away.'

'May twenty-second, technically speaking,' Phaedra corrected without hesitation. 'I'll need every week I can get.'

Bram had no argument there. Heavy training had just begun for most stables in preparation for racing season opening in April. If Warbourne was the usual horse, it might be enough.

'Has your brother approved?' He seemed to recall Giles Montague being a bit reserved on the subject when it had come up yesterday. He could understand why. Warbourne was that rare commodity of the known and unknown and a female trainer was rarer still. Her reception in the racing world was not guaranteed. Giles Montague was right to worry. His sister could be a scandal in the making.

Phaedra shrugged noncommittally. 'He will once he sees what Warbourne can do.' Which might be a polite way of saying she'd cross that bridge when she came to it…if she ever came to it. Bram saw the merit of her strategy. Why argue with her brother until she absolutely had to have his permission? If Warbourne wasn't ready, or if he failed to qualify, what would be the point?

'No one just shows up at Epsom,' Bram prodded. Maybe she didn't know, maybe she hadn't thought about the precursor races. He wasn't sure what she knew about the horseracing world.

She gave a curt nod. 'I know.' But he could see from the little crease between her eyes she was in deep thought. She was still trying to manage the logistics. He could guide her on that point if she'd let him. Many of his connections and obligations in London had centred around the turf.

'I'd love to race him at the Two Thousand Guineas in Newmarket but I don't see how I'll manage it. I think we'll have to simply risk it all on Epsom,' Phaedra said at last.

'I admire your tenacity,' Bram began, hoping he didn't sound patronising. She would not respect condescension. But she had to be made to understand the enormity of her goal. 'To take a colt like Warbourne all the way to Epsom is a difficult task even if there was more time.' Bram shook his head. For all she knew, Warbourne was past his prime, ruined. 'To do it in a single spring borders on impossibility.'

'But just borders,' Phaedra said staunchly. Her

gaze returned out over the water, stubbornness etched in the tightness of her jaw.

Bram let out a deep breath. He could add *annoying* and *obstinate* to the list of adjectives describing Phaedra Montague. 'I don't think even I could do it.'

That did bring her gaze back to him. She raised perfectly arched eyebrow. 'Not too proud, are we?' She tossed his words back at him from yesterday.

Bram chuckled. He could play that game. 'Not proud. Just honest. Sound familiar?'

'Honesty's been quite the theme today,' Phaedra said. Her hands were on her hips, emphasising the slimness of her waist. Bram's hands ached to take their place. 'While we're being *honest* about preferring shirts to no shirts, and who can or cannot train a colt in time for Epsom, let me say this. I am not interested in whether *you* can train him in time. I am only interested in whether *I* can.'

If there had been doubt about her seriousness, Bram would have laughed, thinking her comment nothing more than sassy words from a spoiled young miss. But she was in deadly earnest and she meant every last one of her sharp words. Why shouldn't she? She was the Duke of Rothermere's daughter. To her, he was nothing more than the latest in a string of temporary grooms.

There wasn't much he could tell her to change that without giving himself away. But there was plenty he could show her. Maybe he couldn't read a horse's mind but she wasn't the only one who could train a champion or ride like hell and he'd start showing her right now.

'You say she's the best jumper in the county?' Bram eyed Isolde, who'd finished drinking and had turned her attentions to cropping the sparse tufts of grass.

'Untouchable,' Phaedra said with her customary confidence.

'Merlin seems to be a prime goer. I'll bet he can give her a run for her money.' Competition sparked in Phaedra's eyes. Bram grinned. It didn't take much to stoke that particular fire. She rose to the bait all too easily.

Phaedra gave one of her shrugs. 'He's fast, tends to tire over long distances, but he'll jump any fence you find in the meanwhile.'

'Then let's go.' Bram winked and tossed her up into the saddle before swinging up into his own. He wheeled Merlin around. 'One point for every log, two points for every fence. First one back to the stables claims a prize. On your mark, get set, go!'

Chapter Five

Phaedra pulled Isolde to a halt a half-length behind Merlin in the stable quadrangle. 'I win!' she crowed triumphantly, sliding off the horse's back and loosening the girth. Isolde was slick with sweat. She'd run hard and jumped harder, *much* harder, than Merlin.

Bram dismounted and shot her a mischievous smile that boded ill. 'You can't possibly think you won?' Phaedra drew the reins over Isolde's head. 'I counted fifteen points for me and only eight for you.' It had been no small feat to keep track of logs and fences for the two of them while flying breakneck over the Castonbury lands.

Bram fell in beside her, leading a lathered Merlin to the stalls. 'I believe the rule was first one back to the stables wins, *not* who accrues the most points.'

'Then why jump anything at all?' Phaedra retorted.

'Yes, why indeed?' Bram's white-toothed grin was insufferable in its arrogance and twice as enticing. It was almost impossible to be angry at a smile like that.

'Next you'll be telling me you only jumped a few things to humour me.'

'No, I jumped a few things so you wouldn't *suspect* anything. Once you told me Merlin wasn't keen on longer distances, I knew I didn't have a chance unless Isolde tired herself out.' Bram called for a stable boy to take the horses. 'Give them both a good rub down. They're sweaty and could take a chill. Put on their blankets and turn them out to their paddocks.' Then he gave her all his attention. 'Now it's time to claim my forfeit.'

'You can't be serious. You cheated. You deliberately implied certain things,' Phaedra argued.

'I'm always serious about winning. I didn't peg you for a sore loser, Phaedra. Are you refusing to pay up?'

That stung. 'Of course not.' But it took all her bravado to admit it. The way he was looking at her right now made her wonder exactly what kind of forfeit he wanted to claim. She probably should have defined those terms as well. She gave it a belated try. 'I won't kiss you for it, if that's what you're thinking.'

Bram stepped closer, making her aware of the sheer maleness of him, a potent combination of muscle, leather and horse, all the things a man should be. 'Why not? I am of the opinion you need kissing.'

'I've been kissed before, if you must know,' Phaedra said in low tones. Good heavens, she hoped they weren't overheard. This was the most unseemly conversation. She tried to end it by walking to her office.

Bram gave a chuckle that sent butterflies to her stomach in warm flutters and followed her. 'I'm sure you have if you count parlour games and mistletoe.'

They'd reached her office door. He should take the hint it was time to part. But he didn't. Instead he rested his arm on the door frame over her head and leaned towards her, his arm, his body, effectively trapping her against the wall before she could go in and escape behind the security of her desk. 'That's not the kind of kissing I'm talking about, Phaedra.' There was a wealth of innuendo and invitation in that short phrase and it sent a jolt of warm heat straight to her belly.

She should tell him to stop using her name. He

was hired help. He should know better. She should be outraged at his bold behaviour, maybe even frightened. Aunt Wilhelmina would be. But all Phaedra could conjure up in response was excitement.

'What kind of kissing *are* you talking about?' Phaedra bit her lip wincing at her words. Had she actually said that? 'Never mind, I don't want to know.'

'Of course you want to know.' His blue eyes dropped to her lips, his mouth a teasing half-smile full of knowledge.

'I think you're the most outrageous man I've ever met.' It was the most sophisticated set-down she could manage under the circumstances and the most true. None of the young bucks she'd encountered could match him in his relentless pursuit of…of what? Of *her*?

Bram stepped back, releasing her from his intimate cage, that ever-present smile on his face when he looked at her as if he could read her every thought. 'Good, that gives us something in common. Now, if you'll excuse me, I have work to see to.'

A little flame of temper flared. How dare he imply she'd been the one keeping him when *he'd* been the one to follow *her* to the office and…and what? Phaedra went inside and shut her door, craving solitude.

He really was most the unnerving man she'd ever encountered. It wasn't because she hadn't met an arrogant man before. She'd met a few, Sir Nathan Samuelson notwithstanding, and she'd routinely found the arrogance completely unattractive. But on Bram Basingstoke, that was not the case. He wore arrogance infuriatingly well. He was confident, sure of himself, and sure of her as if he knew all along what she'd do next before she knew it herself.

Phaedra slumped in her chair, getting her racing pulse under control. Admittedly, she had little practice with this sort of man, with *any* man. He'd had it aright when he'd guessed her kissing had been limited to party games and holiday traditions. He'd been right, too, when he'd suggested she wanted to know about his kind of kissing. Just because she hadn't been kissed, didn't mean she didn't want to be. There just hadn't been the right opportunity, or maybe there just hadn't been the right man. She was twenty, after all, and girls younger than she were married with families.

Phaedra fiddled idly with the paperweight on her desk. Bram Basingstoke thought he could be the right man. Was he crazy? She was a duke's daughter. It raised the question of whether or not he knew better. He acted like no servant she'd ever met. There was a bit of irony to the idea that a lady took a groom out riding with her as protection, as a chaperone, but who protected her from the groom when he came in the form of Bram Basingstoke? In no way did he meet Aunt Wilhelmina's terms of an ideal chaperone. He was far too handsome, and far too exciting with his brash brand of conversation.

Phaedra gave a heavy sigh. If the truth be told, she was disappointed he hadn't kissed her in spite of her scold. It might have been nice to know once and for all what the mystique was all about. She was tired of being twenty and having never been kissed, at least not really kissed by a real man. Perhaps there was still hope. Bram had left without claiming his forfeit. Until then, she had Warbourne to think about. Phaedra grabbed a lunge line from a hook on the wall. It was time to see what her colt could do.

Phaedra looked up at the clock on her wall and rubbed the bridge of her nose. Quarter past six already! The afternoon had sped by in an enjoyable flurry of activity. Warbourne had not disappointed. She'd worked with him until late afternoon and then buried herself in her office writing copious notes about the day's training. It was all very promising and she was tempted to send to the house for supper instead of going back. But that was the coward's way. It would accomplish nothing. If she didn't show up for supper, Giles would seek her out down here. If he meant to have a talk, nothing would stop him.

Phaedra rose and stretched, her stomach rumbled. She'd worked through lunch and tea. Supper sounded nice but she'd have to hurry if she was to be on time and dressed to meet Aunt Wilhelmina's exacting standards. Even though no guests were present, Aunt Wilhelmina expected the family to dress for dinner. One never knew who might arrive at the last minute and while *they* could have bad form in showing up unexpectedly, the Montagues could not. A duke and his family must always be prepared to look the part.

Phaedra arrived in the drawing room promptly at seven o'clock dressed in a cream dinner gown of Spitalfields silk woven with blue and red flowers, her hair put up in a twist with a few tendrils left down to frame her face. Her maid, Henny, had been prepared, a gown laid out and a pitcher of warm water already waiting in anticipation.

Lumsden summoned them for dinner with a

properness not to be outdone by any London household. Phaedra thought it was all a bit silly since everyone was gone but Lumsden had been with the family for years and, like Aunt Wilhelmina, he had his own ideas about the importance of standing on ceremony even if it was just the three of them.

That importance extended to where they dined. The long, stately dining table dominated the centre of the room; eight-armed candelabra of heavy silver graced the table length atop a snowy white cloth. Lights from the candles played across the delicate Staffordshire china and crystal wine glasses. Every night, the room was turned out to perfection, much like its three guests, and every night, the room remained mainly empty with only a few to enjoy its beauty.

It had been different in the fall. Kate had been home and Cousin Ross had come to visit with his sister, Araminta. Phaedra had enjoyed their company.

Ross had made dinners lively, discussing local news with Giles and Kate. Even Aunt Wilhelmina had been charmed by him right up until he'd been discovered having a little romance with the maid, Lisette. Aunt Wilhelmina hadn't minded the romance—'it was what men of his station did'— but she had minded greatly that he hadn't wanted to end it. Now Ross was gone and Araminta had married and gone to live in Cambridgeshire.

'Perhaps we could invite Alicia to dine with us again some evening,' Phaedra suggested, taking in the empty expanse of table. Alicia must hate dining alone.

Aunt Wilhelmina, her iron-grey hair pulled back into a tight bun, shot her a quelling look as if she'd spoken blasphemy. '*That woman* has not yet earned a regular place at the table with the Montagues, no matter what name she calls herself.'

That woman, Alicia Montague, had been relegated to the Dower House with her little son and stuck in limbo since autumn waiting to prove to them all she was truly Jamie's widow, waiting for acceptance. Phaedra felt sorry for her. Alicia had been up to the house a few times. Phaedra knew her father liked seeing the little toddler when he was well enough. But for the most part, the family liked to pretend she didn't exist whenever they could. Alicia Montague was awkward to say the least, a reminder that not all was settled.

Phaedra opened her mouth to respond but Giles cut in. 'Phae, let's not bring any unpleasantness to the table. The kitchen has prepared roast pheasant tonight. We should enjoy it. Why don't you tell us about the colt? Did you take him out today?'

'Giles, he's splendid. You should come down and watch him tomorrow.' Phaedra managed to keep up a steady stream of chatter about Warbourne and the stables for most of dinner. She began to hope Giles would forget the talk he wanted to have. But by the time the raspberry crème was set in front of them for the last course, Giles brought the conversation to his subject.

He fixed her with a friendly, brotherly smile. She was not fooled. 'Phae, I mentioned at breakfast that I wanted to talk with you about this spring.' He nodded in Aunt Wilhelmina's direction. 'We would like to give you a Season. It's long overdue and you deserve it. Tucked up here in Derbyshire, you've had very little chance to meet anyone your own age or station.'

Phaedra put down her spoon. She hated when he did that. It was a nasty strategy, making the command seem like a gift. He *wanted* to give her a Season. 'That's very generous of you both.' Phaedra returned Giles's smile with one of her own, picking her words carefully. Aunt Wilhelmina was a grand proponent of the Season. She and Kate had gone around about it when it had been Kate's turn to come out.

'I think it would be a burden and an expense.' Aunt Wilhelmina might like the Season but she liked to save a pound whenever she could. Phaedra hoped the money argument would appeal to her. 'We're just getting the money back in line, Giles, after father's bad investments. I don't want to undo your hard work by straining the coffers over something as unnecessary as a wardrobe and opening up the town house.' To say nothing of the cost of keeping the horses and the carriage in town and all the other expenses of simply being in London.

It was Aunt Wilhelmina who answered. She sharply dismissed Phaedra's concern. 'If we're worried about cost, we can stay at Lady Grace Mannering's, Araminta's aunt. Not much to be done about the wardrobe though. We can't have you go looking like a pauper. People will talk. There's frugality and then there's stupidity. The money has to be spent in the right places.'

Giles covered Phaedra's hand with his own. 'Don't worry your head about money.' There was a glint in his eye that warned her not to press the argument further. He knew very well she hadn't been worried about money in Buxton when it came to Warbourne. He understood her argument now was just a polite subterfuge to avoid the real issue. If she was going to get out of a Season, she'd have to tell the truth, the real reason she didn't want to go.

'I can't leave the stables,' Phaedra said bluntly. 'When I left in January to visit the new stables at Chatsworth everything fell apart while I was gone.' She'd come home to find the stables in disarray, hay orders not placed and horses not shoed.

'We have a reliable man in place now. Bram Basingstoke is quite accomplished, Tom Anderson said as much today when I spoke with him,' Giles answered her evenly.

Giles had come to the stables? 'You came down and didn't come to see me?'

'I came this morning. I was told you were out riding,' Giles said firmly. 'Now, don't change the subject. You know I'm right. You rode with Basingstoke this morning and you know he's capable if he handled Merlin. Besides, Tom Anderson is on the mend. He's able to keep a better eye on things than he was in January.'

'It's not just the stables,' Phaedra hedged. 'I can't leave Warbourne. I won't.'

Aunt Wilhelmina exploded. She pointed her spoon at Phaedra. 'That is enough, young lady. You're twenty and you've never come out properly. You'll never catch a husband, you'll be nothing but a burden on this family.' She paused to draw a breath before continuing.

'I promised my sister on her deathbed I'd look

after you girls and see you settled. Your mother worried about what would become of her precious girls. It's so much harder to raise daughters. The world takes care of its men but it doesn't take care of its women. That's a family's job and one I accepted willingly. Out of love for my sister, I've devoted my life to seeing the six of you raised. You will not fail me at the last, Phaedra.'

Phaedra rose and shoved back her chair, tears of anger and guilt burning in her eyes. She had to get out of the room before she embarrassed herself. 'No, I won't go. Not this year. I most respectfully refuse.'

She shot her brother one last look. 'I'm sorry, Giles. I can't do it. I simply can't.'

Phaedra didn't stop to change her dress or to grab a shawl. She headed out into the night, to the stables. Where there would be peace and there would be no more talk of Seasons and husbands and promises to keep to mothers she didn't remember.

Chapter Six

Bram couldn't sleep. The idea of being in bed at this early hour was still an utterly novel idea. It wouldn't seem so novel in the morning. Still, that didn't change the fact he couldn't recall the last time he'd gone to bed before ten. Usually he headed to bed when the sun was creeping up over the horizon. In London, evening entertainments would barely be under way. But nothing he'd done today had resembled any of his London activities, why should going to bed differ in that regard?

Instead of sleeping away half the day, he'd risen early and seen to morning feeding, following Tom Anderson around and making notes about the various dietary needs of the horses. He'd broken his fast with the other men on the simple but hearty fare of thick porridge. After breakfast, the grumbles had begun over who had to take Merlin out to exercise and he'd quickly assigned himself the task. If there was a difficulty, he wanted to address it immediately and personally.

Then Phaedra had arrived and he'd spent the rest of the morning riding out with her, which had been insightful. She was proving to be an enticing mixture of strength and innocence that was as responsible as the early hour for keeping him up tonight.

He'd made a tactical error today. He should have kissed her, claimed his forfeit and been done with it. Past experience had taught him the best way to deal with unmitigated desire was to address it head-on, much the same as a difficult horse.

Bram gave up and rolled out of bed. There would be no 'addressing' of the Phaedra issue this evening. She was safely out of reach up at the house. But perhaps a little exercise would help him sleep. He reached for breeches and a shirt. He'd do a quick patrol through the stables and see if the horses were settled.

Halfway down the stairs, he heard it, the sound of someone in the stables. The sound could be anyone, a stable boy checking on a horse or Tom Anderson up and about. A sound wasn't necessarily cause for alarm. But the lantern light coming from the vicinity of Warbourne's stall was, especially this time of night. Phaedra hadn't made any friends with her purchase. Bram wouldn't put it past Samuelson to attempt some chicanery.

Bram slowed his steps and approached cautiously. He tensed his body, ready to take the intruder unawares if there was one. It seemed there was. The outline of a figure became evident in the light—a figure wearing skirts. Tension ebbed out of Bram. It was no thief in the night at Warbourne's stall.

'Good evening, Phaedra.' He'd been careful to keep his voice quiet but she startled anyway. She turned to face him, a hand at her throat.

'It's not polite to sneak up on people.'

'It's more interesting though.' He gave her an easy smile. She was dressed oddly for a late-night visit to the stables. Still in an expensive evening gown, she clearly hadn't *planned* to come. She shivered a little and he noted she hadn't come with even a shawl for protection against the damp night. There were only two reasons for such an impromptu visit.

'Is Warbourne all right?' He'd personally checked the colt before he'd gone upstairs for the night and the colt had seemed fine a few hours ago.

'He's fine,' Phaedra said shortly.

'Are you all right, then?' On closer inspection, she did appear upset, although she'd not admit it.

'I'm fine.' Phaedra crossed her arms against the cold, unable to suppress another shiver.

'No, you're not.' Bram stripped out of his jacket, a plain woollen hacking jacket that had been in the pile of clothes he'd borrowed from Tom Anderson. He swept the coat about her shoulders in a neat gesture, the simple garment a stark contrast to the richness of her own attire. In London, he would have had an expensive jacket of superfine or his long riding coat of heavy cloth to wrap about her. His favourite riding coat would have dwarfed her. Here, he had nothing so fine to offer her. It was something of a first for him. But Phaedra shrugged into the cheap coat gratefully.

'Now, are you going to tell me what you're doing out here freezing?' He leaned against the wall, studying her. She was elegant tonight, dressed in a gown of oyster silk that rivalled the styles of London's dressmakers, her hair piled on her head instead of hanging down her back in a thick braid. At her neck she wore a thin gold chain with a charm shaped like a horse dangling from it. She looked beautiful, delicate.

Almost.

With a face like that, a man could easily mistake her beauty for fragility. Tonight, there was nothing of the spitfire who'd raced him neck or nothing across the winter fields. But he *had* seen that woman and Bram knew better. Something had stirred her inner fires enough to make her flee the house.

'How was dinner?' Bram tried again when she said nothing. That got a reaction. Her eyes turned stormy. So that was it.

'They want to send me away.' She shot him an accusatory look.

Bram sat down on a hay bale left between stalls for the morning. 'Where to?' The way she said it made it sound like she was being shipped off to a convent or the wilds of Scotland.

'London! They want me to go have a Season.' Phaedra waved a hand in outraged dismissal. He ducked in time to avoid being hit. 'You'd like that. You'd have the stables all to yourself.'

It was on the tip of his tongue to say she was a lucky girl but to argue it would make him look complicit in her assumption that he wanted her out of the way. He'd love to be back in London with all the comforts it provided. But obviously Phaedra didn't want to go and, contrary to her beliefs, it didn't suit his plans to have her go. London was the one place he couldn't be right now. 'A Season is very generous.' Bram hedged his comments. Inspiration struck. 'Have you been before?'

Some of Phaedra's anger faded when she realised he wasn't going to argue. He could see her body relax beneath the overlarge shoulders of his coat. 'No. I was supposed to but that was the year my brother, Edward, died. He was nineteen.'

He'd heard as much from Tom Anderson. 'And the next year?' The family would have been out of mourning by the following spring.

She shrugged, a gesture he was coming to recognise as a distractor. She shrugged when she wanted to appear nonchalant, a sure sign she was hiding something of greater value. It was a delightful gesture. He wondered if she knew she did it. 'There were a lot of things going on with the family last spring. Giles had just come home and I didn't feel like leaving, not for London anyway.'

Another set of mysteries to solve about the Montagues, Bram thought. It was odd indeed for a ducal family not to send their eligible daughter to London. 'Did your sister go?' Phaedra wasn't the only one who would have been itching for a Season.

The reference brought a slight smile to her lips. 'You don't know Kate. The last thing she ever wanted was a London Season. She went once for her debut and she never went back.'

He was starting to understand. Perhaps her sister's poor debut had coloured her own perceptions. 'Just because your sister had a bad experience, doesn't mean you will.' That would hardly be the case. London's bachelors would stumble over themselves to get to her; an attractive duke's daughter was quite a catch indeed. Something raw and primal knotted in his stomach at the thought of London's bucks competing over Phaedra as if she were a prize to be won. If there was any winning to be done, he'd be the one to do it. After all, he saw her first.

Phaedra shook her head impatiently. 'I can't possibly leave Warbourne. If I go to London, I'll lose my chance to race him at Epsom.' She paused and watched him, her blue-grey eyes holding his. 'Aren't you going to laugh or are you simply going to ignore the statement the way Giles does and pretend you didn't hear it?'

They were back to that again. The lantern light cast an intimate glow over the stables, limning Phaedra's delicate profile in a soft rosy glow. In the loose box, Warbourne had settled to sleep. Bram let the words hover between them before he ventured into the conversation.

'Warbourne's a good horse. There's nothing to laugh about there. But why Epsom? There are other races. There are even other races *at* Epsom he can enter next year as a four-year-old. Why is the Derby so important to you?' The personal nature of her quest for Epsom had not been addressed in their earlier conversation.

'It's the most prestigious. It secures a horse's reputation for stud.' She looked at him as if he were an idiot. Any horseman worth his salt would know that. Bram had met women who were patronesses of the sport but they were not duke's daughters. They were women of a middling rank or less who had made a hobby-cum-livelihood out of it. They dabbled in breeding and racing. Phaedra didn't need a livelihood. It begged the question, what did she need?

'Why is it so important to *you* though?' he pressed, knowing full well he was treading on unexamined territory. Bram could not recall the last time he'd had a real conversation with a woman, where he'd actually listened, where it actually mattered what she said next. Maybe he'd never had one. But he was having one tonight, and he was beyond curious about her answer. For whatever reason, *her* answer mattered. He wanted to know what drove this neck-or-nothing beauty. This was

unexplored territory indeed. 'Well, Phaedra, why?'
He repeated softly.

Whatever her ambitions, she'd not had practice
in articulating them. He could see her mind debating if she should tell him, if she could trust
him. She shot him a hard look, her defences up
in the tilt of her chin, apparently unaware what a
watershed event this was for him. Lord, that look
of hers made him hard. Phaedra in full defiance
made him want to haul her up against the wall.

'I need something of my own. This isn't just
about the Derby. That's only the beginning. I want
to create a grand stud, a breeding and training facility that rivals any in England, north or south.'

Bram let out a low whistle. That *was* an enormous ambition and an exciting one; it was something *he'd* like to do if he could ever raise enough
funds or settle down long enough. 'Does your
brother know?'

'He knows. He doesn't understand, not really.
It's different for a woman.' Phaedra played idly
with a piece of straw but Bram could hear the un-
told story behind that sentence. A man like Giles
wouldn't fully understand. Montague had his military career. He had been in charge of his life. Now
he had this property to oversee and a dukedom
coming his way eventually. As a man, Phaedra's

brother took his independence for granted, a natural assumption of his life. But Phaedra could make no such assumption.

'I'm not a baby any more, not a child. I can do things,' Phaedra said with no little frustration. 'I just have to make Giles see that.'

She was the youngest. Bram had forgotten. When he looked at her, he didn't see a child but a lovely young woman. Naturally, Giles would want to protect her; young and female, a man like him would see her as someone to shelter, especially after the other losses Tom Anderson had mentioned.

'And Warbourne is the key to this dynastic vision of yours?' Bram asked lightly.

Phaedra pulled her gaze from the straw she'd been twisting. 'Yes.'

'Just yes? That's an awfully big risk to take with an untried colt.' He remembered with clarity Giles handing over the pearl set to the auctioneer. Warbourne had cost Phaedra dearly.

'Not really, not if you know what you're doing.' Phaedra rose and brushed off her skirts, bringing the conversation to an abrupt, regretful end. Bram could have kept talking to her all night, another revelation. Usually by now he would have…

well, never mind that. He pushed his more erotic thoughts aside with a hard mental shove.

'I shouldn't be telling you all this, I hardly know you and you hardly know me. You're probably thinking I'm a spoiled little rich girl. I have all of these horses to play with and yet it isn't enough.' She was back to not trusting him. He wanted to change that. He wanted to tell her he had no desire to see her retreat from the stables or from her dreams but she wouldn't believe him, not yet.

Bram's hot thoughts shoved back. She looked irresistible in the lantern light, the upsweep of her hair setting off the curve of her jaw to delicate perfection, the slope of her shoulder leading the eye to the low bodice of her gown and the soft swell of her breasts beneath.

'I'm not thinking that at all, I'm thinking what could possibly drive this beautiful woman to such lengths? To want things it's not usual for a woman of your background to want, especially when it means giving up something as enormous as a Season.' He knew London and its intrigues intimately. The Season was her gateway to marriage, security and respectability, three things a woman treasured as much as her virginity. Even a duke's daughter understood the necessity for a good Season, a good match. Finding a successful match would be easier than getting Warbourne to win the Derby.

That got her attention. 'You think I'm beautiful?' she whispered in surprise.

'Mmm-hmm.' Bram rose and stepped towards her. He watched her pulse catch at the base of her throat as he caressed her cheek with the back of his hand. He cradled her face between his hands, gently tipping her head back, her pink lips already parted ever so slightly, the dark pupils of her eyes wide with curious desire.

'I think it's time to claim my forfeit.' His voice was husky as he bent to take her mouth in a slow kiss.

So this was what he'd meant by a real kiss. It was more than a kiss, more than lips meeting lips in a fleeting buss. Phaedra was blissfully conscious of his hand at the back of her neck, warm and caressing, guiding; of her lips opening to him; of the decadent strokes of his tongue inside her mouth; of her own tongue responding in kind until they were engaged in a seductive duel.

Their mouths weren't all that was engaged. She was acutely aware the kiss had aroused more than her mouth. Heat pooled in her stomach, low and hot, while the core of her burned for more, helped along by the intimate press of his body to hers. She'd seen the glorious muscle of him revealed that morning, but to feel a man, to feel *him* against one's own body, was far headier than the visual.

He was a granite wall against her, all planes and firm muscle, generating an erotic male heat. The wanton in her longed to stroke those planes, to run her hands down the contours of his torso. He danced her backwards to the wall, their duel becoming more insistent, inspiring her own boldness. Her hands were in his hair, then at his shoulders, gripping the muscled expanse of them beneath the fabric of his shirt. His mouth moved to the curve of her jaw, nipping ever so lightly at the column of her throat. She gasped at the pleasure of it.

'Does that feel good, princess?' Bram feathered a breath against her ear and she shivered delightfully for an answer. His hands were more adventurous now, casting away the coat he'd draped her in and pushing down the scooped bodice of her gown. Every last thought she possessed was centred only on the present, on the wicked caress of his thumb across her nipple, on the heat building in her body, and the hardness of him where their bodies met, that unmentionable part of a man pressed against her.

'Do you feel what you do to me?' he asked, his

own breath ragged at her ear now, evidence that he was enjoying this as much as she.

'Yes.'

He kissed her hard one last time and stepped back. 'That's why we have to stop this right now.' He gave her one of his teasing half-grins. 'If we don't, in a half minute or less, I'll have your skirts about your ears and your legs around mine.'

Phaedra flushed and tried to gather her hauteur as she straightened her clothing. '*Your* ears? I doubt that's possible.'

Bram leaned forward and adjusted the shoulder of her gown. 'I assure you it is, princess.'

She grimaced, doubtful. 'Sounds uncomfortable.'

Bram laughed. 'Sounds like a challenge.'

Goodness, the man was arrogant, a fact she'd conveniently forgotten when he'd kissed her. She couldn't believe she'd let things go so far or that she'd told him so much on such short acquaintance. She must be missing Kate more than she thought, but that didn't change the fact she'd enjoyed it—all of it, the conversation and the kiss.

Phaedra gave a regal sweep past him with a pointed '*Goodnight*, Mr Basingstoke.'

He gave her a short bow. 'Goodnight, Lady Phaedra.' She didn't have to turn around to know he was laughing again. She could hear it in his voice. She kept her shoulders squared until she was out of sight. Aunt Wilhelmina would say she'd gotten exactly what she'd deserved for sitting in the stables late at night with a man who so casually ran around shirtless. Unfortunately for Aunt Wilhelmina, her just deserts were proving to be quite delicious.

Chapter Seven

Kissing Phaedra Montague was *not* an antidote for sleeplessness. If anything, it was the cause, that and her infernal ability to talk without telling him anything at all. He was well aware she'd not fully answered his question.

She was dead set on Epsom but she'd not given him one clue as to why. There had to be more to it than merely a consideration of Warbourne's age. What had she said at the last? *It wasn't that hard if someone knew what they were doing?* She had a secret, at least she thought she had a secret, that she knew something about Warbourne others had overlooked. A beautiful woman with a secret was a potent lure indeed and one he knew he'd take in spite of the potential risks.

Bram pushed a hand through his hair and strode out into the courtyard of the stable quadrangle. He breathed in a healthy dose of the night air, letting the cold bathe away the heat of his body.

In all fairness he hadn't done this by himself. She'd been a veritable fever of passion in his arms, an untried wildfire burning out of control. And he'd stoked it, knowing full well what it was doing to him and to her. But Lord, how intoxicating it had been! Bram could not recall the last time an encounter of that nature had aroused him so completely, so beyond control.

Bram paced the quadrangle, squaring it in long, fast strides, trying to rid himself of excess energy and other manly excesses too. Usually, he guided these encounters, took what he wanted, gave what was required, chose when it started and when it ended. That had not been the case tonight. Tonight, he'd barely been able to exert enough influence to bring it to a close before he'd taken things too far.

This boded ill for his plans and he was only one day in. When he'd first spied her, he'd not planned on desire riding him quite this hard or so soon. Tonight, she'd been an irresistible picture of loveliness and vulnerability, mostly because she hadn't tried to be either of those things.

Bram laughed out loud to the sky. He suspected Phaedra would hate to be called vulnerable. It was the last thing she wanted to be. That tilt of her chin, the nonchalant shrug that masked the importance of what she felt, the haughtiness that did little to mask the passions within her, were all telling attributes attesting to her strength and the efforts she took to cultivate it.

She *was* strong. Her strength was not a facade but that did not mean she was without susceptibilities. Neither was he, and that was a problem. Bram stopped his pacing and breathed easier, his body sweat-slicked from the exertion but feeling the better for it.

This physical-mental attraction to Phaedra and her wild dream presented something of a conundrum; it required him to behave honourably, not a practice he was used to exercising. Most of his women didn't demand it. They were women who understood the rules of their liaison—short, physical and with no future expectations. These were not rules he could apply to Phaedra.

Bram climbed the stairs to his quarters, a dissatisfying solution having suggested itself. There was nothing for it. Until he could figure out which rules *did* apply, or until he could convince his body to subscribe to her charms a little less ardently, he would simply have to stay away from her. He hoped he'd come up with a better answer sooner rather than later because kisses like that were the gods' own ambrosia and the devil's due. It would be impossible to stay away for ever.

Phaedra let out the lunge line, slowly leading Warbourne through his paces, letting him learn her signals. The shorter line asked for a walk; slightly more meant a trot, and at full length a canter. In the fourteen days since she'd brought Warbourne home, he'd made remarkable progress. True, he had undergone training before but it was hard to know how much he'd been taught and where the mastery of those skills had broken down. She'd started her regimen from the beginning, wanting to assess his ability and his obedience from the start.

Warbourne pulled on the lunge line, wanting to canter at his own behest instead of hers. Phaedra held firm, tightening her grip on the line instead of letting out the slack. He *would* listen to her, or rather to her signals. Above all else, a horse had to believe his master's hands and his master's legs.

Warbourne returned to a collected and obedient trot. She was starting to see where the problems might have occurred. He was a wilful colt and wilful colts were easily spoiled, usually by accident. She'd seen it happen a time or two with the younger stable hands working with their first horses, their own minds not strong enough to comprehend what it took to truly master such intelligent creatures.

Phaedra let out the lunge line, asking for a controlled canter. Not just any canter would do. Warbourne could not run around her willy-nilly in a circle. This would be a canter on the right lead and at her pace. Even well-trained horses could spoil without a strong, consistent hand. Merlin was proof enough. Without Jamie's strong hand, Merlin had put his own strong personality into action. It had worked until Bram Basingstoke had come along and reasserted mastery.

Of the two of them, Merlin was seeing far more of the elusive Mr Basingstoke than she was, however. Since that night in the stables, she'd caught only glimpses of him. Most of his messages to her were conveyed through Tom Anderson, whose hip kept him confined to the stable block. Tom thought the arrangement was working out admirably. Mr Basingstoke could do the heavy exercising and any business with the horses that required leaving Castonbury. These days there was plenty of business to arrange. Breeding season was beginning and there was always interest in the Castonbury broodmares.

This morning, Tom had informed her Bram had

taken one of the mares over to Gordon Weston's to be covered by the Weston stud, a gorgeous seventeen-hand bay hunter. The match was technically very welcome, but there was resentment too. She'd tried to arrange something earlier in February but Gordon Weston had politely refused. She highly suspected he simply hadn't wanted to do that sort of business with a woman.

Phaedra drew the line in on Warbourne and walked towards him. She gave the horse a rub on the shoulder and slipped him a piece of apple. 'Good boy.' She smiled to herself. Warbourne was coming along nicely, even if she was taking it slowly. But she would show them all, from Sir Nathan Samuelson and his overt dislike of the Montagues to Mr Gordon Weston and his mannerly reserve on the subject of female abilities. Tomorrow, she would trade the lunging halter for a bridle and a bit.

'Time for some grooming.' Phaedra led him outside the riding house where they'd been working and to the stables. This had been their routine: lunging work, paces and grooming. She wanted him to be fully used to her hands and her voice before she put anything on his back. Tomorrow she would add the saddle pad too.

The stable yard was busy with horses being

brought in for the end of the day. The 'supper feeding' would get under way within the hour after the horses had been settled and brushed for the night. A stable boy ran up, offering warily to take Warbourne for her but she shook her head. She wasn't ready to trust anyone with her colt yet even for a simple grooming.

She nearly had Warbourne settled in his loose box when a light commotion in the courtyard drew her attention. A rider had arrived and the stable boys jumped to take his horse. For a moment she thought the rider must be Giles with all the fuss his appearance had commanded. But it was an assumption immediately discarded. The horse wasn't Giles's, but one of the geldings kept in the general string. There was no mistaking the rider for anyone other than Bram.

He swung off the horse with the fluid ease she recognised from their ride and barked a few commands. 'Rub him down good, boys, and give him a hot mash tonight. He's ridden a long way today.' He tossed the reins to one of the waiting grooms and quartered the yard, looking for someone. Her, perhaps? Her insides fluttered irrationally only to be disappointed. His gaze landed somewhere else. 'It's done, Tom. I'll come by and tell you all about it.'

Phaedra stepped forward. 'You can tell me about it first. We'll want to get everything written down in our records. Come by my office after you get cleaned up. I'll expect you in ten minutes.'

Bram shifted his gaze to her, his eyes narrow and cold, making her rethink the order. Perhaps her order *had* sounded a bit high-handed but he'd left her no choice. He'd assiduously avoided her for two weeks now. While he may have personal reasons for doing so, she did worry about the professional implications of the avoidance. If everyone thought they could simply go through Tom Anderson, she would quickly be ignored in the chain of command.

Ten minutes later to the second, Bram presented himself at her office in a fresh shirt, his hair slick from a good dousing at the pump. 'Lady Phaedra, I've come to give my report.' His tone was stiff and slightly mocking as he stood in the doorway.

'You're prompt.' Phaedra decided to pretend she didn't hear his subtle scold.

'You gave me an order.' His eyes flicked to the chair in front of her desk. 'May I sit?' She'd forgotten how blue his eyes were.

'Stop it, obeisance doesn't suit you,' Phaedra snapped. 'I had to do something. You've been ignoring me.'

Bram folded his arms across his chest. 'I disagree. I've been busy. If you needed to see me, you know where to find me.'

Phaedra's temper flared at his surliness. The man was positively arrogant. She rose and leaned across the desk for emphasis, hot words tumbling out of her mouth before she could think them through. 'You kissed me. That was all. Don't flatter yourself that I would spend my days traipsing around the stables behind you in hopes of getting another. You report to me, not the other way around.'

Bram rose, meeting her across the desk, his expression hot with his own agitation. 'I work for myself, Lady Phaedra. Your brother might have hired me but I'll decide how long I'll stay. I'm not a creature of service like Tom Anderson who's devoted his life to the high and mighty house of Rothermere.'

She held his gaze steady, her body remembering the potent masculinity of him. Her stomach quivered with a trill of butterflies. 'That does not give you permission for insolence and insubordination. If others see you circumvent my authority, they will do the same.'

'Then keep the damn door shut because I'm about to "circumvent your authority" right now.'

Bram stretched a booted foot behind him and kicked aside the chunk of wood holding the door ajar. The door slammed closed with a resounding thunk. In that moment, everything changed; Bram reached for her, his hand rough at her neck, his mouth covering hers in a bruising kiss that both punished and aroused.

Phaedra matched him, nipping at his lower lip in retaliation and in desire; this was rough play indeed and not entirely unpleasant. He growled against her neck, his hands yanking her shirt from the waistband of her trousers, his fingertips on her bare skin beneath the fabric, cupping her breasts, thumbing her nipples into wanton truancy. This was not the time for exploring the desires he awoke in her. She shoved hard at his chest. 'I will not be mastered like this.'

'Neither will I, princess. You can save your orders for the common servants.' Bram's eyes glittered dangerously but he let her go, let her take a step backwards.

She would be wise not to push him any further. Phaedra pulled at her shirt, tucking it back in, and sat down with all the dignity she could rally. 'Tell me about the Weston stud.' She hoped her tones were appropriately convincing. She'd put the incident behind her, he should too. Phaedra pulled down the ledger in which all the breeding records were kept and opened it, another suggestion that their conversation had moved on.

Bram sat too, and talked as she wrote, offering a physical description of the Weston stallion for the record. 'It went well. We should know in a couple of weeks if it was successful. It's still early. Weston said we can try again if it doesn't take.'

Phaedra humphed at the news of Weston's generosity and shut the book. 'That's more than I ever got from him. I proposed the exact same match back in February and he turned me down.' It was unfair. Bram had been here a handful of weeks and already Weston had been eager to set up a match.

Bram gave her a wry smile. 'I imagine most men feel uncomfortable discussing breeding with a female. It's a fairly blunt conversation, to say nothing of the act itself.' He chuckled. 'Gordon Weston's a nice enough man but I can't exactly picture him standing at the fence with you calmly watching his stallion take your mare while you discuss the weather.'

Phaedra blushed, this time more from the scrutiny of his blue eyes than the forthright nature of his language.

'For that matter, Phaedra, could you?' His voice

was a rough whisper. 'Could *you* watch and not get just a bit excited?'

'Now you're being shocking on purpose.' She rose and put the book back on the shelf. It was time for him to go. She had to get ready for dinner, had to regain her equilibrium. Whenever she was around Bram Basingstoke, she was constantly off balance.

Bram stood. 'Maybe I am. Let that be lesson number two, Phaedra. Never tempt a man who's watched a stallion breed all day.' He fixed her with one of his hot gazes and melting smiles, his voice a low caress in the quiet privacy of the little room, before he slipped out the door. 'Do you want to know what I learned? I learned that sometimes a lady likes a bit of rough.'

Likes a bit of rough. The thought plagued her all through dinner. Bram was the most arrogant, most attractive, most irritating, most exciting man she'd ever met, and the most inappropriate. In all practicality, she could not think of fixing her sights on him. He was a groom, for heaven's sake. After Kate's marriage to Virgil, the family couldn't take another shock. One of them had to marry decently.

Phaedra pushed her potatoes around her plate, letting her thoughts wander down the most obvious path. Marriage? Did she think that's where this hot and cold adventure with Bram was headed? There was no possibility of it happening in truth. Status differences aside, one did not marry for hot kisses alone. Every governess she'd ever had had neatly outlined the duties of a duke's daughter when it came to marriage. Apparently they'd done their job well.

To marry a man who was practically in service would make her a laughing stock among her social set, and her husband too. Everyone would know he'd married for enormous advantage and for no other reason. A marriage couldn't survive under those circumstances. The doubt would kill any genuine feelings all too soon.

Well, if one couldn't marry handsome grooms, one could still kiss them, came the rebellious thought. If Bram was flirting with her for his own nefarious purposes, perhaps she could turn those purposes for her own good. What had Kate told her once? Men don't 'buy the cow when they get the milk for free.' The adage could work both ways. She didn't want to buy Bram's 'cow' as it were, if *she* could get kisses for free. She just had to be careful not to get caught.

'Are those potatoes to your satisfaction, Phae? You've pushed them around the plate five times now and haven't taken a bite.' Giles intruded on her thoughts after the roasted beef had been set in front of them.

Phaedra looked up from her food. Did she look guilty? Did a person look a certain way after they'd had their mouth thoroughly ravished? More important, would Aunt Wilhelmina *know* that look? She tried to remember if Kate had looked a certain way. Giles and her aunt were staring at her expectantly.

'The potatoes are fine.' Phaedra smiled and forked a mouthful to make her point.

'How's Basingstoke working out?' Giles asked, clearly eager to draw her into the dinner conversation.

'He's working out just fine.' *Kisses like a dream, looks wonderful with his shirt off, likes to work the horses half naked, oh, yes, he was working out fine.*

'Good, Anderson seems to like him,' Giles replied, obviously hoping to have more of a conversation with her on the subject. Of course, with only Aunt Wilhelmina to talk to, anything would be welcome. She really ought to say more or Giles would think something was wrong, especially when she usually gushed about the stables at supper. 'He took one of the mares over to Weston's today for breeding.' Phaedra gathered her thoughts, dragging them away from the other things Bram had done today. Giles would be less pleased with Bram if he knew what had gone on behind the closed door of her office today, or at the round pen, or in the stables late at night.

'Breeding is not a suitable conversation for the dinner table or for a young woman anywhere at any time!' Aunt Wilhelmina scolded.

'It's breeding season, it's what horse owners talk about in March, Aunt,' Phaedra protested gently.

'You, miss, are not a "horse breeder." You are a duke's daughter and it's time you remembered it.' Phaedra repressed a sigh. She *never* forgot it. How could she with Aunt Wilhelmina reminding her every day?

Wilhelmina turned her attentions on Giles with a wave of her fork. 'This is why she needs a Season. She can't even hold a proper conversation. Who will want a wife who is vulgar?'

A lady who likes a bit of rough, Bram's voice whispered naughtily in her head. Phaedra fixed her eyes on her roasted beef, a little smile playing on her lips. She knew one man who might. Good heavens, Bram Basingstoke was going to be the death of her. Or the life.

Chapter Eight

Bram watched Phaedra work the colt from the shadows of the entrance to the riding house. Whoever said absence made the heart grow fonder forgot to mention it made other parts grow harder. Two weeks of trying to avoid Phaedra hadn't resolved anything. If yesterday's heated altercation was anything to go on, avoidance had simply made things worse. It was time for a more direct approach.

There were other things he should be doing this afternoon. His trunk had arrived, finally, from the inn in Buxton and he needed to find a place to store it where it wouldn't be noticed, most especially where it wouldn't be noticed by Phaedra. She was curious enough to look inside and that would be akin to opening Pandora's box.

But he'd caught sight of her leading Warbourne

to the indoor arena and after a half-hour of pretending he had no curiosity whatsoever about the progress she was making, Bram had given in.

There was a stable hand with her, a gangly young lad named Bevins, who was no more than thirteen. Bram could hear Phaedra giving Bevins instruction, her voice bordering on impatient. 'You have to take the lead rope firmly. Don't back away when he tugs, it just proves to him that he's winning.' Apparently this had happened before, Bram mused.

It wasn't just anyone who could get near Warbourne though. He'd heard the boys in the stable talking about the horse in wary tones and drawing straws. None of them were especially excited about taking on the responsibility of caring for the feisty colt. So far, everyone was relieved Phaedra had decreed only she would care for the beast. Everyone except him.

Bram was aching for a crack at the colt. But Phaedra's position on the colt was absolute.

'Now, we're going to see if he'll take a saddle pad.' Phaedra handed the lead rope to Bevins. 'You have to hold him. Make eye contact and talk to him. Let him get used to your voice. I'll settle the saddle pad.'

Bram chuckled to himself. Poor Bevins had obviously drawn the short straw. From the slouch of the boy's shoulders Phaedra had decided he'd be having a lot more contact with the horse.

Bram held his breath in anticipation. He was actually impressed Phaedra had gotten this far with the colt. The pad would be the first step towards taking a bit and eventually a saddle. This would be interesting.

Phaedra approached from the near side but Warbourne sidled away, Bevins making no move to stop him. She tried again to no avail. Each approach made Warbourne more skittish. After a fifth attempt, Phaedra gestured the boy away. 'Go sit over there. You're upsetting him.' She took the lead rope herself and spoke softly to the colt, stroking the white blaze running the length of his face. It was nothing short of miraculous to watch the colt settle at her touch, the signs of nervousness disappearing almost instantly. Bram's respect for her went up another notch.

She fed Warbourne a piece of ever-present apple from her pocket, her other hand moving to take long soothing strokes along the horse's neck, the rest of her body moving subtly to the horse's side so she could manoeuvre the saddle pad on the colt's back. Then suddenly it was there, the white fleece pad was on the colt's dark back and Phaedra was back at the horse's head, calming and soothing. The whole process had been masterful and magical. He'd hardly noticed the moment she'd put the pad on and neither had Warbourne until it was too late.

Warbourne didn't like it but he didn't revolt. He shook his long mane and protested but Phaedra held the lead rope close to his halter until he relented. 'Did you see how I did that?' she called over to Bevins. 'He's just testing you. He's been without a real master for too long. He has to learn some things again, that's all.'

Bevins merely nodded, his face pale. Bram made a mental note to have a word with Bevins. Bram pushed off the door frame and came forward. 'Well done!' He could hardly stand by; the excitement rising in him at the potential of the colt now that he'd passed this milestone was too great. Perhaps, too, this would be a perfect opportunity to teach young Bevins by example. He would test the waters and see what sort of reception awaited him after yesterday.

'Lady Phaedra, your colt is coming along nicely.'

'Thank you, *Mr Basingstoke*.' He saw a secret mocking laughter in her eyes over the formality—a good sign that she wasn't holding yesterday against him. Perhaps it was even a sign she was eager to forge ahead with their relationship, such as it was. The idea made her all the more enticing, a reminder of the fact that she was the most forbidden of fruit. He had no doubts Tom Anderson would dismiss him on the merest suggestion of rumour if anyone even breathed the idea he harboured inappropriate intentions towards Phaedra.

Bram stretched a hand out to Warbourne's lips and let the horse root at his empty palm. 'Tease,' Phaedra admonished playfully in quiet tones that excluded Bevins. 'He thinks you have a treat.'

'Only because he thinks everyone carries apples in their pockets.' Bram gave her a little smile. 'Bevins, come here.'

'Yes, sir.' Bevins approached warily, drawn forward only out of his desire to please the temporary stable master.

'You want to work with horses, do you, boy?'

'Yes, sir.' To his credit, Bevins straightened a little.

'Might as well start with the best.' Bram fixed him with a serious stare. 'You should see working with Warbourne as an opportunity instead of a duty. You can learn a lot from Lady Phaedra. It's your lucky day. Here's a lesson for you. If you want a horse to know you, blow in his nostrils, let him get used to your scent.' Bram blew softly into

Warbourne's nostrils. 'Now, you try.' He stepped back next to Phaedra to watch Bevins.

'You have a soft spot for the boy,' Phaedra said.

'I've noticed he's a hard worker but he hasn't been around horses much.'

'He hasn't been here very long,' Phaedra said softly. 'His folks died from fever and he's been living with his grandmother in the village. He's very conscious of providing for her. I know he visits her on his half-day off and he gives her most of his wages.'

'*I've* got a soft spot for the boy?' Bram joked, but he was impressed she knew that much about the boy. She had a good heart for horses and for growing boys, it seemed. It spoke well of her, but Bram wasn't surprised. Phaedra was a woman who wore her heart on her sleeve for the entire world to see—an admirable trait and a trusting one.

'You haven't tried a bridle and a bit yet,' Bram couldn't resist.

Phaedra shot him a grey look of incredulity. 'I had thought to. Yesterday, that had been the plan, but he's skittish today. It might be too ambitious given his mood. I've been taking things slow with him. It minimises failure and maximises success.'

Bram raised an eyebrow and shrugged, noting the irony of the proposed strategy. So far, it hadn't worked all that well with Warbourne's mistress. He opted for innuendo. 'Maybe. However, Warbourne is in a receptive mood at the moment. Now might be a perfect time to push forward. We can always stop.'

Bram let Phaedra digest the double meaning of his content and decide what she wanted to do with it. He turned to Bevins. 'Go to the tack room and get the three-jointed snaffle bit.'

'You just couldn't stay away, could you?' Phaedra challenged after Bevins sprinted off to get the bit.

'The colt's exciting, I confess.' Bram fixed her with a stare entirely different from the one he'd used on Bevins, making it clear the colt wasn't the only thing he couldn't stay away from.

Phaedra put a hand on one slim hip, calling him out. 'Are we talking strictly about horses, Mr Basingstoke?'

'Are we?' He flashed her a wicked grin. 'That's for you to decide.'

He bent, running a hand down the horse's leg, pleased the horse stood still for him. 'He has good lines, that has never been in question. He's unruly but he's come quite a way in a fairly short period. I haven't seen a horse of this quality for some time. It's hard to pass up the treat.'

She looked away, a slight blush staining her cheeks. Ah, she *did* understand they weren't simply discussing the horse. Bram stood up from his examination of Warbourne's leg and brushed his hands on his breeches. He stepped forward, his voice low. 'What shall it be, Phaedra? I've signalled my availability and you've responded with your willingness.'

She looked a horseman's dream standing there with her long braid and tight breeches, her eyes more grey than blue today and wide with expectancy. She wanted him to kiss her no matter how much she might deny it. He might have if Bevins hadn't chosen that moment to return breathless holding the snaffle bit in one hand, the bridle and more gear in the other.

'Ah, impeccable timing, Bevins,' Bram said wryly, stepping away from Phaedra with a private smile that said this wasn't over.

'Rogers said you'd need a stronger bit on that beast,' Bevins explained, jingling the extra equipment, completely oblivious to the sensual tension simmering between Bram and Phaedra.

Bram felt Phaedra's eyes on him as if this were a supreme test. 'Rogers is an idiot if he thinks a strong bit is a good idea.' Bram reached for the snaffle without hesitation. 'The snaffle allows for direct reining, Bevins. It's better for younger horses. Don't let Rogers tell you differently.' He could feel Phaedra relax. He'd passed the test.

After three tries, they'd managed to successfully get Warbourne to take the bit while Bevins watched in slack-mouthed amazement from the gallery of the riding house.

Phaedra passed the reins over Warbourne's head and their eyes met across his back. Sheer, unadulterated delight radiated in the wide smile she tossed him in celebration. Her horse was bridled. Ahead of schedule. He knew the very thoughts running through her mind. Epsom loomed large and possible on the calendar. He knew, too, that he would not forget the look on her face right now, the pure joy of success shining in her eyes.

The next hour passed companionably as he and Phaedra worked with the horse, *together.* They took turns with the lunge line and leading the horse through a series of exercises until Warbourne was lathered. Bram was fairly well lathered too. Holding Warbourne was no mean feat. He marvelled that Phaedra could do it. But always the unanswered question hovered, potent, between them.

'Bevins, do you think you can take the colt back to the stable and clean him up?' Bram called, reeling in the lunge line. Phaedra protested but Bram held up a restraining hand. 'Warbourne needs to get used to other people caring for him. He's had you exclusively now, Lady Phaedra, for a few weeks. He's ready to experience another groom.' He turned to Bevins. 'Ask Tom to help you if you're worried.'

'Perhaps I should go with him,' Phaedra offered. He would not let her get away so easily.

'No, let him do this. We all had to start somewhere. We can't build his confidence if we don't give him any.' But Bram kept a careful eye on Bevins and Warbourne until they were out of range. It wouldn't do for him to be wrong now. He'd made headway with Phaedra *and* the colt today.

'Thank you for your assistance. I wouldn't have pushed him,' she said as Bevins disappeared from sight.

'It wouldn't have been a wrong choice, just a different one.'

Phaedra nodded. 'Bits and saddles aren't unfamiliar to Warbourne. He knows them, he's been down this path before. He doesn't need to be tamed as much as he needs to be trained. I am trying to balance the concepts. He's not a wild horse, but a high-spirited one and one that people have not worked with in the right way.' She shot a look at the discarded bit lying on the railing. 'Too many trainers would have opted for the stronger bit. Why didn't you?'

'My experience has shown me a stronger bit creates all nature of problems—steering difficulties later on if the horse learns to run through the bit, health problems like dry mouth.' Bram didn't let her get another word in. With Bevins gone, he could turn his attention to other issues. He was done with horses for the moment. He stopped her at the entrance with a gentle grip on her arm. 'We have unfinished business, Phaedra. I am waiting for your answer.'

I have signalled my availability and you've responded with your willingness. Phaedra could not pretend he meant anything else, not with those blue eyes lingering on her lips in the most suggestive of ways. But what to say? Should she take his invitation and satisfy her curiosity or should she say no, the answer she'd been raised to give?

He tipped her chin up, the pad of his thumb stroking her bottom lip, his voice a sensual murmur at her ear. 'I can show you pleasure beyond your wildest imaginings, Phaedra.'

He kissed her then, a long slow kiss that caressed her mouth and warmed her body. But it was his hands that nearly sent her over the edge. He raised her arms over her head and held them there, shackled in the grip of one strong hand against the wall, her body deliciously exposed to the long muscled length of him. His other hand was at her breast, kneading, arousing through the cloth of her shirt.

His body pressed lightly against hers and she revelled in the strength of him, the power and prowess of him, as he moved against her ever so provocatively. Her body clamoured for more, ached for it with an intensity that drove all other cares to the far reaches of her mind. She would have been his entirely in that moment, all good reason abandoned, if he had not released her.

'Do you believe me, Phaedra?' he whispered in husky tones.

Pleasure beyond her wildest imaginings. Phaedra nodded, her legs barely able to keep her upright. She was thankful for the wall at her back.

'Come to me when you're ready.' Bram stepped out into the stable yard, the evening dusk already swallowing him up. 'Come soon.'

Phaedra leaned into the wall, and expelled a deep breath. What had just happened? The question was hardly worth asking. She *knew* what had happened. She had just given him her answer without saying a word.

Chapter Nine

An affair with the head groom. Was that what she wanted? Phaedra leaned against the rails of the paddock, watching the horses nip and play. She couldn't tolerate going inside yet when there was a chance she'd run into *him*. She was no coward but facing Bram after their last encounter seemed the height of awkwardness. What did one say to a person who'd just propositioned them? *And* whom she'd rather implicitly accepted.

There was no pretending she wasn't interested. In many ways, Bram was the perfect antidote—handsome, willing and more than able to translate his promises into actions. Those actions would be irrevocable and they would not be without consequences. It wasn't the social consequence she was worried about. There would only be those if she got caught and she didn't plan to. It was the emotional.

Could she stay detached enough to let him go if she pursued the flirtation to its ultimate conclusion? It would be too easy to fall in love with Bram. There were lots of reasons to, reasons that surprisingly went beyond the physical.

She'd *liked* talking to him that night in the stables. He understood her. Unlike Giles, he had not merely ignored or glossed over her idea of racing Warbourne at Epsom and he'd seemed genuinely intrigued about the horse trailer others had laughingly called Phaedra's Folly. He was good with horses. She'd been suitably impressed when he'd chosen the snaffle bit the other day. Those reasons, coupled with the fact that he roused her with a single touch, a gentle stroke of his hand against her cheek, and challenged her in ways no one ever had with his honest addressing of passion, made him exciting. More than that, the combination made him irresistible.

Was it really so wrong? Convention was rankly against accepting such an offer but her curiosity was not. Phaedra simply had to decide what she wanted. Did she want a few stolen hours of pleasure from a man who would be moving on once Tom Anderson took back the reins of command?

The very idea was scandalous and delicious all at once. Phaedra shivered at the thought. If she let this opportunity slip away, where would she ever find a man like him again?

And yet she was a product of her breeding. All of her life, she'd been taught to reject an offer such as his. It was hard to thwart the teachings of childhood.

Not for the first time, Phaedra wished there was someone she could talk to. Usually, she'd take her concerns to Kate but Kate was gone now and she was on her own. That left Giles. Phaedra could hardly imagine discussing this with her brother. *'Giles, I'm considering taking a lover and he's the head groom.'* Even the words sounded wicked when she thought them in her head.

Giles would side with convention because he was a man of honour, but Phaedra was certain Kate would not. Kate had been no shy virgin when it came to men. She was missing her sister more than ever. What would Kate make of the handsome horse handler whose every kiss conjured up a penchant for sin? She knew what Aunt Wilhelmina would make of him. There'd be no sympathetic advice from that quarter.

Phaedra watched the horses nipping at one another, playing, flirting. It would be easier to be a horse. Phaedra wished she understood men as well as she understood horses.

Across the field, a slender figure came into view leading Makepeace, the even-tempered grey gelding from the general string. His leg must be better. The figure waved and Phaedra waved back. It was Alicia, Jamie's widow. An idea came to her. Maybe she *did* know someone who could help her. After all, Alicia had married her brother. Jamie had courted her; they'd fallen in love against the tempestuous backdrop of a war. Surely *she* knew something of men.

'Is this your idea of riding?' Phaedra teased good-naturedly as she strode towards Alicia. 'You're supposed to be on the horse.' Phaedra took the reins from the petite blonde. It had been something of a surprise to discover Jamie had married a woman who didn't ride. Phaedra had always imagined her brothers marrying avid equestrians like themselves. But neither Giles nor Jamie had been inclined that way. Instead they'd both chosen vicars' daughters.

'Did you have a good outing?' Phaedra asked, trying to make small talk before launching into her preferred topic of discussion. She didn't know Alicia very well and the family had not encouraged familiarity. Perhaps Alicia would think it odd that she'd suddenly sought her out now.

Alicia smiled a soft, happy smile that lit her face. 'I did. I returned some mending to Mr Everett and we shared a cup of tea. He's a kind man.' Her gaze darted away and her next words rushed out as if she'd said too much and was anxious to cover them up with explanations. 'I think Mr Everett understands how seldom a mother with a baby gets out. I enjoyed the chance to talk with another adult.'

But the light blush tingeing Alicia's cheeks suggested there was more to it than that. Phaedra tipped her head to peer at Alicia, sensing there was more left unsaid. 'Of course you did. It's perfectly understandable. It must get lonely in the Dower House.' Mr Everett, the estate manager, *was* a nice man. He'd lived at Castonbury his whole life and had taken over from his father. But Phaedra sensed the 'nice' she associated with Mr Everett was not the same sort of 'kind' Alicia perceived. It was almost as if she *liked* him in a manner that transcended an acquaintance. Or, Phaedra thought, she was imagining things simply because Bram had stirred up all nature of crazy sensations.

'I hear you have a new colt in the stables.' Alicia turned the conversation away from herself. 'And a new groom to help out Tom Anderson. I caught a glimpse of him when I came for Makepeace today. In fact, he was the one who recommended the gelding.'

Phaedra nodded. Alicia had given her the perfect conversational offering, but how to start? 'Mr Basingstoke has made himself quite useful. He's been exercising Jamie's horse, much to the relief of the stable boys.' Phaedra laughed a little here but Alicia gave her a vague smile, uncertain of the humour. Phaedra had hoped talking about Jamie would open up the conversation. It looked like she'd have to try harder.

'Merlin's a handful. Jamie was the only who could ride him. He wouldn't tolerate anyone, not even Edward or Giles. Did you ever see Jamie ride?'

Alicia shook her head, her pale blue eyes suddenly sad. 'Only at a distance.' She put a gloved hand on Phaedra's arm. 'I am sorry, my dear. You all have counted on me to bring you precious memories of Jamie and I have failed you miserably. We were together such a short time and our courtship was a wartime whirlwind. For better or for worse, we didn't know each other well in the sense that we didn't know each other's histories, our likes and dislikes. I could no more tell you his favourite colour than you could tell me mine.'

She had one of those expressive faces that showed every genuine feeling. There could be no doubt she felt her regret deeply.

'What made you fall in love with my brother?'

Alicia looked out over the fields, thinking, perhaps remembering. Phaedra hoped she hadn't conjured up too much sadness. Perhaps it was still too painful for her to talk of Jamie. 'We met at a dinner party,' Alicia said after a while. 'I think it was his laugh, his smile, the way it didn't stop at his mouth but went all the way to his eyes. He understood himself. There was a confidence about him because he didn't take himself too seriously. Duke's son or not, he understood he was a man like any other when it came right down to it.'

That sounded like her brother—confident and laughing. It was good to know her memories were intact, that she hadn't made up a person to fit her fading recollections.

'Around here, everyone has known everyone all their lives and their families' lives,' Phaedra ventured. 'We don't marry for smiles or laughter. We marry because we know each other's histories and place. There aren't a lot of secrets between a couple.'

'Like Giles and Lily?' Alicia said kindly.

'Yes, like Giles and Lily, although the match

wasn't planned and they certainly hadn't spent their lives falling in love with each other. I don't think Lily liked Giles very much at all until now. But they knew each other.'

'I think there must be a great comfort in that.' Alicia sighed. Was that wistfulness she heard?

'Or great boredom,' Phaedra said, thinking of Bram and how he didn't fit the conventional standard. She had no idea where he'd come from, what place he called home. Was that part of his novelty? The idea that he was new?

Alicia laughed. 'Boredom is underrated, Phaedra. Many a good woman has been led astray by the promise of something exciting and new.'

Like Aunt Claire's first marriage, Phaedra thought instantly. Aunt Claire had married away from Castonbury and that had been a disaster. She hadn't known her husband well at all. As a result, she had fallen victim to his good looks and smooth charm, a cautionary tale against falling in love with a stranger. Better to marry as Giles was doing and taking a mate who'd shared your life and your land.

'Jamie was exciting and new,' Phaedra argued. 'He would have taken care of you. There would have been no risk.'

'You're wrong. There has been tremendous risk.

He died, Phaedra, and now my life is in limbo. People doubt me, doubt that I am who I say I am. And truly, I don't know what will become of me or my son if I am not believed.' It was the first time Phaedra had ever heard Alicia break from her quiet calm. She was always so composed. Not even Giles's questioning had ruffled her when she'd first arrived.

Phaedra's heart went out to her. Whatever suspicion surrounded Alicia, it could not be doubted that she suffered. It was there in her blue eyes, that constant shadow of sadness or perhaps despair. Phaedra had not fully realised until that moment how precarious Alicia's situation was.

Since her arrival in the fall, Alicia had been part of the problem, part of the devastating tragedy that had haunted the Montagues: two sons dead, one of them the heir. And *her*, a woman the family had no knowledge of, Jamie's widow and mother of his son, who would become the future duke. All of them, herself included, had treated Alicia as if she was the calamity, a woman not to be trusted. Somehow Alicia's claims had made her the enemy.

But today, Phaedra began to see a new depth to the dangers and risks from Alicia's point of view. By her own admission, she'd married a man she hadn't known well. She'd known even less about his family and still she'd come. Alicia was brave, just as Kate was brave to sail off into the unknown. But Kate had Virgil by her side and once Alicia must have counted on having Jamie to help her navigate the new world facing her as his wife. Without Jamie, the world must have seemed bleak indeed.

Beside her, Alicia took a deep breath and regained her composure. 'I'm sure this isn't what you wanted to talk about,' she said.

Phaedra hesitated. 'What makes you think I wanted to talk about anything in particular? I saw you across the field, that's all.'

Alicia smiled. 'You saw me across the field and decided you'd suddenly start asking questions about how to attract a man's attention, is that it?' She gave a friendly laugh. 'Do you have a young man?'

'No,' Phaedra said hastily and firmly.

Alicia wasn't convinced. She said nothing for a moment, a finger pressed thoughtfully to her lips. Phaedra could practically see her thinking. 'It's not Mr Basingstoke, is it?' she asked, a hint of caution evident in her tone.

Phaedra's silence condemned her.

'He's a dangerous sort of man, I feel compelled to warn you,' Alicia offered quietly.

A cold knot formed in Phaedra's stomach. Had she been naive enough to think his attentions were exclusive? 'Has he made improper advances? If so, I shall dismiss him,' Phaedra said with admirable calm.

'No, it's nothing like that,' Alicia assured her. 'It's just that he's such a handsome man with the devil's own dose of charisma. It's obvious he's a complete rogue when it comes to women.' Alicia paused before adding, 'I've known men like him before. They're absolutely charming, they make your insides melt and they make you promises they don't intend to keep, only that's not so clear at the time.'

'I shall be sure he doesn't interfere with any of the maids,' Phaedra said stiffly, hoping her aloof demeanour would fool Alicia.

Alicia persisted. 'I don't mean to dash your hopes, but I would think twice about getting involved with Mr Basingstoke. Truly, my dear, what do you know of him? Do you know where he's from? Who his family is?'

Phaedra shrugged. 'It hardly matters, he's only here for a short time.'

Alicia smiled gently and took back the reins. 'It's best you remember that. I have to get back to young Crispin. I'll have a groom look after

Makepeace. Thank you for the walk, it was nice to have some company.'

There was more Phaedra wanted to say as they parted. Alicia seemed like a good person to whom bad things had happened. She wanted to invite the young woman to the house for dinner, wanted to offer to give her riding lessons, but all of that was out of the question. 'Alicia,' Phaedra called out as she moved off with the gelding. 'Thank you for your advice. I wish things could be different.'

Alicia nodded. 'I do too. Have a good evening.'

It would have been wonderful to be able to look upon Alicia as a sister. She would have been able to if Jamie had lived. He would have brought Alicia home with great fanfare. Aunt Wilhelmina would have planned a grand party. Instead Alicia had been tucked away as an embarrassment. What would Jamie think of the way the family was treating his wife?

Sometimes Phaedra wondered why Giles remained suspicious. Alicia was a decent human being, a good mother to her son. It was impossible to fathom why a thoughtful, lovely woman would be capable of such an enormous duplicity. To claim to be married to a future duke was an enormous lie to tell, one that could see her imprisoned or transported, perhaps even her child taken from her. Phaedra could not conceive of a reason someone would take such a risk.

Other times, Phaedra wondered how Alicia knew so much of the world. She'd told Giles she'd been raised as a vicar's daughter and that she'd found genteel employment as a lady's companion. Those were not worldly positions and yet Alicia had seemed quite worldly today about the nature of men, as if she had personal experience with less than honourable gentlemen on more than one occasion. *I've known men like him before. They're absolutely charming, they make your insides melt and they make you promises they don't intend to keep.*

The question was *how* did she know them? Surely Alicia didn't classify Jamie among their number, which suggested this roguish calibre of men were men she'd known before. Again Phaedra was back to how. How did a discreet lady's companion meet gentlemen of questionable repute and not only meet them but consort with them enough to know their true colours? It did make one wonder if Giles's suspicions were not completely misplaced.

Chapter Ten

Phaedra cantered Isolde across the fields, enjoying the rare warmth of an early-spring day. The heather was starting to show its purple colour and the grass was looking green instead of brown. Winter was fading at long last. But spring brought its own sense of urgency. April meant racing season opened in a month. In the south, it would open in a matter of weeks and she had yet to ride Warbourne. Until she could mount him and put him through his paces without fail, she couldn't begin to look for a jockey.

Tomorrow. She'd mount him tomorrow to celebrate the end of the first week of April. One week closer to Epsom and one week closer to Aunt Wilhelmina's party, the compromise to a Season. If she wouldn't go to London, she had to at least tolerate a party—a party with dancing. Ugh.

Giles had drawn the line at that and Phaedra knew it was the best she could hope for. But she wasn't looking forward to it. The dress-fitting this morning had delayed her time in the stables, hence this late-afternoon ride.

The lake came into view and Phaedra reined Isolde to a halt. A quick look about her confirmed she was alone. She grinned and slid off the mare's back. After all the pins and poking she'd endured for her party gown, she deserved a treat. She'd go for a quick swim. The water was bound to be cold, but it would be private. No one else would be mad enough to dare the chilly waters.

Phaedra made a quick picket for Isolde and headed towards the lake shore, pulling her shirt tails from her waistband as she went. At the lake's edge, she bent and pulled off her boots. That's when she noticed. She wasn't as alone as she'd thought on first glance. There was a horse picketed on the west edge of the lake, out of her initial view, a tall chestnut that looked remarkably like...Merlin.

Phaedra switched her gaze to the lake's grey surface but she knew what she'd find before she saw him. It wasn't as if there'd be a stranger out there. This was Castonbury land, after all.

There was someone else mad enough to brave

the lake. Bram was striking towards the west shore with long easy strokes. Was there anything he *wasn't* good at? He could ride, he could swim and he could kiss. Lord, how he could kiss! Every time she was with him there was something new and exciting to explore. He was the kind of man mothers warned their daughters about and he made no apologies for it.

Phaedra debated making a quiet exit. No good could come of being out here with him and one of them naked! Especially after his proposition in the riding house, a proposition she'd yet to officially answer.

Phaedra bent to pick up her boots and took a step backwards, hoping slow movements wouldn't catch his eye. But luck was in short supply. He caught sight of her and changed his direction. So much for making a quiet disappearance. If she was gone when he reached shore, he would know she'd run. There was nothing to do but stand her ground.

Phaedra crossed her arms and assumed a stance she'd seen Giles use when he wanted to promote his dominance. At least she'd noticed Bram before she'd taken off any significant piece of *her* clothing which was more than she could say for him. The angel on her shoulder hoped he'd have the decency to stay in water that covered him.

The devil on the other hoped he wouldn't. An illicit trill ran through her at the prospect of what might be revealed.

Bram reached the shallows and began to wade towards shore, the water receding to showcase his muscled chest and lean hip bones before he stopped, making Phaedra well aware that the downward angle of his musculature pointed the way to the unknown beneath the water.

'Coming for a swim?' His gaze landed on her bare feet where they squished in the mud.

'I was but you stole my lake.'

'It's still your lake. No one's stopping you. Come on in. I'd say the water was fine but it's not. It's absolutely frigid.' His blue eyes dared her to join him.

Water dripped from his dark hair and he looked like a veritable Adam in the garden, primal and handsome. For a moment her wilder side was tempted. But then she recalled other things that happened in the garden, other things like sin.

'It looks like you're not sure though,' Bram challenged good-naturedly. 'If you want to swim, you should. Really, Phaedra, what's the worst that can happen?'

'You tell me.'

Bram threw back his head and laughed. '*Worst*

is not one of the words ladies use to describe what happens with me.'

'Well, it might be one of the words Giles uses to describe you. If he knew half of what we've done, you'd be finished here.'

Bram shrugged. 'Then it hardly matters what we do now. The damage is apparently already accomplished.' He held out a hand. 'Come on in, Phaedra. You know you want to.' He cocked a dark eyebrow, looking irresistible. 'Unless…you're afraid?'

Phaedra fixed with him a thunderous glare, curiosity getting the better of her by a long shot. '*Those* are fighting words.' She stripped down to her undergarments—a modified chemise that came to her waist and custom-made smalls she wore beneath her breeches—and strode into the icy water. She was Phaedra Montague. She wasn't afraid of anything, certainly not of Bram Basingstoke's hot blue eyes, and she was going to prove it.

Lucifer's stones, she'd actually done it! Bram grinned in appreciation. Phaedra's adventurous spirit had not failed him. Phaedra splashed at him as she strode past, the movements of her lithe body reminding him that the thin garments she wore offered very little real protection from male eyes.

Once she was wet, there'd be no protection at all. She executed a shallow dive, striking out for deeper water. 'Race you to the island!'

Bram dove and followed. He was a strong swimmer but Phaedra had a head start and hadn't already spent herself swimming vigorous laps in the lake. The island was about two hundred yards out in centre of the lake and Bram pushed hard to catch her but Phaedra reached the shore a body length ahead.

'Remember, we have to swim back.' Bram started to pull himself out of the water, weighing the disadvantages of full emergence. Now that the excitement of the race was over, his own nakedness had not escaped him. Did he risk freezing in the lake and stay decently covered to play the gentleman or did he walk up on shore in all his glory and venture making a bad first impression? Admittedly, the cold water had affected his 'glory' somewhat. The devil in him wanted to stalk out of the water and see what Phaedra made of his altogether, even if it was slightly less than standard at the moment.

In the end, Phaedra decided for him. She faced him squarely on the beach, hands on hips, either not caring or else oblivious to the way her undergarments clung to her skin. 'Are you going to stay in the water all day? I wouldn't have you freeze for modesty's sake. It's not like I haven't seen a pizzle before.'

Bram laughed, his body rousing in spite of the cold. He loved a vibrant woman who was sure of herself, even if she shouldn't be, and Phaedra was as vibrant as they came.

'A horse and a man are two different things,' Bram warned with a wicked smile, coming closer. He fully intended to call her bluff. If she wanted him to stop, she'd have to ask after having made that bold statement.

'I know,' she shot back. 'I have brothers.'

'If you're sure?' Bram gained the shore, thankful to be out of the water. The island was quiet, unaffected by the wind that blew along the shoreline. Bram was thankful for the small bit of warmth the stillness afforded. 'You know what they say, "once revealed, never concealed."'

Phaedra gave a most unladylike snort. 'That sounds like one of Aunt Wilhelmina's sayings.' But she wasn't indifferent, Bram noted with satisfaction. For all her vaunted experience with stallions, her eyes had a hard time focusing elsewhere in spite of her valiant effort.

This was definitely one of her more endearing qualities—supposed worldliness mixed with untried curiosity. He'd not been wrong about her in Buxton. She was exciting.

Her hair hung in a thick wet plait over one shoulder, her undergarments clung, outlining the delectable fullness of her breasts and the slim curve of her hip. She was every man's dripping-wet fantasy, which was rapidly being confirmed by signs of life in his nether regions. Bram could set aside concerns of making a bad first impression and worry instead about the very opposite.

She'd not mentioned his proposition. He could only assume she'd stumbled on him by accident. That being the case, he hoped they wouldn't stay long. There was no reason to linger on the island considering the weather and the state of their garments or lack of them. Unless, came the thought, she'd sought him out deliberately. Perhaps she'd decided on her answer.

'Too bad there isn't a fire waiting for us,' Bram joked, not nearly as at ease with the situation as he'd thought he'd be. He was used to women watching his body, women seeing him naked, seeing him in various states of arousal, but Phaedra's untutored gaze was proving to be far more arousing than the jaded eyes of London's fast widows and wives.

'There is, if you want to make one.' Phaedra

busied herself pushing aside a clump of foliage, revealing an old wooden chest with iron bindings. She lifted the lid with a grunt. 'In the summers, we'd spend the day out here, my brothers, my sister and me. We've never really outgrown keeping a few supplies out here.' She tossed him an old quilt and took one for herself. 'There's dry wood and flint in the trunk too.'

Bram took the quilt and wrapped it about his waist. 'You're a regular Robinson Crusoe.'

'It's hard not to be when you have four brothers who were mad for all the adventure stories.' Phaedra sobered and corrected herself. 'Had. I mean, *had* four brothers. Now I guess I just have two.'

Bram set to work laying a small fire. 'You have a good family, one that loves one another. You're lucky.' He struck the flint, watching the sparks ignite. 'I don't know about Aunt Wilhelmina, of course, but your brother seems devoted.' Phaedra might not recognise how fortunate she was on that account. He'd seen too many young women compelled to marry simply because their family demanded it or were forced to it, exiled out of the family home because the males hadn't provided for them. His own sister had been a victim of the former. He doubted Giles would ever compel Phaedra to unwillingly take a husband.

'Aunt Wilhelmina means well but her ideas about life are a bit limiting and archaic.' Phaedra tugged her quilt about her, covering up her curves. 'She's been with us since my mother died. She's really the only mother I've known, for whatever that's been worth. Raising us was a labour of duty to her, not necessarily a labour of love.' Phaedra gave a telltale shrug beneath the quilt and stared into the little fire. 'I was only four when she came to live with us. I don't remember my mother.'

It bothered her, Bram thought, settling beside the fire. She'd given one of those shrugs of hers meant to communicate complacency when it implied the opposite. She cared very much that she didn't remember her mother.

'What happened?' Bram probed gently, his own curiosity piqued.

'When I was younger, I was told it was a fever. But later, Kate hinted it might have been a miscarriage.'

'Childbed fever, perhaps.'

Phaedra gave him a soft smile. 'Perhaps. All I remember now are nuances—a smell, a gesture, a tone, just shadows really. There are portraits, of course, but those are someone else's memories imposed on mine. She was beautiful and kind and father doted on her.'

'Ah, it was a love match, then?' That would be something rare indeed in the high echelons of dukes. Dukes seldom had that luxury.

Phaedra shook her head. 'Not love but something very close to it. My father is like any other man of his rank. He has his bastards. But he and mother dealt well together and he was affectionate.' Hope and disappointment warred in that comment. Hope that something more than an arranged marriage was possible and disappointment that the one marriage she knew of had fallen short of that.

'We don't talk about her very much any more.' Phaedra gave him a long considering look, her head tilted to one side. 'I think you're the first person I've ever told. I wonder what that means? I feel like I've packed her up and put her away somewhere but now I can't remember where that is.'

Phaedra began undoing the long braid. It was an entirely feminine gesture. The quilt slipped from one shoulder as she raised an arm and she shivered.

'Here, let me do that for you,' Bram offered so she could stay warm. 'Turn sideways a little.' He unravelled the long strands and drew his fingers gently through them in a combing motion. The fire was growing hot now and the little beach was actually comfortable. They could stay awhile longer.

'What about your family?' Phaedra asked, her train of thought still running along that same line. It wasn't his favourite topic.

'I have a sister and a brother, both older.' If he'd been born second, there'd have been no need for a third child. But his father had been adamant he have his spare. Bram's sister had not been enough.

'And your parents?' Phaedra prompted.

'Both still alive. Your hair is much darker wet. It looks like wild honey.' He tried to redirect the discussion. His family was not worth the conversation. But Phaedra would not be deterred.

'Do you see them often?'

'No, my father is something of a…well, suffice it to say that we don't get along.' That was putting it mildly. He'd never quite lived up to his father's expectations. It had become something of a game to see just how disappointing he could be before his father cut him off entirely. This last escapade which had landed him in Derbyshire had nearly done it.

'You shouldn't speak of your father like that,' Phaedra said, clearly shocked he'd be so irreverent.

'Why not if it's the truth?' Bram's answer was harsher than he intended. 'You don't know him,'

Bram amended. His father had revered his older brother to the exclusion of him and his sister. Eloise had been brought up to think of herself as a nuisance to the family, an expensive flower to decorate another's garden. She'd married the first decent match to come along to appease their father and get out.

'I didn't exactly fit into my father's plans for me.' He didn't dare say anything else for fear of giving himself away.

'What was that?' Of course she'd want to know. But Bram had other things on his mind than his father. He was sitting beside a fire on a deserted island, never mind it was in the middle of an estate, with a mostly naked woman of delectable proportions. It was amazing they were still just talking.

Bram leaned in close to Phaedra's ear, breathing in the scent of her. She smelled of water and wind and ever-present apples. 'The church,' he ventured. Perhaps she would think his family were gentleman farmers. It wasn't out of the realm of possibility his father had 'aimed high' for his son. He feathered a breath past her ear, his hands kneading her shoulders. 'That's why I know so much about sin.'

'I bet you do.' She gave a soft laugh and leaned against him, her head lolling comfortably on his shoulder. The fire and the intimacy of their situation were starting to work their magic. She was feeling safe and comfortable.

'I wish we could stay here for ever,' Phaedra confessed drowsily.

Bram reached with one arm and threw the last of the kindling on the fire. They would have to go soon. 'Aside from the swim back, why would you want to stay here? We are lacking in amenities.'

Phaedra stretched against him. 'Aunt Wilhelmina is planning a party for me in lieu of me going to London for a Season.' Apparently that issue had been resolved with a compromise.

'Don't you like parties? Pretty dresses?' Bram encouraged. He'd yet to meet a woman who wasn't swayed by the promise of a new gown.

Phaedra laughed and turned to face him, a little smile flitting on her lips as they sat cross-legged. 'Do you want to know a secret?' she said in low tones. 'I can't dance.'

'You can't?' He had a hard time believing it. Phaedra was athletic. She could swim, she could ride. How was it that she couldn't dance? He loved dancing; the feel of his hand at a woman's back was one of Society's permissible pleasures.

'It's not for a lack of trying. Aunt Wilhelmina hired countless dancing instructors for Kate and me but apparently the males in the family got that talent.'

'Maybe you simply haven't found the right partner?'

'Maybe I simply can't do it,' Phaedra replied honestly.

'Maybe you haven't had the right instructor,' Bram argued. He'd not met Aunt Wilhelmina but from Phaedra's description, he could imagine the sort of dance master she'd hire. One of those prim and prudish gentlemen in a cheap black suit, who thought dancing was the stiff performance of figures and patterns. Dancing was anything but that. It was passion and life, energy and motion, an exquisite form of human expression.

'Stand up,' Bram urged, rising and brushing at the sandy dirt on his quilt. He shifted his quilt to his waist to free his arms.

'What are you doing?' Phaedra rose, uncertain, clutching her quilt about her.

'Not me, *we. We* are dancing.' He took her hand and placed it on his shoulder.

'Oh, no, *we* are not doing this.' Her quilt slipped to the ground and Bram moved her into his frame, his hand at her back, feeling her skin through the damp silk. His other hand closed over hers and he moved them into position. 'Ready? One, two, three, one, two, three.' He guided them into motion, dipping and swaying as he counted. 'You're doing fabulously,' he said, slowly taking them through a turn on the other side of the dying fire. 'Don't look down. Look up, at my eyes.' He held her firmly against him as they moved, their proximity much closer than a ballroom would allow, her hips flush against his, their bodies keeping no secrets.

She was liquid in his arms, her pulse starting to race at her throat, her pupils dark with desire. Her body knew what this was even if her mind didn't. Dancing was sex. Public sex, the kind of intercourse Society permitted on the dance floor.

Bram brought them to a halt, brushing her lips in a slow kiss, desire heating him as thoroughly as the fire. 'I want nothing more than to lay you down right here on the quilts.' His voice was raw with want, his body driven past the point of control.

'Alicia warned me about men like you. You make promises you can't keep,' Phaedra protested in a hoarse whisper, but her breath was coming fast and hard, evidence that she'd been as affected by their dance as he had, that desire was riding her as well. He was not alone in this.

Bram nipped hard at her ear, his hands moving to take her breasts in his palms, his thumbs

stroking the nipples erect. 'She's vastly underesti-
mated me. I never make promises about pleasure
I can't keep.'

Phaedra's hands were at his waist, fumbling with
the blanket, her voice a mixture of sultry seduction and trembling need and in her eyes there was
wildness. 'Then do it, Bram. Make me a promise.'

He had to make himself some promises as well,
starting with a promise not to take this too far.
There was pleasure they could have and then
there was the pleasure they couldn't. Bram lowered her down, spreading his quilt on the ground
for a makeshift mattress, conscious only of the
moment, her mouth on his, her hands in his hair
and the pleasure that would follow.

Chapter Eleven

She was being reckless. She'd been reckless the moment she'd stepped into the water. She should have stopped long before this. She should have stopped before they'd built a fire. Even before that. She should have stopped before he'd stepped out of the lake, glistening and naked, a woman's most carnal fantasy. The point was, there'd been several opportunities to stop and she'd heedlessly ploughed past them, her curiosity getting the better of her by far.

Now her hands were tugging his quilt loose, her curiosity a step closer to being satisfied. He'd pegged her aright the other day. She'd watched too many stallions cover mares not to wonder about her own sexuality. Why not solve that wonder with a man like Bram who knew what he was about?

The quilt slipped from his hips and he knelt

down on the blanket, gesturing for her to join him. 'It's time for those undergarments to come off, Phaedra. Wherever did you find such things?' His eyes roved her body as she sat beside him.

'I made them. Actually, my maid, Henny, and I did them.' Suddenly self-conscious, Phaedra fingered the lace trim at the hem of the chemise. 'I needed something I could wear under breeches and shirts. The usual chemise was too long. I took a pair of Edward's old smalls, cut them down and used them for a pattern and we bought more suitable fabric. It was Henny's idea to trim them.' She was rambling. She couldn't help it. Bram was tracing the tiny lace on the smalls with his index finger, sending a delicious shot of heat to her belly.

'Silk is more suitable for stable work or for the wearer?' Bram laughed and stretched out beside her, propping himself on an elbow. He resumed his intimate tracing, knowing full well what he was doing to her. 'I will like thinking of you roaming the stables in your breeches and silk smalls.' His voice was husky, his eyes dark with desire.

'You most certainly will not!' Phaedra protested in embarrassed alarm.

Bram laughed down at her softly. 'I most certainly will and while I am thinking of that, you can be thinking of this.'

His hand slipped beneath the undergarment. Phaedra gasped against the thrill and the shock of his hand against her most private parts. He stroked her and all shock was forgotten in the wake of the sensations his touch roused. Phaedra arched up against his hand, her body seeking more. As wondrous as they were, the sensations were incomplete.

He sought her core with a finger and she shut her eyes against the wave of pleasure sweeping over her like a tide, crashing and building against the shores of her sensibilities until she could not bear the exquisite pain of near-fulfilment any longer. She arched against his hand one final time, Bram's voice soft at her ear at the crucial moment. 'Open your eyes, Phaedra. Let me see your pleasure.'

She managed to oblige as the tide took her, gathering her up in a whirlpool before she crashed, her eyes locked with Bram's, his blue gaze her only anchor in the sea of passion. She was breathing hard when she had enough sense to take stock of such things. Bram's hand was in her hair, pushing it out of her face.

'No wonder Aunt Wilhelmina says it's a sin.' She sighed. 'No one would get anything done if they thought they could do that all day. Kate hinted at it, but...' Phaedra shook her head. This was what Kate had tried to tell her. No wonder words had failed her usually erudite sister. Words were failing her now.

'Amen.' Bram smiled.

Phaedra glanced down the length of his body. His member jutted hard and thick against his stomach. Inspiration struck. 'Can I do that for you?' She reached down to take him in her hand.

Bram sucked in his breath. She'd take that as a 'yes.' Phaedra slid her hand the length of him in exploration, noting the heat, the long ridge, the soft tip. She paused in wonderment at the new sensations.

'Don't stop, don't stop now,' Bram said through gritted teeth, obviously frustrated by her distraction. Each word came out with great effort, his mind and body engaged elsewhere. Then came the wonderful moment when she felt him tense beneath her hand, his body gathering itself right before he released.

A smug smile split her face. She'd done this to him, the master of pleasure.

'You seem mighty pleased with yourself.' Bram chuckled.

'As do you.' Phaedra nestled closer, her head on his chest, her hand tracing light patterns on his torso. 'So,' she began, wondering if her next words would spoil the mood or enhance it. 'If you don't want to talk about your family, perhaps you'll tell me about yourself. Where do you come from, how is it that you know horses so well?'

'You're not going to give up, are you, minx?' Bram sighed reluctantly into her hair. She could feel his hesitation in the altered rhythm of his breathing.

'It's only fair,' she said gently. 'You know a lot about me but I know hardly anything about you.' *Except that you give pleasure beyond compare.* Maybe that was enough to know. Maybe she didn't need to know any more. It would make letting him go easier when the time came. 'Where did you work before you came to Castonbury? Surely that can't be an enormous secret. I'm starting to think you have something to hide.'

'Most women like a little mystery in a man,' Bram teased, but Phaedra would not be dissuaded. She sat up and faced him.

'I'm not most women,' she said baldly. 'You have nothing to hide from me, nothing to be ashamed of.'

A shadow passed across his eyes ever so briefly Phaedra thought she might have imagined it. 'All right, I used to work at Nannerings, it's a riding school in London. My students were young dandies who fancied themselves candidates of the *haute école* and young ladies who thought it romantic to learn to ride there.'

'I'm sure you had something to do with the last,' Phaedra said wryly. Every young lady in London would want to ride if he was their instructor.

'I was heavily sought after,' Bram admitted obliquely, but it told Phaedra enough. He was more than a groom, more than a stable hand with good looks and rakish charm. She knew how Society worked. Nannerings would have been a meeting place where the *ton* would encounter those less *tonnish*, perhaps the sons of gentry who'd come to make their fortunes in the big city.

There would have been invitations, a chance to briefly elevate one's social standing, especially if one was as charming as Bram. Hostesses would find him quite the handsome novelty to parade around their musicales and soirées. It explained why he danced so well even in a quilt and several other things about him that didn't fit, like his expensive boots, why he'd not been afraid to take a swing at Sir Nathan Samuelson, why he'd not been afraid to pursue a duke's daughter. He didn't see himself as their inferior. He saw himself as a man who might claim to be their equal in some ways.

'You're staring,' Bram broke in.

'I'm *thinking*,' Phaedra corrected. 'It all makes sense now.'

'What does?' His eyes began to crinkle into the lines of smile.

'You do.' She could be as oblique as him. Let him be tortured by his own device for a bit.

Bram shook his head, grinning. 'Minx. I won't even ask because you're not going to tell me.'

'Why tell you?' Phaedra tossed her hair over one shoulder. 'You already know who you are.' A man between, neither highborn nor low. She envied him that limbo. It enabled him to craft his own life.

'I'm the man whose going to have to swim back to shore.' Bram groaned. The fire had effectively died. It was their cue to end the interlude. 'I don't suppose you have a row boat stashed on the island?'

'What would you do if I said yes?' Phaedra rose, gripping her blanket tight about her. There *was* a boat on the other side if the weather and rot hadn't gotten to it.

'Why, honey, I'd love you for ever.' He was only joking, of course, and they both knew it. But still, the sentiment was nice. To be loved by a man like Bram Basingstoke would be a worthy prize indeed. But a difficult one to claim.

It would be folly to speak out loud the question

looming in her mind. They had done a most intimate act together. Did it mean anything to him or was she just another of his Nannerings students? Was this nothing more to him than an exercise in physical release, not all that different than his cold water swim?

For her, it was impossible to walk away from this encounter, or swim away as the case may be, and not be honest about the fact that he was laying siege to her finer feelings whether he wanted to or not. Those were questions she didn't have the courage to ask, not now, for fear that she was not ready for the answers.

The boat was where it was supposed to be and Bram rowed them back to shore wrapped in a quilt. Phaedra hoped there was no one on shore to mark their progress—two quilt-clad refugees from the island in an old wooden row boat.

'You know,' Bram said, pulling the boat up to the shore. 'We'll have to take everything back out there.'

'When the weather's warmer. Don't forget, we'll have to swim back,' Phaedra countered coolly, trying to pretend she wasn't already thinking of the next time they could be together.

'Only if you want to wait that long.' Bram gave her a naughty wink. The dratted man had read her mind yet again. If today had decided anything, it was that she was going to take Bram's offer. How could she not when it had only heightened her desire. There was more pleasure to be had and she would have it with him.

Phaedra gathered up her clothes and began to dress, watching Bram saunter over to his pile on the west side. Even at a distance, she enjoyed watching him bend and flex his way into his breeches. But then suddenly the bending and flexing stopped.

Bram dove into the tall reeds, parting them like Moses, beating at them as if he were flushing out prey. Something, no, *someone*, emerged and ran, fleeing to a horse tethered in the distance with Bram giving naked chase after him. Whoever it was had enough lead on Bram to get away with a vault into the saddle and a vicious kick. The intruder had fled.

Phaedra covered the distance to Bram at a run. 'Are you all right? What happened?'

Residual anger rolled off Bram in sheets while he dressed. 'He was here while we were out on the island. In short, the stranger saw us,' Bram said grimly, squatting once more. His hand traced a heavy boot print in the sticky mud, perfect for holding an impression. 'I suspect our visitor was waiting for our return.'

Phaedra shaded her eyes and looked out to the is-land, a clearly visible landmark in the not so far-off distance. It would not have been difficult to see them if one really looked. This was bad news indeed. If the stranger went to Giles with what he'd seen, it would be devastating. 'Did you get a look at him at all?'

Bram shook his head. 'The horse was nondescript, brown with a black mane.' A bay, then. There were countless bays in Derbyshire. That was of no help.

'Hair colour?' Phaedra quizzed. It would be a long shot. Most riders would be wearing a hat.

'Maybe red? I wasn't paying attention.'

Phaedra froze.

'You think you know who it was,' Bram said grimly.

'Hugh Webster.' Phaedra sighed. The only red-head she knew of was Captain Hugh Webster, the very worst person to be seen by, in her estimation. 'He's been paying visits to Alicia.' If he went to Giles with this… The thought didn't bear completing.

Bram read her mind. 'I think he'll come to us with an offer of blackmail first once he regroups. It gets him nothing if he tells Giles except a duel and that can hardly be what he wants. If he comes to us, he might think he'll make some money.'

'I have nothing of value.' Phaedra shrugged.

'You have Warbourne,' Bram said succinctly,

'and you have yourself.' Then he paused, debating what to say next.

A cold pit was growing in Phaedra's stomach. She wouldn't give up Warbourne. She'd rather have the whole world know she'd been alone with Bram than give up the colt. 'Go ahead, say it.' If there was worse, she wanted to know.

'This piece of information might gain him more if he sold it to someone else instead of coming back to us. Who is he friends with?'

Phaedra swallowed hard, the bigger risk becoming self-evident. 'Sir Nathan Samuelson. Webster was with him in Buxton, if you recall.'

'I don't, I was busy elsewhere, punching his friend.' Bram offered her a mischievous grin that made current circumstances seem less serious. 'Perhaps the best option is to sit tight. We'll see what he does and not worry about it until then. There's no sense jousting with ghosts.'

'I think you mean windmills.' Phaedra smiled in spite of her misgivings.

Bram grinned. 'Well, of course not windmills. They would hurt. Those blades are fairly sharp, you know.'

Sir Nathan Samuelson was tired of being the Montagues' doormat to rejection. It was about time the tides turned in his favour and it seemed they had. The promise of a juicy titbit of news from Webster was welcome indeed. He needed a wife, a rich one, and fast. He poured a drink for himself and for Captain Webster. Webster sprawled in a chair near the fire.

'That Basingstoke has overstepped himself this time.' Webster took the glass and gulped a healthy swallow.

'Really? Do tell,' Nathan replied. 'There's a man who needs to come down a notch or two in the world. He doesn't understand his place. He's a groom, a horse handler. *I* am a peer of the realm and you're a captain. We're both far above him in station.'

Sir Nathan loved nothing so much as knowing his place in the world was loftier than someone else's. However, status only meant something if everyone agreed to the rules. He didn't care much for equality. It was a value he had little use for. What was the point of it? If everyone had status, then no one had status. Equality ruined everything.

'For starters, are you sure he's just a groom?' Webster shifted his position in the chair and sipped from his glass. 'Something doesn't strike me right about that. What do you know about him?'

Sir Nathan shrugged. 'He was in Buxton at the horse auction along with everyone else. But he's not from around here. That's not a Derbyshire accent he's carrying.'

Webster shook his head. 'How many grooms do you know with such high-class tones?'

Sir Nathan warmed to the idea. Not only would it be revenge against the Montagues but it would satisfy his personal need to bring Basingstoke down a peg. 'Do you think we have an impostor in our midst?' Webster could always ferret out a fraud. It was one of the traits Sir Nathan admired about him.

'Couldn't hurt to make an enquiry or two,' Webster mused. 'We'll rough him up regardless. But it would be nice if we knew who we were beating up.'

Sir Nathan gave a harsh laugh. 'Damn, but you're a cold fellow, Hugh.'

Webster raised his glass in response.

Sir Nathan took a hearty swallow of brandy, one of the few pleasures he could still afford. If he didn't resolve his finances quickly, his French brandy drinking days would soon be over. He broached the second item he wanted to discuss with Webster.

'I've been thinking I have picked the wrong

Montague in the past.' Sir Nathan clasped his hands over his beefy stomach where it was starting to strain against his waistcoat. Too much ale, his housekeeper told him, but the welcoming ladies at Mrs Taylor's Gentlemen's Parlour in Buxton assured him they preferred a heartily built man.

They both knew Sir Nathan had tried unsuccessfully to interest Lady Claire, Rothermere's young half-sister, in a proposal last autumn. She'd gone as far as inviting him to dinner and he'd invited her to the assembly at Buxton, but ultimately, she'd preferred the company of Rothermere's French chef. Then there'd been the debacle with the duke's shrewish daughter Katherine. That chit had had no excuse to refuse him. She was ruined and everyone knew it. She'd been lucky to receive his attentions. But she, too, had snubbed him, opting to marry a black man. An ex-slave at that! Her rejection still stung particularly.

'You can't mean to marry Giles.' Webster laughed at his crude joke, his eyes gleaming with evil excitement. 'And you know Alicia is mine.'

'Yes, you've made that clear.' Nathan dismissed the notion hastily. 'I'm not interested in her anyway, a widow with a brat clinging to her. She's not my taste, too delicate by far. She'd probably break after a good ploughing. I don't know what you see in her.' Webster had visited her twice in as many days this week.

Webster smiled faintly. 'The keys to the kingdom, my friend.'

'Unrelinquished keys, don't forget. Giles won't go easily. He means to be the duke, not spend his life working for that little tyke of hers,' Nathan scolded. Webster was playing a deep game there, gambling on marrying into the ducal family through Alicia's claim, a claim Giles Montague had not officially acknowledged. Nathan preferred a more direct game himself.

'That leaves Phaedra, you old devil,' Webster said with a grin.

'Phaedra. She's my kind of game,' Sir Nathan confirmed, rubbing his hands together with glee. 'Giles would hate it.'

'He wouldn't be the only one. So would Basingstoke.' Webster hung his bit of news out there like a carrot. So this was what he'd come to share. Well, it was about time. They'd talked around the juicy titbit now for the better part of a half-hour.

'All right, I'll bite. Tell me why Basingstoke would care who she marries? He'll be gone by summer.' Sir Nathan stretched out his legs on the fender of the fireplace ready for a naughty story.

'Basingstoke's hot for her.'

'Well, that's a given. A saucier derriere in breeches I have yet to see. Makes the rest of her tolerable.' Phaedra was all spit and fire. Sir Nathan shifted in his chair to dislodge the growing bulge in his trousers. He was already imagining the games he could play with her, ropes and whip at the ready.

'Listen.' Webster set aside his glass and leaned forward, hands on his thighs. 'She and Basingstoke went swimming today, out to that little island, you know the one. I caught sight of their horses on my way home from Alicia's.' Hugh Webster winked. 'They left their clothes on the shore.'

Hot images of Phaedra Montague rose in Sir Nathan's mind, along with jealousy. How dare that scrapper of a groom take such liberties…how dare *she*? But he knew how she dared. She was as hot-blooded as they came, she probably couldn't help herself.

'Better yet,' Webster was saying, 'there was smoke coming from the island. They stayed long enough to build a fire.'

He didn't need to explain the implications. If they'd stayed long enough to build a fire, they'd stayed long enough to engage in other activities too. Nathan's mind was running rife with what those activities might be. Marrying Phaedra would provide a perfect way to strike back at Basingstoke for the public humiliation he'd meted out in Buxton and to get back at the Montagues and their high-handed rejections of his very decent offers of marriage. At the least, maybe he could use this to steal her colt from her, perfect retribution for the humiliation of outbidding him in Buxton.

There was still the issue of acceptance. He had to ensure Phaedra took his offer. The invitation for the ball at Castonbury that had arrived in the afternoon would be an ideal opportunity to make his intentions known.

'It looks like we have the perfect *ménage-à-trois*: revenge, blackmail and a wife in the bargain.' Sir Nathan rose. 'Let's go down to the village and celebrate. Must celebrate while we can, you and I won't be bachelors for ever.'

Chapter Twelve

She was going to have illicit sex with Bram Basingstoke. Phaedra climbed the steps to Bram's rooms over the stable, humming a little tune under her breath. If today's events had proven anything to her it was that she could not wait for ever. The threat of discovery had not deterred her. In fact, it had heightened her need to act. Exposure meant Bram would leave, either under his own free will or be forced to it by Giles's sense of honour and Aunt Wilhelmina's attempts to hush up the incident.

She might have come anyway, Phaedra reasoned. The lake had been too much temptation and she'd wanted to even before then. The moment he'd made his proposition, she'd thought of nothing else. Phaedra smiled to herself. Bram had probably known she'd accept. He just didn't know when. That part would be her surprise.

Light peeped out from under Bram's door at the top of the stairs. She'd thought of this moment all through dinner, letting talk of Aunt Wilhelmina's party roll over her without effect. Let them talk about marrying her off. Tonight she didn't care. Tonight she'd have her fun.

Phaedra smoothed her skirts one last time. She'd dressed carefully too, selecting a simple evening gown of blue sarcenet that would easily come off. She raised her hand to knock.

'Come.'

She pushed open the door and stepped inside, shutting it firmly behind her. Bram sat at a small table acting as a makeshift desk, dressed in breeches and a shirt open at the neck. He was writing, his tanned forearms exposed beneath his rolled sleeves. It was a sexy scene and it held Phaedra's attention. Bram Basingstoke was literate.

She should have guessed sooner. He'd made that joke about windmills at the lake but she'd been too caught up in the issue of discovery to take note of what it might signify.

He looked up, his surprise genuine. 'Phaedra, what are you doing here?'

She smiled, pleased she'd caught him off guard for once. All too often it was the other way around. Phaedra put a hand to the loosely arranged curls atop her head in the French style, pulled a pin and let her hair fall. 'I have come to accept your invitation to sin.' Seconds later she was treated to the rare sight of Bram Basingstoke rendered speechless.

His mouth went dry, his body went hard at the sight of those wild honey tresses cascading over Phaedra's shoulders like a waterfall in motion. Was there anything so lovely as Phaedra Montague offering to be his? God knew he wanted her, consequences be damned. After the lake today, he'd not thought she'd come. He should have known better. He could see now he'd misjudged her. Nothing would deter Phaedra if she wanted something.

He rose and went to her, letting a slow smile spread across his face. 'I'm glad.' He took her mouth in a lingering kiss, tasting the sweet remnants of wine, savouring what it meant: she'd come to him straight away. She had not dithered and worried over her decision. She'd known what she wanted without hesitation. He liked a lover who seized what she wanted.

'Why tonight, Phaedra?' he whispered, moving

his attentions to the curved shell of her ear. She might not have hesitated but he didn't want her coming as a reaction to something else. He didn't want her driven here because of a quarrel with Giles, or pressure from Aunt Willy, as he liked to think of the aunt he had yet to meet and probably never would. 'It's not because of today, is it?' Bram feathered a breath past her ear.

'Of course it is.' Phaedra's own breath hitched in response. 'How could you tease me with such pleasure and think I wouldn't want to claim all of it?'

Bram laughed. Good. That was the only reason he wanted her in his arms, the pursuit of pleasure. Her arms were around his neck, her body pressed to his as if to demonstrate her point. He kissed her again, his hands buried in her hair, his nose taking in the apple-cinnamon scent of her, his arousal growing.

He pushed at the delicate puffed sleeves of her gown, moving them down over her shoulders. 'You chose well,' he murmured against her neck, feeling the excited race of her pulse beneath his lips. The bodice gave easily and it was the matter of two well-placed gyrations from Phaedra's hips and the gown fell to her feet.

The thin cambric of the petticoat with its white-on-white embroidery was an aphrodisiac in itself.

'You're a veritable angel.' Bram could hear the huskiness in his own voice. The lamplight teased, bathing the fabric in transparency. He could see the tantalising outline of pink nipples beneath the square-cut bodice of the undergarment, the dark shadow of wild honey curls between her thighs beneath the thin skirt.

He spun her around in his arms, dancing with her like they had danced on the beach until they reached the cot. He laid her back on the narrow bed. 'Maybe not an angel, maybe Sleeping Beauty.' He smiled down at her with her hair spilling across his pillow.

She laughed up at him and scolded, 'There will be no sleeping tonight.'

Bram stepped back from the bed, his eyes never leaving hers. 'Watch me, Phaedra.' He stripped for her then, pulling his shirt over his head and tossing it to the room's one chair. He pulled off his boots, noticing her gaze travel the length of his thighs. He revelled in her perusal. His Phaedra was bold.

He rested his hands at the waistband of his breeches. 'Are you sure?' He had to ask one last time, prodded to it by his rusty conscience. He hoped she was.

She grinned. 'I've seen it before.'

'But you'll be meeting him in truth tonight,'

Bram said gently. He wanted her to understand to-night would be different than the encounter at the lake. That had been spontaneous and unplanned. This would be deliberate and the results would be for ever. They'd been playing at the lake.

She reached for him, pulling him down to her. Her eyes danced with mischief but she was serious. She knew exactly what she was doing. 'I know, Bram. I want you.' She let him go.

The words were a heady ambrosia. Bram felt his need ratchet up another level. He slipped off his breeches and knew a moment's pleasure as Phaedra's eyes roamed his body as they had at the lake.

'I didn't know a man could be so...so...beautiful,' Phaedra said appreciatively, looking her fill before he slid onto the cot beside her. She ran a hand down the expanse of his chest, coming to rest on his soft tip. She rubbed her thumb across it. She reached lower and squeezed lightly. Bram sucked in his breath. Untutored or not, Phaedra instinctively knew how to touch a man. 'You like that,' Phaedra said.

Bram decided to reassert his authority. If she kept this up, they wouldn't get much further and he'd be spent. 'It's the equivalent of what I can do to you.' To demonstrate, he took her breast in one hand and stroked the rosy tip beneath the fabric until it pebbled beneath his thumb. Phaedra's breath came on a sharp intake, signaling her pleasure.

'Bram?' Her voice was shaky.

'Hmm?'

'It's time for this petticoat to go.'

He couldn't agree more.

At last they were naked, together, skin against skin, and Bram revelled in it. He took her breasts in his mouth by turn, sucking and nipping, Phaedra arching against him with a moan, her own pleasure mounting. He moved his worship lower, blowing softly into her navel, holding her firmly by the hips as she pressed against him. Then he was at the apex of her thighs, the scent of her indicating her readiness.

Bram kissed her damp curls, foreshadowing what was to come. Phaedra was not shy, she opened for him, and he took her gently with his mouth, his tongue bringing her to the brink. Her hands fisted in his hair, her body a riot of sensations as she shattered beneath him, her breath coming hard and fast in the aftermath. She was ready for him, ready for more. His body was not inclined to wait any longer. The exquisite agony of foreplay had heightened his senses beyond all logic.

Bram moved over her, covering her with his length, his dark hair falling forward in his face, giving him the look of a Celtic warrior of old, wild and primal and possessive. Oh, how she wanted to be possessed! Her body was primed for it, driven to matchless lengths of pleasure by all that had gone before. He probed for her entrance as he settled between her thighs. Her legs bent, her hips lifted towards him invitingly, her body intuitively knowing how they would fit together in this most intimate of joinings.

He entered her with a swift thrust, meeting with little resistance. He stilled within her, letting her body adjust. She felt herself stretch, felt him push forward, felt herself take the whole of him. Was there anything more divine than this feeling right now?

There was. Bram moved back and then forward, establishing a rocking motion. She found the rhythm and joined him, creating a heady friction that mounted with each thrust. They were climbing, careening towards an unseen peak. Bram's breathing came hard and fast, her own came in unmitigated gasps. If they could go a little harder, a little faster, they would reach the great unknown.

And they did. Just when she thought they could do no more, something deep at her core fractured, shattered into a brilliant release. Bram collapsed against her, his own release achieved in a final, powerful thrust.

She was spent, absolutely spent. She wanted to sleep, Phaedra thought drowsily. Beside her, Bram rose. Where he found the energy for movement was beyond her. Everything that had happened tonight was beyond her. She hadn't known, she'd leave it at that. The simple phrase said it all.

The lamp had burned out long ago. In the dark of the room she could see the outline of Bram's form as he splashed water into a basin. She heard the clank of an ewer being set down and the wringing of a cloth.

Bram returned to the bed and pressed the cloth between her legs. She jumped a little, slightly self-conscious now that the heat of their intimacy had passed.

'I'm sorry it's not warmer, still, it will do.' A skilled lover and a considerate one, Phaedra thought, looking up into Bram's face.

'What was that? At the end?' Phaedra ventured.

In the dark she could see him smile. '*Le petit mort*, the little death.'

Bram set aside the cloth and lay down beside

her, wrapping his arms about her for warmth. 'Every culture has its own name for it. It refers to the release that comes with completion.' Bram played with her hair. 'The Egyptians felt that part of a woman's life force was expended in intercourse.'

'I feel boneless enough right now to believe it.' Phaedra laughed softly. 'All I want to do is sleep.'

'That's natural,' Bram murmured softly. 'Some scientists, physicians and so forth hypothesise that the orgasm is necessary for pregnancy, it keeps a woman lying down long enough to let the sperm penetrate her womb.' His hand stilled in Phaedra's hair and she knew a moment's concern.

'You needn't worry on that account,' Bram assured her. 'I withdrew in time. There will be no consequences to our pleasure. I know it's not romantic to speak of such things, but it must be done.'

Phaedra lay in silence after that, savouring the warmth of Bram's arms, piecing together the remnants of what they'd done. She had to go back. She couldn't spend the night in Bram's room but the thought of making the journey up to the house was singularly unpalatable at this point.

'You can sleep awhile,' Bram said, drawing a blanket up over both of them. 'I'll wake you in time to get you back, and who knows, maybe we'll have time for an encore.'

Phaedra hoped so. Her last thought before drifting off to sleep was that Bram was a man of his word. He'd most definitely kept his promise.

Chapter Thirteen

It was a promise Bram kept repeatedly in the weeks that followed. Spring had proven true and Phaedra spent every minute she could spare riding out with Bram. There were picnics by the river, swims in the lake; they returned the boat and replenished the firewood on the beach. There were rides along the forested trails of Castonbury and up into the heather-covered hills. Always, the outings ended in the same way, with her in his arms, their clothes atangle, their passion replete. Bram was a tireless lover and an exciting one. Phaedra had not dreamed anything could be like this.

'It's like flying across a field on Isolde, the wind in my face, knowing no one can catch us, only better,' Phaedra tried to explain one afternoon as they lay on a blanket looking up at the blue sky, her head on his chest.

Bram laughed. 'I'm glad to know I'm a better ride than your horse.'

Phaedra laughed too. She could always count on laughing with Bram. 'Why is it that everything is so easy with you?' Phaedra traced an idle pattern on his chest where his shirt fell open. 'You don't need dances and manners. Why can't it always be like this? No pretensions, no complications.'

Bram's hand caressed her hip in a familiar manner as he thought. 'I don't want anything from you that you're not willing to give.' There was sense in that. Giles and Aunt Wilhelmina wanted things from her she was not willing to commit.

'May I assume from your comment that things are not "easy" elsewhere? How are things at home? How's Aunt Willy?'

The way he said it, as if he had great familiarity with her family, when in actuality he'd not met any besides Giles, made Phaedra laugh again. *'Aunt Willy?* I dare you to call her that to her face.' She could just picture the shade of red her aunt would turn if someone called her that.

Bram shrugged beneath her. 'I've been calling her that in my head for some time now. Seems natural enough. It will be our secret name for her.'

'Secret name or not, she's awful. Aunt *Willy* is obsessed with her party plans. I'll be glad when the party is over.' The gala, as her aunt insisted on calling it, would be futile. She wasn't interested in anyone but Bram. 'She and Giles are probably up at the house right now deciding who I'm going to marry.'

'Any news from Captain Webster? Still nothing?' Bram asked tentatively. It had been two weeks and nothing had materialised from the incident at the lake. They were starting to feel safe, or at least safer.

'Nothing,' Phaedra affirmed drowsily, letting the sun work its magic. There would be nothing better than falling asleep with Bram. The only thing that marred her happiness was the reality that it was finite. This affair with Bram would have to end and her happiness with it.

She was living on borrowed time as it was. Warbourne had come down with a minor bout of lameness in his left leg, not uncommon when a horse's diet changed from winter grain to fresh spring clover. But it had put her off mounting him and continuing his training. As soon as Warbourne was healthy, she'd have to decide on a departure date for Epsom. She had no illusions Bram would be there when she got back. Tom Anderson had fully recovered and was able to take over his responsibilities.

'You're a million miles from here, Phaedra,' Bram prompted. 'Thinking about Warbourne? He's fine. I checked on him this morning. You should be able to mount him tomorrow.'

Phaedra sat up slightly. Bram would be surprised to know she thought about him more than she thought about her horse these days. She didn't want to think about tomorrow or any of the tomorrows that were to come. They would only be one step closer towards heartache. 'What about you?' Phaedra said playfully. 'Are you fine?' She slid a leg over his hips and straddled him with a knowing smile. 'I'd like to mount you today.'

Bram grinned up at her, banishing her worries. 'Me today, Warbourne tomorrow. I'm moving up in the world.'

Phaedra reached a hand between them to stroke his member where it rose against her. 'You certainly are.'

'I'm losing her.' Giles pulled back the heavy fabric of the curtains, watching Phaedra and Bram lead their horses into the stable yard as dusk fell over Castonbury. They didn't look like a groom and his charge. They looked, well, they looked 'together'. That disturbed him greatly.

Lily came to stand beside him, a soothing hand

at his arm. 'You're not losing her, Giles. She's just growing up, finding her own way, as we all do.' She'd come up earlier in the day to help Aunt Wilhelmina take care of some details for the gala and he was glad she was here. Her presence was a piece of calm, an anchor, in his very chaotic world.

Giles shook his head, unwilling to accept Lily's verdict. 'He's not the sort she should be finding her way with. I regret hiring him. My only consolation is that Tom Anderson is up and about now. I won't need Basingstoke any longer.'

He'd made a mistake when he hadn't asked for references. He knew nothing of the man except that he was good with horses and a handy man in a fight. For a temporary worker those qualities had seemed enough. But Giles had seen the way Basingstoke had looked with Phaedra. There were other things too, when he thought about it. They had ridden out on several occasions Giles knew of. He'd thought nothing of it. He'd been thankful Phaedra was following protocol at last and riding with an escort. Now, he wasn't so sure that was the safest course of action, the two of them alone out in the vast Castonbury lands.

Lily smiled up at him. 'You're a good brother to worry about her but she'll be fine.'

'I'm not a good brother. I'm a man, and I'm re-

membering what you and I got up to on our rides.'
He and Lily had gotten up to plenty but *that* was
different. He was a man of honour. He was going
to marry Lily. More than that, he *loved* Lily.

Giles hugged Lily to him and returned to his
desk where mounds of paperwork awaited him.
Phaedra confounded him.

He knew how to lead men through the bloody
fray of battle but what did he know of shepherd-
ing young women into adulthood? Of helping them
make matches that would see them well-settled
and happy with a family of their own? That was
women's work. Women instinctively knew how to
arrange these things. He hoped Aunt Wilhelmina's
party worked. More than anything, he wanted
Phaedra settled and fast.

Phaedra needed a husband to protect her, a husband who understood her as well as the ways of
the world. She didn't need a fortune-hunter or a
man who would use her for her connections. What
she didn't need was the handsome likes of Bram
Basingstoke, a no-account bounder with nothing
to his name but his good looks.

Giles picked up a report and tried to focus. It
was good news, he should be glad. Finances were
starting to stabilise but other things at Castonbury
were more unsettled than ever, primarily Alicia's

claim that she was his brother's widow and this child of hers the rightful Rothermere heir.

Giles spread his hands on its polished surface. Alicia had been all that was patient and kind since her arrival in the fall. He doubted he would have managed the protracted situation with as much *élan* if it had been him. But then again, the cynic in him spoke, she could afford to be patient. She had a roof over her head, a very nice roof too. The Dower House was no mere cottage, and she was playing for high stakes: a dukedom.

Giles started through the reports, glossing over the first two which he was already familiar with. He hated thinking of Alicia 'playing for stakes,' as if he'd already decided she was a fraud. But the implausibility of the marriage was ever at the fore of his thoughts. The timing fit but Jamie knew his duty. A whirlwind war romance was *not* his duty no matter how pretty the chit was.

Giles couldn't fathom Jamie doing it and Alicia had on occasion fed his doubts with a few little 'slips,' things she'd said or done that seemed out of place, like that bit at Kate's wedding. One way or another, her situation had to be decided.

For himself, he'd never coveted the dukedom for his own, but he did care for his family. Harry could take care of himself and Kate was settled in Boston with Virgil. But Phaedra was young. She'd been raised to privilege. If his father died and Alicia's son inherited, who knew what would become of Phaedra. Phaedra was not entitled to anything the new duke did not want to give her and that included the stables and her horses. That was why Phaedra needed a husband.

'You're worrying again,' Lily said softly from her chair. 'You've been looking at that same sheet paper for the past twenty minutes.'

'Of course I'm worrying. What will Phaedra have if Castonbury betrays her? My father won't live for ever.'

'She'll have us, Giles,' Lily answered simply. 'Family doesn't change even when circumstances do.'

Lily was right. As usual she'd seen to the heart of matter, looking past the peripheral issues. That was why he loved her. But it still couldn't hurt to have a word with Bram just to be sure.

Bram stepped out bare-chested into the stable quadrangle and took a deep lungful of the fresh morning air. It wasn't supposed to be like this, beautiful mornings, days filled with the satisfaction of hard work, passionate nights, even passionate afternoons. If life got any better, he'd think he'd died and gone to heaven, the one place his father had assured him he would never go.

Bram sought out the pump and doused his head with a healthy gush of water. He'd be dirty by the time the day was over but he'd at least start clean. It had been six weeks since he'd come to Castonbury. He should be tired of Phaedra by now, tired of his little rustic sojourn. He should be elated that Tom Anderson was back to work. It meant he could leave. Indeed, he'd probably be asked to leave any day now. That had been the agreement.

Only he didn't want to go. He didn't want to return to being the idle Bram Basingstoke whose days were fundamentally useless. More than that, he didn't want to leave Phaedra. Not yet. He was sure a time would come when he would want to leave; it always did with his affairs.

He reached for his towel and began drying, his eyes looking past the stable yard to the rows of paddocks and beyond to where the heather was starting to show some colour against the land, his mind fixed on the business of the day. It was either think of that or think about how many precious days he had left. There was no doubt about it though, those days were numbered.

Bram shook his head free of the last of the water

droplets and draped his towel about his neck. Today would be a perfect opportunity to exercise the more vigorous mounts who didn't do well constrained to the riding arena and the turn-out paddocks. The boys wouldn't mind. Everyone was feeling spring in their bones, even him.

Spring had made him reckless. He'd let his intrigue with Phaedra grow, something he'd not expected. He had a weakness for a pretty face, to be sure, but it was a short-lived one easily satisfied and overcome after a period of regular association.

Like many things in his life, pretty faces could only hold his attention so long. Phaedra and horses had proved to be the two exceptions in a long list of items that conformed most disappointingly to the standard of brevity. Both of them were also likely to cause him trouble. He could leave and get away with his masquerade. But Phaedra and Warbourne kept him rooted here in spite of his gambler's common sense.

He was also rooted by a disturbing sense of honour that hinted at deeper emotions. Phaedra may need him yet. He could not walk away while the situation with Captain Webster lay unresolved. He would not let Phaedra face that danger alone. In this case, Giles would be of no protection. Giles Montague couldn't shelter her from things he didn't know about. If he and Phaedra chose not to tell Giles about the incident, Giles could not stand between Phaedra and Samuelson's threats when they came, *if* they came.

A loud whinny from the riding house drew Bram's attention. That was unmistakably Warbourne. *She hadn't waited.* Bram reached for his shirt and tugged it over his head in a hurry. Phaedra would be foolish enough to mount that colt alone. Visions of Warbourne tossing Phaedra and stepping on her in his rebellion urged Bram into a run.

He wasn't too late. The horse was saddled and prancing under the weight but Phaedra had things well in hand. Bram eased himself into the shadows of the doorway. He would be there if she needed him. He watched, body tensed with expectation, as Phaedra approached the colt and swung up in a fast, fluid motion. She was seated before the colt began to shift under the unfamiliar weight, the reins tight in her hands for control, her heels jammed down in the stirrups for balance.

Warbourne turned in circles but Phaedra was in command, her words floating across the arena in snatches. 'You remember this, don't you, boy? You know how to take a rider.' On it went, the soft pattern of her voice, the rigid control of her feet and hands at his neck and sides, until she had him patrolling the arena in a collected trot. Bram laughed to himself. He'd been a fool to have worried.

Bram stepped out of the shadows, careful to wait until she brought the colt to a halt. He didn't want to take a chance that Warbourne would spook. 'I don't think I could have done any better.'

Phaedra tossed him a smug smile and urged Warbourne towards him. 'That's high praise indeed.' She brought the horse to a halt. 'Things will happen fast now. I'll take him down to our training track and see what his reaction is to being outside. As soon as that's settled, I can do some race training.' Bram noticed the singular reference. She was determined to do it alone. He'd have to change her mind about that. Warbourne wasn't a horse one rode alone.

Bram stroked Warbourne's muzzle. 'Have you picked out the races you want to try him at yet?' Another man would have argued with her audacity but there'd be no stopping her. Only Phaedra would stop Phaedra.

Phaedra gave a small shake of her head. 'I'll go straight to the Derby with him. There's really no time to do otherwise.'

Bram nodded. The days were passing. In the southern part of England, the early-spring race season was under way at Newmarket. Up here in the north, there wouldn't be any great meets until the end of the month. 'Don't leave it too late, we still have to find a rider.' She had to know finding a rider might prove to be the biggest obstacle of them all. The Jem Robinsons of the world wouldn't be lining up to ride Warbourne. That calibre of rider was likely already claimed by the big breeders like Egremont and Grafton. The Duke of Grafton, both father and his son after him, had owned the Derby winner more times than not and had the trainers and riders to keep the streak up.

Phaedra slid off Warbourne in a graceful motion and shot him a condescending look. 'I know. First things first.'

'Where are you taking him?' Bram fell into step with her.

'Down to the track. It's a good morning to see how he runs.'

Bram shot her a surprised look over the horse's muzzle. 'So soon? You just mounted him.' When she'd mentioned it, he'd not understood it to be quite so immediate. A queer sense of foreboding took up residence in his stomach.

'There's no time like the present and time is slipping away.' Phaedra reached up and patted Warbourne's neck. 'Besides, he knows what to do. He's just been taking his time remembering. Right, boy?'

The Montague track was an oval three furlongs in distance not all that unlike the training tracks at Newmarket. Bram had learned from Tom Anderson that Giles's great-grandfather had designed the track in the early 1700s as a testimony of the Rothermere wealth. But recent generations hadn't shared his extreme love of the turf and little had been done with it beyond using it as a place to exercise.

'Give me a leg up,' Phaedra said once she'd walked the track and made sure it fit her specifications for safety. Bram cupped his hand for her boot and tossed her up. Phaedra settled into the saddle while he adjusted her stirrups and checked the girth. He checked the girth twice, unable to shake his apprehension.

Bram gave Warbourne a pat of approval before moving away. 'Not too fast, Phaedra, just see what he can do, see what he responds to.' She was going to bark at him for that and then she was going to forget his advice. Bram pulled out his pocket watch and flipped it open, prepared to be ignored.

'I know what I'm doing,' she said tightly. Phaedra steered the horse onto the track, gathered herself and then with a kick she was off, her body poised in perfect form over the saddle and Warbourne's neck, Warbourne's dark mane flying.

Heavens, the horse was beautiful, the very personification of speed. Whatever else could be said of her, Phaedra had a good eye for prime horseflesh. Warbourne was the epitome of the modern thoroughbred. Bred for speed, he was taller through the withers than the previous generation of racers, and stronger, able to exert great speeds at a shorter distance. Bram shot a glance at his watch. For raw speed and an amateur rider, Warbourne was doing well. With a trained jockey on board who knew how to navigate a course, who knew how to get every last ounce from a horse, Warbourne could approach record speeds.

Warbourne was flying and Phaedra was flying with him. For a moment everything was perfect and then it went terribly wrong. In an instant, controlled perfection morphed into chaos.

Chapter Fourteen

Bram saw it all in slowed motion. Warbourne's stride broke from its collected rhythm, his muscles bunched, his ears went back and he was off in a bolting gallop. They flew past Bram on their second lap, Warbourne clearly out of control, a full-blown runaway. For an awful moment he watched the reins slip out of Phaedra's hands and his stomach fell. It would only be a matter of time before she was thrown and he was helpless to stop it.

A fall of that magnitude could be deadly unless by some miracle of strength, the miracle of simply being Phaedra Montague, she could hang on long enough to outride the colt's spook. If she'd been in the riding house she could have run him into a wall, the tried and true method for stopping a bolting horse. Out here on the open track there were no walls. Bram cursed his oversight. He should have saddled up Merlin. If he'd brought a horse to act as an 'outrider' he could have ridden after them and perhaps pulled Warbourne over.

Still, Phaedra's form was magnificent. Her hands fisted in Warbourne's long mane, her thighs clenched tightly around his barrel, her only remaining point of real contact with the horse. But Warbourne continued to surge. It would have been an impressive display of stamina and speed if Bram hadn't been so worried about Phaedra.

Then it was over. Bram watched in amazement as the muscles of her thighs went slack and Warbourne slowed to a trotting halt. The crisis had passed. Bram ran onto the track to take hold of Warbourne's bridle as if he could hold back a thousand pounds of horseflesh single-handedly.

Phaedra laughed, a little breathless, atop her sweating steed. 'He won't bolt again. He's well-spent.' She leaned down and patted Warbourne's shoulder. 'I thought that might happen.'

Bram gave her an incredulous look. 'Don't tell me you enjoyed that?' It had been torture for him watching Warbourne dash around madly with her on board and she'd been having fun?

'It's the clenched thighs,' Phaedra explained, showing no desire to dismount. Most people he knew would have jumped off that horse straight away. But now that the crisis had passed, admiration was warring with his anger. She'd been extraordinary and he couldn't help but appreciate it.

'Care to explain?'

'Tightening your thighs signals him to run. The tighter the thighs, the faster he goes. It's why he's thrown his jockeys at the starts.'

'How did you know? How did you guess?' It had been risky to give up her last point of reliable contact. If she'd been wrong, she would have been thrown most definitely.

'His dam's grandsire, Brave Warrior, had the same problem.' Phaedra gave him one of her smug grins. 'He turned out great foals but had a checkered racing history himself because of his little problem. Oh, look, here comes Giles.'

She waved to someone behind him and Bram turned to see Giles Montague approaching.

'Did you see him, Giles?' Phaedra called out.

'I saw some of it,' Giles said with a tight smile. He leaned on the railing beside Bram. 'He's magnificent, Phae. You've done a good job. No one will be able to touch him at the October hunts.'

Bram thought for a moment Phaedra might contest the omission of racing but Phaedra simply smiled and moved away from the railing. Warbourne was still pulsing with adrenaline from his run and needed some light work, which was just as well. Whatever Giles Montague had come down to say, Bram would prefer to hear it first. He hoped news of their indiscretion hadn't reached Phaedra's brother.

'Were you the one who taught her to ride like that?' Bram asked casually. If they'd met at a club in London, he and Giles might have been friends. Right now, the perceived differences in their stations prevented that familiarity. Giles wouldn't get too close, or too friendly, with an itinerant horse handler.

'No, I can't take credit for that. I think growing up, Jamie and I were more like uncles to her than brothers. She was so much younger. I was off to school and into the military before she was ten. It's mostly Edward's fault. He was around the house longer and, being the two youngest, they were close.' Giles's jaw tightened. 'It should be *you* on Warbourne. He's not Isolde. It's one thing when you're riding breakneck on a horse you know. It's another when the horse isn't as familiar.'

'Better my neck than hers, eh?' Bram paraphrased bluntly. Phaedra would not like that verdict.

Giles gave him a sharp look. 'She's all I've got left. I don't know if you've looked around my family lately, but it's in tatters. There are too many people I've failed to save. My baby sister won't be one of them.'

Bram heard the protection there, heard the concern and the affection. Phaedra wouldn't. She would see only a curtailing of her freedoms.

'She's not a baby,' Bram ventured, meeting Giles's gaze evenly as if he had a right to such a frank exchange with a man his superior. 'Sisters grow up. They marry, they start families of their own. Be sure you don't mistake protection for suffocation. Phaedra's wild. She won't take kindly to being reined in.'

'You mean Lady Phaedra,' Giles corrected with an assessing look full of speculation.

'Yes, my mistake.' Bram looked out over the track. He'd gone too far there.

'Make sure it's your only mistake, Mr Basingstoke. I'm a man, I know how men think. I'll tell you right now, she's not for you. She's a duke's daughter.'

Giles paused and fixed him with a gaze of stone. 'She refused to go to London. Did you know? I believed at the time it was on account of this horse business. Now I'm starting to wonder, Mr Basingstoke, if it had anything to do with you? I hope not. I would be very disappointed to learn it had. Her aunt and I are hosting a party tomorrow for the express purpose of giving her a chance to meet eligible young men.'

'You mean *suitable* young men,' Bram corrected.

'Yes, I mean suitable. Are we clear? She's not meant to throw herself away on itinerant horse handlers, especially those who will only be here for two more days.' Giles's grey eyes were hard. He would brook no argument, certainly not from a groom, although he needed to be argued with. Giles Montague was making a huge mistake.

The man meant well but he didn't know his sister at all. His attempts to protect her would only result in firing her rebellion. The last thing either he or Giles needed was an angry Phaedra storming off in the middle of the night and taking her colt with her out into a world where neither of them could protect her from the scandal that would inevitably follow.

'When she brings the horse in, tell her Aunt Wilhelmina's dressmaker is waiting for her up at the house.' Giles turned on his booted heel and headed back to the house.

Phaedra stood still, arms held out to her sides, aching while the dressmaker gave the gown a final look-over. She'd spent the morning holding

Warbourne accountable with those arms. Holding them out for the dressmaker all afternoon was sheer torture. She knew it could have been worse. Giles could have heard about the island, or any of their numerous indiscretions, and come to force some ancient code of justice on them. Or he could have come to tell Bram his services were no longer needed.

Phaedra turned on command and distracted herself with thoughts of the workout. Warbourne had speed aplenty but it was one thing to run on an empty track devoid of horses, another to run in a field of twelve or twenty. Epsom was known for its large fields of contenders and the track wasn't an oval either. Nor was it six furlongs, the distance she'd raced Warbourne today on his tear. The Derby was a mile and a half of ups and downs.

Still, that didn't undermine the day's successes. She'd stayed on! With Warbourne's reputation for throwing riders, she'd fully expected to spend much of the day in the dirt and much of the evening in a soaking tub.

'Shall we add some of the lace to the bodice?' Aunt Wilhelmina asked. The dressmaker held up a length of the Brussels lace.

Phaedra had to protest. 'Any more trimming and I'll look like one of Monsieur André's fondant cakes. We have quite enough lace.' All she wanted to do was get back down to the stables. She had a map of the Epsom course somewhere down there. But she was kidding herself if she believed that was her only reason for wanting to go back. Bram was there. She'd be looking for him as much as she was looking for a map. He'd become her port in the storm. She wasn't quite sure how she'd let him go when the time came but she sensed that time was coming. She'd known from the start that it would but there was little consolation in that.

Phaedra didn't make it to the stables until after dinner, which had turned into an awkward affair full of pronouncements made by Giles, none of which she was planning to adhere to. She wasn't giving full training and riding of *her* colt over to anyone simply because Giles thought Warbourne was too much horse for her at this point.

Phaedra made her way towards Warbourne's stall. The colt could always raise her spirits. She reached Warbourne, glad to see the colt was still awake. He came to her, his nostrils seeking out any treats. Phaedra laughed softly and stroked his muzzle. 'Sorry, boy, I don't have any treats to-night.'

'What about me? No treats for me either?' Bram materialised beside her, leaning on the half-door of Warbourne's stall. He was dressed in shirt and breeches, a jacket thrown on against the chill. His words were light but his tone wasn't. Something unpleasant lurked beneath the words. Phaedra stood in silence, stroking Warbourne's muzzle, and waited for Bram to speak.

'I spoke with your brother today. He thought Tom Anderson could use an extra hand for the party and all the guests' horses but he'd like me to leave afterwards.'

It wasn't really a surprise but hearing the words spoken out loud made it all so much more final. Phaedra swallowed hard. She tried to discern Bram's reaction. Was he disappointed? Or was he glad to be moving on, glad not to have to be the one to break this off? It was easier to lay this decision at Giles's feet, their affair a result of circumstance.

'Is that satisfactory to you?' Phaedra summoned her old hauteur.

Bram's hand covered hers where it lay on the door. 'It's not an issue of being satisfactory or not. We both knew the limitations and we both know I cannot offer you anything more than the time we've had together, no matter how much we might want that to be different.'

She looked at him. 'Do you want it to be different?'

'Phaedra, honey, you of all people know if wishes were horses beggars would ride.' It wasn't an answer but perhaps it would be best not to know. She preferred to believe she wasn't in this relationship alone, that it meant something to him too.

He elbowed her, some of his usual playfulness returning. 'But that's two days from now and two nights.' Bram's hands were at her shoulders, turning her so that her back faced him. His strong fingers kneaded the tight muscles of her shoulders. The pressure of his hands felt wicked and wonderful all at once. His hands moved to her neck and she gave a little moan of delight. The tension began to seep from her. She laid her head back on Bram's shoulder and let his arms come around her, enfolding her against the strength of his chest.

She let her eyes flutter shut, let Bram kiss the curve of her jaw, his hands rising above her ribcage to take her breasts in his palms. Phaedra gave a soft sigh, her tension gone, replaced by something else, something primitive and wild that wanted only this, only Bram.

'Give me pleasure, Bram.' Beggars couldn't ride, and neither could they be choosers. If she couldn't choose, then at least she'd take her last pleasures where she could. Phaedra turned in his arms, taking his face between her hands and kissing him full on the mouth. She kissed him again, this time slowly, her hands in his hair, breathing in the scent of him, the taste of him in her mouth, the hardness of him against her stomach. It was not enough. She wanted release. She hitched her leg at his hip, letting her skirts fall back and his hand slide up, warm on her bare thigh.

He wouldn't last long at this rate. He'd hated telling her the news tonight, hated not being able to tell her he regretted leaving as much as she did. But he didn't dare say anything for fear of giving her false promises. He knew better than she that she was better off without him. His hand was at the core of her, finding her slick and ready.

'Touch me again like you did on the island,' Phaedra whispered, her head thrown back, her neck exposed to his mouth.

'You liked that, didn't you?' Bram murmured.

Suddenly Phaedra froze against him. Her eyes riveted on something past his shoulder. 'Oh, Lord! Bram, *stop*!' That was not the typical response. Usually it was, *Don't* stop. Then he heard the reason for her urgent whisper.

'Touch her again in *any* way and I'll see you dead on the duelling field.' Giles stood in the aisle, arms crossed and angry. 'Now, who would like to tell me exactly what is going on here?'

Phaedra stepped away, her hands pushing wildly at her skirts in a belated bid for decency. Instinctively, Bram moved in front of her, a shield from Giles's wrath, the primal instinct to protect surging strong within him. Whatever Montague wanted, the man would have to go through him. The best he could do for Phaedra was to get her out of here until Montague's anger had cooled or been directed towards him instead. He'd welcome it. He wouldn't mind explaining a couple of things to Giles Montague even if it had to be done on the knuckle end of his fists.

'Phaedra, go up to the house,' Giles instructed, attempting to speak around Bram's broad-shouldered blockade. 'I will sort everything out.'

Bram could feel Phaedra bristling at his back. 'Like you did my horse?' Great, now he was caught in a sibling crossfire.

'Phaedra, please go up to the house,' Bram tried. This time she obeyed, but not before she shot Giles a hard look that would have melted stone. Bram didn't relish being Giles when he returned to the house. He had no illusions Phaedra's departure made things better. Giles would not take well to disobedience from his sister when she gave another man acquiescence.

'Is this your idea of heeding my warning?' Giles growled. 'Was I not explicit enough this afternoon?' He eyed Bram with speculation. 'Or did my warning provoke you to speed ahead, thinking you'd lose her to a *worthy* gentleman?'

Bram lunged, catching Giles by the lapels of his coat and hauling him against the wall. 'You know nothing about her. If you did you'd realise I'm not the one losing her, you are. Let her race her horses, Montague. She's going to do it anyway.'

Bram's breath came fast and hard. Giles Montague was a strongly built man. He wouldn't be held for long. To prove it, Giles gave a hard shove that sent him sprawling backwards, his shoulder knocking against a tack cupboard.

'Don't tell me about my sister! You're a bounder and a cad to take advantage of an innocent young girl.' Giles leapt for him but Bram rolled away and regained his feet. Innocent young girl? Phaedra was a woman full of passion, not that Giles would want to know that.

They were grappling now, their hands at each other's throats. This time, it was Bram against the wall, Giles's face a savage red. He would hear no wisdom in Bram's words. Why should he listen to the man who wanted to seduce his sister? 'You don't have two days, Basingstoke. Get your hands off my sister and get your sorry self off my land.'

Chapter Fifteen

'You look a treat, miss.' Henny stepped back from the mirror to examine her work. Phaedra dutifully turned her head side to side, showing off the brilliants pinned in her coiffure. Henny *had* outdone herself but that didn't make Phaedra any more desirous of going downstairs. The day had been a disaster from start to finish.

She had fought with Giles, or at least she'd *tried* to fight with him. She was spoiling for a good argument, but Giles had refused. He'd been aloof and chilly, hardly responding to her hot words. She'd called him stubborn and controlling, drunk on his own power. She'd railed at him about the colt, about curbing her own freedoms, but mostly she'd railed at him over Bram. Bram had been dismissed and now he was gone without so much as a goodbye.

She should be thankful. Bram's very unsuitability had been the saving of him. If Bram had been a gentleman of any standing, Giles would have seen them married with all due haste. That didn't change the fact she was reeling from his desertion.

She'd only begun to realise last night when she'd fled to the stables how much she'd come to depend on Bram's presence.

She'd spent most of the day at the stables, avoiding Giles and party preparations and hoping to catch sight of Bram, hoping they could talk. But Bram had left early, before first light according to Tom Anderson, and the stables felt the emptier for his absence.

There was no question this affair which had started as a physical experimentation had become much more for her. Yet she was left wondering in the end, what had she meant to him? She hated herself for caring what that answer might be. She'd not wanted this to become anything more and yet it had.

Henny was staring at her with a funny look. Apparently she was expected to say something. Oh, yes, they'd been talking about her hair, a rather minor subject when her life was falling apart.

'It looks lovely, Henny, truly it does.' Phaedra reached for the heart-shaped locket on her dressing table. 'Help me with this, we'll have to hurry if we don't want Aunt Wilhelmina breaking down the door.'

Aunt Willy. She wouldn't be able to hear that name again without thinking of Bram. Aunt Wilhelmina would be in alt tonight. The whole day had been spent in preparation for the evening, most of which Phaedra had thankfully avoided. Phaedra had no doubt the house had bustled with workers arranging flowers and decorating the saloon where the party would be held since sunrise. A London debut wouldn't be any more elaborate than Aunt Wilhelmina's 'simple party.'

The whole countryside was invited, from the magistrate, Sir Rufus, on down to Reverend Seagrove. Aunt Wilhelmina had condescended to invite Alicia for the sake of appearances. Even Sir Nathan and Captain Webster had been on the guest list.

Phaedra had disapproved of their inclusion but Aunt Wilhelmina had been adamant: if there was to be any slighting it wouldn't be on the Montagues' part. It would be too obvious an oversight to leave them off the list when appropriate guests were a bit thin on the ground in this part of the world. Derbyshire, Aunt Wilhelmina had reminded her, wasn't exactly brimming with peers.

Henny helped her with the clasp and Phaedra studied the effect of the simple gold jewellery against the bare expanse of bosom on display. Phaedra tugged at the low bodice. 'Do you think necklines will ever go up, Henny?' It was hard to condemn a man for ogling a woman's bosom when fashion demanded it be practically thrust in his face.

Henny laughed. 'Lord, no, miss. Necklines aren't going up any time soon unless fathers and brothers decide to petition for some decency on behalf of their daughters and wives.'

The maid winked mischievously. 'But I don't see any men complaining.'

Henny sobered. 'Speaking of men, I hope I am not too bold. We were sorry to hear about Mr Basingstoke. The girls at the house liked him. He was always full of manners and a bit of the devil.'

Phaedra blushed. News had certainly travelled fast. She hoped not all of what had transpired last night had made its way through the servants' grapevine.

'Phaedra!' Giles called impatiently through the door. 'You can't be late to your own party.'

Henny gave her a smile. 'Go on, there are lots of nice young men downstairs who'd consider themselves lucky to have a girl like you.' She gently pulled Phaedra's hands down. 'Stop with your fussing. You look lovely even if we had to rush.'

The rush had been Phaedra's fault. She'd stayed too long at the stables trying to make the event disappear by ignoring it. Her strategy hadn't worked. Here she was at half past seven, hair pinned up, and dressed in a gown of worked Union silk, a fashionable confection of blush pink trimmed with expensive blond lace. No London modiste could have done better. Matching slippers with tiny satin bows peeped from her skirts and a scarf of China crêpe embroidered with pink flowers at the tails waited on the bed to grace her shoulders. No lamb led to slaughter had ever looked finer.

Phaedra took one last look at her reflection. The woman in the mirror was a lovely liar, the epitome of a perfectly turned-out debutante. There were no telltale signs she'd spent the day in breeches working her colt or that she'd been caught in the arms of a most unsuitable man the night before. The woman in the mirror looked entirely innocent of such heated wrongdoings. That would make Giles happy. She couldn't promise she could make him happy after tonight. If she meant to be at Epsom for the Derby, she'd need to leave soon.

Giles knocked again, the short rap indicative of his impatience. 'Phaedra, are you ready? Auntie will have my head if we're not downstairs in five minutes.'

Phaedra opened the door and played the ingénue. 'Is it time already?'

'Father wants to see us before the guests arrive.' Giles flicked his cuffs in a quick inspection.

'Father's coming tonight?' Father kept to his rooms these days. He hardly came to any social events. The last one had been a disastrous dinner meeting with Kate's husband, Virgil.

Phaedra took the silk scarf from Henny and settled it about her shoulders, trying to cover up the bare bodice.

'It's your big night, Phae. Of course he'll be there.' It was the nicest thing Giles had said to her since last night. She fought the urge to wince and failed. She didn't want this to be her 'big night.'

Giles gave her a placating smile, the kind big brothers perfect for cajoling stubborn little sisters. 'It won't be that bad. There will be dancing and food. It will be nice to have a party. We haven't had one since Kate's wedding.' He squeezed her arm affectionately. 'Maybe it's time we started having parties again. Maybe it's time you start meeting nice young men. Lily tells me Mr Chesterton will be here tonight. He's a poet. He's just published a volume of poetry dedicated to Prinny, studied literature at Oxford. His father's a baronet from Wessex. He likes to travel.'

Phaedra listened half-heartedly to Giles's well-intended recitation of Mr Chesterton's fine attributes. She didn't want a *poet*, she wanted a man who smelled like wind and spices, whose chest was a granite slab of strength, who could waltz divinely in nothing but a haphazard kilt made from a quilt. She wanted Bram.

Aunt Wilhelmina assembled the family in the little-used music room at the front of the main house. The Montague children, one and all, had preferred outdoor pursuits to the elegant, polished harpsichord Aunt Wilhelmina had imported from Italy years ago for the 'betterment of their musical instruction.' Lumsden was on hand with flutes of iced champagne. 'Lady Phaedra, would you care for a glass?' He offered her the tray. 'Your aunt wants a toast.'

Phaedra dutifully took a cut-crystal flute. She understood. This was her penance, the price of her indiscretion. She'd ventured outside the prescribed behaviors for a girl of her rank and birth. Now the family was united in its attempt to salvage her virtue.

What there was of it. By that she meant the immediate family, not her virtue. The family assembled was made up these days of Aunt Wilhelmina, a frail duke, one older brother and another brother's widow. Out of a family of eight, only four of them were gathered. She felt the absence of the other four keenly, even more so when she saw her father in the big green armchair by the fire. He was thin and pale, a shadow of the man who had gamboled on the Castonbury lawns with his children in the long summers of her youth.

'Come here, Phaedra.' Her father held out a papery hand to her. 'Come let me look at you.' His grey eyes were bright and alert, unclouded by medications. He stared hard at her as if he had never seen her before. Then he smiled. 'You look like your mother. You've got her hair and her face. You and Edward got the best of her.' His eyes misted for a moment and then he was off on another tangent. 'I hear you have a new colt in the stables.'

They talked a few minutes about Warbourne. She told him about the colt's speed and the ebony sheen of his coat but nothing that would upset him. There was no mention of Bram, no mention of Epsom. Since Jamie's death, the implicit rule had been 'say nothing to upset father.' Their father had done a good enough job of that on his own, retreating into a world of memories where his two dead sons were still alive.

Alicia touched her lightly on the arm, looking pretty in a plain ball gown of pale blue. 'Excuse me, I don't mean to interrupt but Aunt Wilhelmina wants to toast now and then you'll need to go with Giles and greet the guests.'

None of which would be Bram.

Bram put the finishing touches on his cravat and thrust an emerald stick pin through its snowy folds for decoration. He consulted the small round mirror in his room at the Rothermere Arms for any errors in his toilette. It felt odd to be wearing his usual clothes after so many weeks without them. The dark evening trousers and the layers of coat and waistcoat over his shirt felt constraining. But the days of Bram Basingstoke the head groom at Castonbury were behind him now, or almost behind him.

He was going to the party. He owed Phaedra that much. He'd left things awkwardly with her the night previous regardless of Giles's intrusion. He'd not offered her reassurance when she'd sought it. She'd been devastated to hear he was leaving and he'd said nothing to assure her he was just as disappointed. Instead he'd acted nonchalant, as if he were ambivalent to the situation when he wasn't ambivalent in the least. Then he flirted with her, promising to make the last two days count. He meant to keep that promise by showing up tonight.

That was a piece of chivalry he didn't want to take out and examine too closely for fear of what he'd find. He wasn't used to women who brought out his finer qualities. But Phaedra had and she deserved to know he hadn't simply walked away from her at her brother's decree.

Beyond that, he wasn't sure what else he could offer her, what else he *should* offer her. He was a rogue and a rake with little to bring with him aside from scandal. His reputation hadn't bothered him before but it was bothering him now that he'd dusted off his little-used conscience.

Bram gathered up a walking stick from the bed. It would be easy enough to infiltrate the party. No one turned a well-heeled gentleman away. No one would be looking for Bram Basingstoke the earl's son, and no one would take this fashionable gentleman for Bram Basingstoke the groom. People saw what they expected to see.

Whistling, Bram headed downstairs to the public room. It was quite convenient to be persona non grata for the evening. He would dance with Phaedra and kiss her goodbye and Giles Montague—and everyone else—would be none the wiser.

Giles Montague needed to be more careful about who he hired to work in his stables. Sir Nathan patted the inner pocket of his evening coat, a fine swallow-tailed affair in black wool that had just arrived from Buxton along with this most important letter. Phaedra Montague was about to be up to her pretty neck in scandal unless she saw her way to obliging him.

Sir Nathan chuckled, stepping down from his carriage and looking up at the impressive facade of Castonbury Hall, light and music spilling from its windows. He'd have to play his cards diplomatically though. He didn't want to advertise this scandal to the general populace. That would only serve to chase Phaedra into Basingstoke's arms— society would require it. He wanted Phaedra in *his* arms. He'd paint himself the rescuing hero, the supportive neighbour willing to take tainted goods off Giles Montague's hands, horse and all. By the time the night was over, Giles Montague would appreciate him as a man of great refinement and discretion.

Chapter Sixteen

The Grand Saloon stood at the south end of the Marble Hall, a testament to refinement and Rome. Lights blazed from sconces of Venetian glass placed strategically around the enormous circular chamber. The room was turned out in its best form tonight. Even in her cynical frame of mind, Phaedra could appreciate the beauty of the room.

Designed originally to reflect the best forms of Roman architecture, the room was round and columned; the walls held niches to act as a sculpture gallery when the room wasn't being used as a ballroom. But obviously, her ancestors had known it *would* be a ballroom and had had the wooden floor 'sprung' especially for dancing.

For the occasion, the columns were wreathed in garlands of evergreens and tea roses as were the arches over the four double doors set at various intervals leading into the room. The only space not bearing the stamp of Aunt Wilhelmina's decorating was the soaring skylight sixty-two feet above the whirling dancers. Like the massive Marble Hall leading to the chamber, the saloon, too, rose the full height of the house, making the room seem even larger.

It was a fairytale setting and Phaedra tried to make the best of it, truly she did. She danced with each of her partners, none of who grimaced when she stepped on their toes. She rather wished they had. After an hour and a half of what passed for chivalry among 'nice suitable gentlemen,' Phaedra had had enough.

Where were they, all those nice young men Henny had been so hopeful about? Phaedra's borrowed optimism had faded considerably. Not one of the young men listed on her card had sparked her attention. In short, not one of them was Bram Basingstoke. Not one of them showed a proclivity for taking off his shirt or swimming naked with her in the Castonbury lakes.

Not that she wanted them to, Phaedra hastily amended her thoughts. She had no desire to see Mr Chesterton the poet without his shirt. It wasn't just Bram's penchant for the daring and indecent that drew her. It was *him*, the devil-may-care grin, the deep blue eyes that looked straight through her, the shockingly honest truths he was wont to exhort. Oh, she knew where those nice young men were, they were right here in the Castonbury saloon and she didn't want any part of them.

Phaedra didn't want to look into one more pair of placid eyes that revealed no flicker of inner fire. She didn't want to engage in polite conversation that gave no hint of a person's true feelings. Would anyone miss her if she slipped away?

A quick survey of the room suggested she might manage it. Aunt Wilhelmina was talking with Reverend Seagrove and her father on the sidelines. Giles was with Lily, getting ready to take their places in the next set starting to form on the dance floor. Her own partner would be coming to claim her any moment. If she meant to disappear, she needed to go quickly.

Framed by four sets of double doors that allowed guests to enter the room at various points of the circular chamber, the Castonbury saloon was relatively easy to slip out of unobtrusively. And that's precisely what she did.

She was in the library, a semi-private location tonight and it had been prepared as such. Low light lit the room enough to keep it from being dark and a fire had been laid for those who might wish a place for quieter conversation. But music from the saloon could be heard through the door, a constant reminder that the occupants were not truly alone. Anyone could burst in at any moment, a potent deterrent for guests seeking a rendezvous of a more clandestine nature. For now, it was empty and that suited her fine. Phaedra breathed a little sigh of relief. Alone at last.

Except for the man rising from the sofa. Oh, dear, she wasn't alone, after all.

'Hello, Phaedra.'

Phaedra stifled an undignified yelp. She'd know that sexy drawl anywhere, but it took a moment to recognise him in the dim light and fine clothes. 'Bram?' It was unmistakably him once her eyes adjusted. He was the last person she'd thought she'd see tonight but not for lack of wishing. 'I—I thought you'd left.'

'I thought you'd be dancing.'

Phaedra shook her head, smiling. Bram was here. He'd come back. He did care, after all. 'I've had enough of dancing for the evening. No one seems to measure up to my latest dancing instructor.' She wanted to do more than stand there and trade banter with him. She wanted to throw herself into his arms and confess how much she'd missed him in just one day. But he wasn't the sort of man who appreciated a clingy woman and they'd made each other no promises. It would have to be enough that he was here.

Bram stepped towards her. 'Perhaps you haven't found the right partner.'

'That's what my instructor tells me.' Phaedra laughed, thinking of the island.

Bram held out his hand. 'Will you dance with me, Phaedra?' His eyes glowed like cobalt flame and he was in deadly earnest. The very propriety of his request made it seem all the more provocative.

'Here?' Phaedra moved into his arms. His hand closed around hers, warm and firm, fitting her to him, his other hand at her back. Phaedra smiled up at him, savouring the clean-shaven jaw, the handsome planes of his face with their high cheekbones and razor-straight nose, the way his eyes looked just before he kissed her.

'Yes, here.' Bram moved her in a slow circle to the strains of the music outside the door. He whispered against her ear. 'If we dance here, no one can count this as one of our dances. We can still have two dances out there.'

Not like this we won't. The ballroom would not tolerate the closeness with which he held her, the intimate way his hips pressed against her, his hand at her back helping her find the gentle rhythm of the dance.

Phaedra knew this dance; it was one of the scandalous waltz-style dances Prinny had introduced in London last summer. One didn't have to be in the capital last Season to know the outrage the prince's choice had spawned. The outrage had drifted up north to Derbyshire with shocking haste.

'We're waltzing. Aunt Wilhelmina would be scandalised.' Phaedra locked eyes with her bold partner.

Bram gave a wicked smile, his eyes laughing. 'Rightly so if one truly understands the dance.'

'And I suppose you do?' Phaedra teased. Her body was finding it easy to follow the movements of his, easy to answer the desire rising in his eyes.

'I do. Are you ready? We're going to turn, this is the top of our ballroom.' He swept through a turn that brought her up against the hard planes of him. 'Does that give you a clue as to the real source of scandal?' He leaned close to her ear. 'It's a metaphor for lovemaking, Phaedra, for courtship. The man is in pursuit and the woman is a coy mistress leading him a merry chase.'

His words, low at her ear, conjured hot images. 'Are you certain?' Put that way, the scandal was understandable.

'I am very certain.' Bram gave a deep, sonorous chuckle rife with wicked mischief. 'Have I succeeded in shocking you?'

He'd like that, the idea that he'd finally shocked her after weeks of trying. Phaedra tipped her head to the side with a considering gaze. 'No, you've merely intrigued me.'

The music came to a halt, he nipped at her ear. 'Good. I'm going to get us champagne. When I come back, let me intrigue you some more.'

'Use the far door so you don't have to go through the ballroom.' Phaedra sighed, reluctant to let him go. 'If Giles catches you...'

'He won't,' Bram assured her. 'He's not expecting me.' With a wink, Bram slipped through the door at the far end leading into the drawing room.

Phaedra sat down on the long sofa, a little smile dancing on her lips. *He'd come back. At risk to himself.* She wasn't sure what that meant exactly but for the moment, it was enough. Perhaps it would be easier to let him go if she knew he cared too. It was as she suspected. Somewhere between railing against his arrogance and dancing in quilts, she'd fallen in love with a most unsuitable man and the best she could do now was mitigate a broken heart. But that would come later. For now, she still had tonight.

* * *

The little minx was up to something. Sir Nathan Samuelson skirted his way along the perimeter of the ballroom making his way to the last place he'd seen Phaedra Montague. He was going to make it very clear to her that she couldn't avoid him all night. Her aunt might have succeeded in keeping him off Phaedra's dance card, but Sir Nathan thought he might have a brand of persuasion that would change Phaedra's mind. It would do his reputation wonders if he was seen dancing with a Montague. It wouldn't hurt his more private agenda either. He could hardly court her if he couldn't even dance with her.

Sir Nathan scanned the ballroom, catching sight of the side doors. With the crowds, he hadn't noticed the doors earlier. He'd already checked the exits leading out to the wide veranda overlooking the south lawn. Many couples strolled out there, taking advantage of the mild evening but Phaedra had not been among them. He'd also checked the Marble Hall where others were admiring the artwork on display in the long foyer. She'd not been among the groups there or in the drawing room where the refreshments were being served.

Sir Nathan approached the doors. He was running out of options which meant the chances were good these doors held the answer. There weren't many more places she could be. Sir Nathan turned the handle and it gave.

Someone was coming, someone who wasn't Bram. Phaedra watched in morbid fascination as the handle on the door from the ballroom turned. Bram would have used the other door. Sir Nathan Samuelson stepped into the room. Phaedra rose quickly from the sofa, eager to keep the furniture and as much distance between them as possible. It boded poorly that he was here at all. How could he have known she'd left the dancing unless he'd been watching her? The thought that he'd made her the focus of his attentions sent an unpleasant chill down her spine. Bram would be back soon.

'My dear, we're alone at last. I thought I'd never find you. You've given your own fete the slip,' Sir Nathan drawled, shutting the door firmly behind him. 'These parties make it difficult to have a decent conversation.'

'There is nothing I wish to say to you,' Phaedra replied coldly, standing her ground. She didn't want to be afraid of him, but he made her so very uncomfortable with his leering eyes, the way they would move up and down her body, so different from Bram's appreciative gaze.

'Splendid, my dear.' Sir Nathan rambled about the room, looking behind curtains for hidden strangers. 'What I really want you to do is listen. I have recently come across some information I think you'll find highly interesting and perhaps even motivating.'

Phaedra crossed her arms defiantly. 'I doubt it.'

'Well, my dear, I don't.' He rubbed his hands together with a hearty chortle.

Chapter Seventeen

Phaedra stepped backwards in answer to his advance, putting the long sofa between them. She wished she were at the stables where there were pitchforks aplenty for makeshift weapons. Libraries were a bit lacking in impromptu weaponry.

'What's this, Phaedra?' Sir Nathan continued to move towards her, hands outstretched in a gesture that supposedly meant he came in peace but his gaze told another story. 'I think you and I got off on the wrong foot in Buxton, and really it wasn't my fault. It was Webster's. He was the one mishandling the horse.' Sir Nathan tsked with fond disapproval. 'Such a wastrel he is. It just proves we're right about outsiders in our part of the world. Like should stick to like, and we are alike, Phaedra, you and I.'

Phaedra swallowed hard, looking about for some

tool of defence. In the semi-darkness her hand groped about the table behind her, closing around a porcelain vase. 'You're nothing like me.'

He smiled, a condescending grin. 'Allow me to argue the point, my dear. We both enjoy the turf, we've both spent our lives in Derbyshire, we're both used to the finer things in life. I would deny you nothing my worldly gains could afford.'

'Which isn't very much from what I hear,' Phaedra interrupted. 'You couldn't even afford Warbourne.'

His eyes narrowed, the silken persuasion gone, replaced by something more predatory. 'You couldn't either as I recall. You sold family jewellery for that colt. Now you listen here, you come on out and dance with me, show the world the Montagues and I are friends, more than friends, and I won't tell your brother what I know.'

'And what is that?' She would not dance with this man, would not tolerate even the most civil of touches from him. Her grip on the vase tightened. A nice cosh on the head would do him an immense amount of good.

'That you and I have something else in common. We both like to go slumming on occasion. In short, I know what you did and who you did it with the day you went swimming in the lake.'

He held out his hands expansively, examining his nails. 'I don't mind really. Slumming can be a bit of fun. Your sister Kate knows all about it. Apparently it runs in your fine Montague blood.'

Phaedra's temper fired. 'Virgil is a prince among men. If anything, she's married above herself.'

'Not in our world she hasn't,' Sir Nathan said smugly. 'Now, come on over here and take my arm. We'll walk back to the ballroom and you can give me that dance you owe me.'

'No.' Phaedra backed up. At her back was the door joining the library to the saloon. If she could reach it, she could slip into the crowd there. Sir Nathan would not risk a scene.

Sir Nathan's eyes flicked behind her, noting the outline of the door. 'I'm not in the mood for "no" tonight.' He growled. He lunged for her in a quick movement that belied his heavier bulk.

Phaedra darted aside but the move took her away from a clear path to the door. He was stalking her now and she had no outlet. He closed in, penning her between the wall and himself. She was going to have to fight.

'Have a care, Sir Nathan.' Phaedra gathered her bravado, her eyes indicating the door to her left. 'Anyone could walk in at any time.'

The reminder didn't have the desired effect. He

was close enough to smell now, his strong cologne overpowering at this range. It was not a subtle scent, not like Bram's spices. 'I wouldn't mind if they did.' He leered. 'In fact, I hope they will. A compromising position is all I need. Your brother would be hard-pressed to deny me after that, and so would you.' He grinned evilly. 'Perhaps you'll think about that before you decide to scream. Do you really want anyone to see you with your skirts up?'

His hand was at her cheek now, his rough knuckles stroking her jaw. His other hand was on himself, caressing the bulge in his trousers. 'How about a kiss for your future husband?' His face angled towards her, his breath rife with the remnants of his dinner, his mouth open. This was her moment. Phaedra raised her arm and swung her vase, catching him on the side of the head. The vase shattered. Sir Nathan stumbled, momentarily stunned from the blow.

His hand went to his head and came away with blood.

'You bitch, you've cut me!' he roared. He lunged for her. Desperate, Phaedra sidestepped his off-balance grab and flung open the door, sending him stumbling into the ballroom where he promptly careened into Bram. Champagne spilled on clothes, crystal shattered on the floor and the music came to an undignified halt while everyone stared. It wasn't every night a man bumbled into a ballroom with blood streaming from his head.

Phaedra sucked in her breath. Bram's eyes flicked over Nathan's shoulder to her. She bit her lip. For a moment she thought Sir Nathan wouldn't recognise Bram. 'Well, look who we have here. It's Lord Bramford.' Sir Nathan sneered in contempt, pressing a white handkerchief to his head.

Lord Bramford? The reference made no sense. What was Sir Nathan playing at? From the corner of her eye, Phaedra caught sight of Captain Webster with Alicia on the periphery of the ballroom.

Webster stepped forward. 'Are you sure about that, Sir Nathan? He looks like the head groom to me, that fellow they picked up in Buxton.' Bram had gone stiff, his jaw clenched.

The crowd drew a tight circle around Nathan and Bram, sensing a noteworthy drama was about to unfold. If she had any sense, she'd fade back into the library and put a discreet distance between herself and the scene. Maybe everyone would forget to ask why Sir Nathan was bleeding. But she couldn't tear herself away any more than the guests could.

'Well, hey, maybe he is.' Sir Nathan squinted in contemplation. 'No, no, I am sure this fellow is Lord Bramford, the Earl of Hartvale's son.'

Earl's son. Phaedra clutched the door frame for support. The little inconsistent pieces reeled like the glass shards of a kaleidoscope in her mind, forming a pattern of truth; the sense of command, his effortless grace in dancing, his reluctance to discuss his family, even the boots she'd noticed the first day testified to what her intuition had screamed all along—Bram Basingstoke was no mere groom. But she hadn't listened.

She'd been too wrapped up in the sensual game they'd played. She'd been duped, absolutely, thoroughly and completely. Phaedra felt sick. Giles was going to kill her for this.

Giles. The full import of Sir Nathan's revelation struck her anew. Not only had she been duped, Giles had too. She wasn't the only one who was going to suffer. Giles would bear the scandal of having hired an earl's son to work in the stables in the first place. After the year he'd had, it was the last thing he needed. She forced herself to concentrate on the scene unfolding.

'I could be wrong.' Webster gave a casual shrug. 'Hard to know really, the last time I saw him he was...'

Naked. The situation which had seemed bad a moment ago was about to get a whole lot worse, proving that all things were indeed relative. Any moment the whole story was going to come out and the district would know of her folly, unless Bram's fist got to Captain Webster's mouth first.

It did, and within an hour the party had disassembled entirely, the last carriage pulling out of the Castonbury drive on the stroke of eleven, an early night even by country standards. The fete had been a complete debacle.

'They're all going home to write letters.' Aunt Wilhelmina harrumphed as Giles gathered the family in the blue sitting room where they'd toasted an evening of success just a few hours before.

Giles shot Aunt Wilhelmina a quelling look, his grey eyes twin storms. 'I think letters to petty relatives are the least of our worries at present.' Phaedra did not think she'd ever seen her brother this angry, except for the other night. But this was a different kind of anger. This anger was boiling under a lid, in an attempt to remain contained, far worse than honest anger given free rein.

Lily put a gentling hand on his shoulder. 'Giles, we should give people a chance to explain.'

'What is there to explain?' Giles ground out,

taking a seat near the cold fireplace. He glared at Phaedra. 'Sir Nathan has a head wound and you were in absentia from your own party at the time.'

Phaedra pleated the thin fabric of her skirt. 'I would hardly call it a head wound.'

'I would hardly call it a coincidence,' Giles pressed. 'I'm not interested in quibbling over the particulars.'

'I had gone to the library. I'd wanted a moment to be alone, but he followed me.' She told the story carefully, leaving out certain elements. She made no mention of Bram or of the information Sir Nathan had threatened to reveal. The rest of the story poured out in cautious bits. Sir Nathan had touched her, had forced her to the wall when she'd resorted to shattering the vase against the brute's head.

'I will call him out over this,' Giles said tersely when she'd finished. 'Scores will need to be settled. I shall call on Sir Nathan tomorrow.'

That was the last thing she wanted. 'Whatever for? *I* settled the score tonight, and an expensive score it was. That was Wedgwood porcelain I broke over his head.' She didn't doubt Giles's prowess with firearms but Sir Nathan wouldn't hesitate to reveal the rest of what he knew. Who knew what Giles would do *then*?

'There are things men should settle between themselves,' Giles insisted. 'Sir Nathan thought to compromise you in your own home. Such an action cannot go unaddressed. Which brings us to you, Mr Basingstoke. Care to explain what an earl's son is doing working in *my* stables?'

Heavens, it was true. If Giles was saying it, there could be no doubt. Phaedra had hoped Sir Nathan had been making wild accusations but those hopes hadn't lived long. She looked at Bram, all nature of emotion warring inside her. Anger over being duped, anger at not seeing what had so obviously been in front of her from the start, anger, too, at herself.

'I'm up here on a repairing lease.'

Phaedra's stomach fell. She knew what a repairing lease really was. Her old worries came back. He'd been passing the time and she'd been a foolish dalliance to while away the hours of his banishment. He clearly wasn't in Derbyshire for his health. There were few reasons young, healthy gentlemen came to Derbyshire other than to mend their reputations.

All the *I told you so's* of the world seemed to be pounding their victory in her head. He had used her and all the while she'd been falling in love. She'd told him her dreams, told him things she'd not shared with another *ever*, and in return, he'd *used* her.

Bram was looking at her. She could feel his gaze but she could not look at him. She couldn't bear to see the truth of it, that this cruel subterfuge had been a game. Bram was about to disclose all his secrets. In a moment she would know all about him. She'd spent weeks wondering. Now that the moment of truth had arrived, she wasn't sure she wanted to know, after all.

He began to speak, his gaze moving away to Giles. 'I told you in Buxton, Montague, that I worked at Nannerings, the riding school in London, and I've mentioned as much to Phaedra as well. I have not lied to you about my qualifications.'

'You left out some pertinent details,' Giles interjected. 'Such as the fact that you weren't just a riding instructor, but an earl's son. And secondly, why were you forced to leave?'

Bram's eyes shifted back to her but Phaedra wouldn't look up. 'A woman,' Bram answered tersely. 'I left over a woman.'

Phaedra's eyes focused on her hands in her lap. Of course it was a woman. He was a handsome man and he'd all but admitted he'd been highly sought after.

'Did you love her?' Phaedra asked quietly. There might have been no others in the room except for the reminder of Aunt Wilhelmina's sharp indrawn hiss of a breath.

'Phaedra, such a question!' she scolded, a bastion of propriety to the last. 'That's hardly appropriate.'

'I think it's very appropriate, considering what you've been up to,' Giles broke in. 'Go on, tell us about this woman.'

'No. I did not love her,' Bram announced to the room at large.

Phaedra *did* look up at that. 'You gave up your job over her and yet you had no feelings for her?' She didn't like where this analogy was leading. The situation was far too reminiscent of what had happened here. He was leaving over *her*.

'I had no choice. I shot her husband in a duel,' Bram said matter-of-factly. 'Many people thought it should have been me who'd taken the bullet. After all, he was a wronged husband and I a mere cuckolder.'

'Did you kill him?' Giles asked with a great amount of sangfroid. Phaedra couldn't help but notice Aunt Wilhelmina leaning forward, careful not to miss a single word in spite of her teachings to the contrary about gossip and rumour.

'No, I did not.' Bram was speaking to Giles now. 'But the incident was enough to make it necessary to leave London. My father thought it best I leave town for the duration of the Season.'

'Your father the earl,' Giles put in.

'Yes. I am the Earl of Hartvale's second son, Lord Bramford Basingstoke.' To his credit, Bram didn't try to deny it, although there would have been little point to it at this juncture. The jig was up and he knew it.

'And now you're here.' Phaedra rose, wanting to pace and spend some of the angry energy she'd accumulated. What had begun as the most marvellous interlude of her life had taken a dark cast. It was ending poorly. 'You're repeating the same pattern. I understand. I was just another student at Nannerings to you.'

Tears burned in her eyes. What a fool she'd been to think this would be special to him, that *she'd* be special to him. What she felt now was her fault. He'd not promised her anything beyond the moment. She'd been warned about the overwhelming persuasion of the heat of passion.

'What is all this talk about?' Aunt Wilhelmina interrupted.

Lily swept forward, taking charge of Wilhelmina. 'I think it's time you and I let the three of them talk.

I'll have your maid fix up some warm milk. You must be exhausted.'

'Phaedra, go with them,' Giles said. 'There are things that need to be said privately and it won't help you to hear them.'

She did go. But she lingered outside the door. She shouldn't have. The moment the door was shut, Giles began to speak again. She pressed her ear to the wood. 'You are an earl's son. You have knowingly misled my sister and me by pretending to be someone else. *Your* masquerade has brought shame to our family, all for the sake of appeasing your boredom, no doubt.

'Additionally, you've compromised my sister. Your rank and a gentleman's honour demands you marry her and restore the family name. The sooner, the better, I think. We can tell everyone it was a fairytale courtship. The ladies will know how to shape the story to make its oddities romantic instead of scandalous.'

Outside, Phaedra clenched her fists. She didn't want a forced marriage to a man who cared not a fig for her. But Bram's response came as a blow.

'No, Montague. I won't do it. I won't marry your sister.'

It was the final nail in the coffin, the absolute death blow. Phaedra put her hand to her mouth and fled. She'd been an abject fool.

Chapter Eighteen

Giles Montague's men had caught up with him in Buxton in much the same place Giles had found him, although in a slightly more inebriated condition. Part of him had expected it, the part that knew Phaedra had meant it when she'd said she'd go to the Derby. But Giles, who ought to have known better, wasn't sure and, as an unpleasant result, Bram found himself standing before a man only two years his senior as if he were a recalcitrant schoolboy caught pranking the headmaster.

Phaedra's brother met his gaze across the expanse of polished desktop. 'She's gone.' To his credit, Montague looked suitably worn. Dark circles suggested the man hadn't slept well in the days it had taken to track him to Buxton and bring him back. 'She and that damned colt of hers are out there, somewhere, alone.' Giles waved a hand to indicate the vast world beyond Castonbury. 'I haven't a clue where she is.' Montague's fist came down hard on the desk, rattling the inkwell. Giles Montague was not a man used to being frustrated. 'I don't suppose you know where she is?'

Now they were getting to the heart of the summons. Giles Montague was desperate. 'If I did, what would you do?' Deuce take it, Bram hated being put in this position. He didn't like the idea of Phaedra and Warbourne roaming around with only each other for protection any more than her brother did. But Bram liked the idea of Phaedra being dragged home, her dream in tatters, even less.

Not even days of endless drinking had been able to soften the image of an angry, hurt Phaedra the way she'd looked that last night. It was no wonder she wouldn't forgive him, he could hardly forgive himself. Now, Montague was asking him to betray Phaedra again.

Montague's jaw tensed. 'If you are holding out on me and she's hurt, I will personally...' Montague's threat didn't make an appearance. Bram's temper exploded. He leapt across the polished surface of Montague's irritatingly perfect desk. Bram unseated Montague and the pair hit the floor, a brawl fully under way. Giles Montague knew how to fight, Bram would give him that; he knew from their previous go-round. But the man was tired and Bram was fully fuelled with righteous anger.

Bram straddled him, pulling hard on Giles's cravat. 'Do not assume you are the only man here who is worried about her,' he said through gritted teeth. He released the cravat and stood up. 'Have I made myself clear?'

Montague rose and brushed himself off. 'She belongs back here where she is safe. She is the daughter of a duke. This is not a game.' Bram tensed, waiting for Montague to take a swing at him. But Montague merely resumed his seat, his grey eyes hard.

Bram shook his head. 'She sold her mother's pearls for that horse, for that chance. I won't sell her out for less.'

Montague thought for a moment. He crossed his arms, having come to a decision. 'All right, what do you propose?'

'I'll go after her. I'll bring her home *after* she races the colt. In the meanwhile, I'll keep her safe.' Although it might be difficult to do that at close range. He'd be the last person she'd want to see.

Montague met the suggestion with a sceptical look. 'And may I ask who will keep her safe from you?'

'You will have to trust me to act on my best judgement.'

Montague snorted. 'Forgive me if I find that a bit hard to accept. To date, your "best judgement" has done nothing short of compromise her.' But Bram thought that was the least of his worries. Phaedra had barely looked at him, too angry to meet his eyes. If he went to Epsom, maybe he'd have a chance to win her back, on his terms and hers, not Giles Montague's.

'Still, it looks like I'm your best choice.' It wouldn't serve to correct Montague on the compromise part.

'You're my only choice. If you know where she is, you'd better find her fast and you'd better be serious about protection. You can take Merlin and the coach if you'd like.' Montague paused. His offer of the best and fastest the Montague stables had to offer said enough. They were men of the world, they knew what sordid underbelly lay beneath the glamour and speed of flat racing. The faster Bram caught up to her, the better.

He'd failed to protect her. Giles waited until Bram Basingstoke had left the room before letting his head slide into his hands. Now he was reduced to desperate measures. It was sheer lunacy sending the man who wanted to seduce Phaedra after her as protection. Lord, maybe he had already seduced her for all Giles knew. He should have gone after her himself like any self-respecting brother would have done. Only he didn't know where to look with any certainty and apparently Basingstoke did. Oh, he knew she'd gone to race the damn colt. The question was where.

Had she gone to the Doncaster spring races in Yorkshire? Had she ventured south, racing her way towards Epsom? Perhaps she would dare the standard classics at Newmarket? The Two Thousand Guineas Stakes were next week. He didn't know and he couldn't very well waste time running from venue to venue, not when he was needed here as well.

Giles pulled open the narrow top drawer of his desk and pulled out a letter that had come just that morning from Harry. It was short and had been written in haste. Harry's excitement was nearly as palpable as the air of mystery. Harry had discovered something. He didn't say what it was, or perhaps he *couldn't* say. But the hint was there. The muddied waters surrounding Jamie's death were clearing. Harry was getting closer to *something*.

He wished he could be there when Harry found the answers, and Harry *would* find them. Harry was thorough and meticulous. He would leave no lead unexplored. And when he had his answers, Harry would exact justice if there was any to be had. Growing up, Harry had worshipped Jamie, they both had. Giles had been just young enough to look up to his brother and just old enough to be his constant companion. He'd never had to follow at a distance like young Harry.

Those had been heady days, striding around Castonbury like young gods. He had a hundred pictures in his head of Jamie, hands in pockets, wind blowing his hair back as he strode across the fields so confident, so immortal, so sure in his knowledge that one day all this would be his.

Giles rubbed at the bridge of his nose. Neither of them had ever guessed Castonbury would skip Jamie and come straight to him. Neither of them had wanted that. If Jamie walked through the door right now he'd hand it all back. Lord, he'd give anything for Jamie to walk through that door.

Giles shook his head. Such imaginings were not worthy of a grown man. They were weak and fanciful. Yet he couldn't help thinking how different things would have been if Jamie had come home. Maybe Kate would still have married Virgil.

Maybe Phaedra would still have run off with her blasted horse. But Father would still be in his right mind instead of withdrawing into the past and 'better days.' *And maybe you would not have discovered Lily*, his conscience scolded mercilessly. *Be careful what you wish for.*

Yet he couldn't help but wonder if things would have been different, *better*, if Jamie had come home. *Edward too*, his conscience railed again. Edward and Phaedra had been close as the two youngest. Perhaps Edward would have tempered her wildness…or aided it. Giles chuckled at the idea. Edward had been the angel-boy when it had come to looks but he'd been wilder than all of them. No doubt, Edward would be with Phaedra right now, traipsing across the country to race that colt and thinking it was a jolly lark to run away from home. He'd have loved Phaedra's new horse travelling cart.

It would have been good to have Edward with her, better than Bram Basingstoke, although what Phaedra really needed was him, Giles, and his voice of reason to weigh against her recklessness. But he could no more be with Phaedra than with Harry, no matter how much he wished it.

He could not leave Castonbury. It would mean leaving Father and who knew what kind of trouble he and that mincing valet of his, Smithins, would get up to if left unwatched. It meant leaving Alicia unsupervised, a thought that sat poorly with him.

To add to his pile of wishes, he wished he felt more comfortable about her claim to be Jamie's wife. In truth, it was Jamie's action in the whole bit that didn't ring true. Jamie *knew* he had to marry better than her. But Giles also knew better than anyone the kind of things being on a battlefront could do to a man, the types of feelings it could engender. Jamie would have not been immune and perhaps he'd been less prepared for those emotions than a man who'd been taught to expect life in the military.

Giles glanced down again at Harry's cryptic note. Short, terse, mysterious, it hardly seemed worth the effort to frank it all the way from Spain with such vague references. But it was the last line he wanted to read over and over, the last line that kept him here, another reason he could not go hunting Phaedra.

Dear brother, there is hope. I will not stop until I've exhausted it all.

Hope for what? That a body had been recovered so funds could be released? Hope that Jamie had had a decent burial, after all? That he wasn't mouldering at the bottom of the Bidasoa? That Harry had incontrovertible proof about the legitimacy of Alicia's marriage so that the family could go forward in certainty about the future of the dukedom?

Or the wildest hope of all that there had been some mistake, that Jamie hadn't drowned that fateful day on the river? Such a hope was sheer madness and Giles pushed it away. No one thought that any more. Too much time had passed and Jamie would never have let them languish in grief-ridden suspense this long, nor would Jamie have forsaken his wife and child, if that's what they were.

Giles pushed back from the desk. He had to get out of this room. He wouldn't get any work done at this rate. He'd saddle up Genghis and ride out to see Lily. When he'd proposed a proper, long engagement, he'd never dreamed it would seem this long. He should have married her last summer and been done with it. He could hardly wait to have her with him all day, every day, even if it was simply to look across a room and know she was there.

'It's official. She's not here, damn it all.' Sir Nathan drained the last of his glass and set it down on the table beside him with a thud. 'My sources tell me Lord Bramford was back at Castonbury today, without her.' He had reasoned the pair of them would be together. It would have made it easier to extract his due revenge for the ball if they had been.

Across from him, splayed out in a chair and still nursing a discoloured jaw, Hugh Webster perked up. 'At least we can get Lord Bramford.' Hugh rubbed the side of his face. 'He packs a helluva wallop.'

'I know,' Sir Nathan replied drily. 'But it can't be obvious. We'll look guilty if anything happens too close to home.' Subtlety wasn't Hugh Webster's strong suit when it came to revenge, although the fellow was plenty crafty.

It was down to revenge now. There was no sense trying to be discreet. Phaedra wouldn't marry him, short of being dragged to the altar by her hair. While that created a rousing fantasy, the actuality of such an event seemed unlikely.

Webster was grinning. 'What did you have in mind?'

'Going after the colt. She'll learn she can't mess with me and not pay. A little nobbling would be just the thing to teach that lesson. The only thing now is tracking her down.'

Hugh chuckled. 'How hard can it be to find a woman and a horse travelling with that odd contraption of hers? I know a couple fellows in the village who would be up for it.'

'Perfect. If anything goes wrong, we can blame them. The Montagues will never be able to officially trace anything back to us, even if the fellows squeal.' Nathan refilled his glass.

Hugh raised his glass meaningfully. 'It's time for revenge.'

'Past time.' The Montagues were about to get what was coming to them.

Chapter Nineteen

Epsom, four days before the Derby

Phaedra anxiously studied the mantel clock in the private parlour of the Waterloo Inn, ticking away the hours of the early afternoon. It was hard to conduct interviews if there was no one to actually interview. She fought back the urge to go to the window and stare out into the courtyard or go to the door and scan up and down the corridor for potential candidates.

Someone had to come. Surely someone would claim the right to ride Warbourne. She had not travelled this far to fail days before the race simply because she didn't have a rider. This was Epsom at the height of spring racing. It wasn't as if riders were thin on the ground.

The former spa town was already abuzz with

race day business. She'd snagged the last room at the popular Waterloo Inn on the High Street, the remaining rooms claimed by other owners who'd made the week-long journey from Newmarket to Epsom after the recently run Two Thousand Guineas Stakes. The stakes winner, Manfred, was already here munching hay in the stall two down from Warbourne. His owner, Scott Stonehewer, was down the hall in the public room playing an afternoon game of cards while his star colt rested.

The innkeeper bustled in and Phaedra's hopes began to rise. 'There's someone here to see you, Lady Phaedra.' He bowed respectfully, doing his best not to give any sign he thought her behavior out of the ordinary. It might be because he was discreetly diplomatic, knowing all coin was worth the same value no matter who it came from and Phaedra had been sure to pay him well. Or because this was Epsom, a town that owed its survival to the thoroughbred racing industry and the reality that standard gender roles were somewhat suspended for a week in May when the country caught Derby fever.

Phaedra smiled, letting relief fill her. 'Send him in, please.' Someone had come, after all.

Phaedra sat up straight, plucked at the bodice of her blue muslin day dress to make sure all was respectable, folded her hands in her lap and was immediately at a loss for words.

'Hello, Phaedra.' The caller was no rider at all, but Bram Basingstoke in the immaculate flesh, looking entirely too handsome for his own good as he leaned in the doorway, dressed in buff riding breeches, a dark jacket and high boots.

She'd thought she'd dealt with her feelings for Bram during the long journey to Epsom. There'd been little else to do during the days on the road. Apparently not.

He'd deceived her, played her for a fool all for the sake of a little sport and the consequences for her had been tremendous. *She* was supposed to pay for *his* indiscretion with marriage. If she didn't pay with marriage, she'd pay with scandal. It was only a matter of time. She knew she was lucky news of the situation hadn't drifted down to Epsom just yet.

It would have been better if he'd remained an anonymous groom. Marriage would have been impossible. It would have been best for it to remain so. There would have been no hurt feelings, no overt rejection, just a whimsical impossibility. Being the son of an earl made it so much worse, because the impossible became possible and she had been rejected.

Bram stood there unfazed. If the same thoughts plagued him, he gave no sign of it. 'I heard all the best horses were in town and thought I'd stop by to see if it was true.'

'Yes, it's true, as you can see.' She wished for an ounce of his sangfroid. It took all her effort to keep her voice calm, as if seeing him again didn't conjure up a host of feelings. She was still over-whelmed by the sheer masculine potency of him, the way he owned a room simply by walking in it, the way he could garner her best affections just by looking at her and use them against her. She couldn't forget that last part.

The Derby was days away. She didn't have time for whatever Bram wanted. She had to find a rider. Bram pushed off the door jamb with his customary ease, took a seat in the upholstered chair across from her and crossed his legs. If she was smart, she would not let him settle in for a long stay.

'I am glad you dropped by but you have to go. I am interviewing riders.' She couldn't very well conduct interviews with him hovering nearby for a lot of reasons, not the least being the havoc he wreaked on her ability to think clearly.

'Ah, yes.' Bram didn't move from his chair. 'I heard. I tracked you down from the stables. I saw Warbourne, by the way. He looks good. Bevins told me you were staying here, alone?' He raised his dark eyebrow in that annoyingly superior way of his when he found something suspect or displeasing.

'Yes, most of the owners are staying here,' Phaedra said sharply. She didn't have to defend her choice to him. The Waterloo was perfectly respectable. 'If you'll excuse me?'

Bram gave her a soft smile that was more alarming than his wolfish grin, the one he used right before he kissed her. 'Face facts, Phaedra. No one's coming.'

She didn't need to look at the clock to know he spoke the truth but she wouldn't show her disappointment to him, the man who thought he knew everything about horses, about her. She pasted on a smile. 'Did you poison the well? I shall have to raise my price. Thanks to the stud fees, I can do that.'

For once Bram didn't rise to the bait of an argument. He shook his head and Phaedra braced herself for the worst. 'It won't matter how much you pay. Everyone knows Warbourne's a risky horse to ride. No one's going to bet their literal necks he's worked out his problems.' Bram paused, a little debate warring in his eyes as he studied her.

'Go on,' Phaedra urged. If there was more, it would be best she knew it.

'Well, and the fact you're a woman. You have to admit, it's a deuced unlikely pairing. A risky colt tamed by a woman no one's heard of. I'm sorry, Phaedra.'

Phaedra stood up and turned towards the window, away from Bram. She swiped at her eyes. The room must be dusty in spite of the meticulous housekeeper. She wouldn't want Bram to misconstrue the tears for something else.

'I'll find a rider. I'll find someone,' Phaedra said resolutely.

'Where? The race is four days away. Whoever he is, he has to have time to practise on Warbourne. You can't just *say* you'll find a rider, Phaedra.'

She did not need to be reminded of that. 'If you have nothing to contribute, I'd like you to leave.' Phaedra stood up, dismissing him, and thankfully he went. She could get back to her lonely vigil.

Bram went only because he'd be back with a much-needed contribution. By virtue of her own words, she'd have to listen to him. She needed a rider and he would get her one. He would turn Epsom upside down if that's what it took to get back into her good graces.

Bram set off towards the stables, whistling a bit under his breath. The sun was out and spring had this part of England firmly in hand. He'd found Phaedra and the little minx had landed on her feet. The Waterloo was in a prime location on the high street, with close access to the downs and the morning exercise runs. For now, all was well in his world.

He didn't lie to himself that it would remain so. Sir Nathan Samuelson could show up and make trouble, someone could recognise him. Even if none of those things came to pass, he would have to reconcile his feelings for Phaedra in short order.

He'd promised Giles to bring her home after the Derby. That meant four days. There would be travel time too, but he didn't want to count on that in case he didn't get back to good terms with her. That left the four days before the Derby—four days to figure out what had motivated him to follow her the length of the country, to protect her against Giles's well-meant restrictions, to risk his own livelihood by breaking his agreement with his father. One did not do such things without a reason. He needed to know his. Once he knew that, he could decide what to do about it.

He might be going insane, becoming a modern-day Don Quixote, years of hard living and womanising having taken their toll on him at last. Or Aphrodite might be taking her revenge for all the hearts he'd broken. He supposed it was not beyond the pale that he was falling in love. It stood to reason, when such a thing finally happened it would be with a woman out of his reach and Phaedra was definitely that. Why would she want a wastrel with no prospects when she could choose anyone?

There was no pretending his father wouldn't hear of this. All of London would flock to Epsom. There would go the allowance. That had been the deal. He had his wages from Castonbury but they wouldn't sustain him for more than a few days in the style to which he was accustomed. Still, when it came down to it, disappointing Phaedra or disappointing his father, the choice was clear.

It had been a certain torture to see her again. His heart had ached at the sight of her sitting at the Waterloo wrapped in her pride, her haughty chin up as if her own stubbornness could make a rider materialise. Well, she might not be able to do that. But he could.

Bram chose to seek out Matt Somerset first. He found the rider whittling on a hay bale in the long barns overlooking the downs.

'Basingstoke, good to see you.' Matt Somerset shook his hand vigorously. 'Where have you been?'

Barely reaching Bram's shoulder, Matt Somerset had the build currently popular among hired racing riders—short, lean and wiry enough to hold a thousand pounds of speeding horse.

'Up in Derbyshire. I had to get away after the business with Fenton.' Bram had known Matt for three years. He didn't mind confessing. Matt was a trustworthy man known for his integrity in a sport that sometimes had none. 'I met a horse up there.' Bram leaned on the fence overlooking the practise oval where some horses were taking their afternoon exercise.

'A horse? Isn't a woman more your style?' Matt joked.

'Well, maybe I met both.' Bram smiled slyly, taking a well-intended elbow in the ribs from Matt. 'Anyway, this horse is fast and he needs a rider.'

'For what race?'

'The Derby.' That would either interest Matt or make him suspicious. Or maybe both. Matt's keen brown eyes looked out over the track, giving nothing away.

'What's the horse? Some unknown, I suppose?'

Bram shrugged. 'Warbourne.'

'Heaven help us.' Matt shook his head. 'So he ended up in the north, did he? With that pretty woman who's been around the stables? Word on the street is that she can't find a rider and with good reason. You do know that horse, don't you?'

Bram stood his ground. He knew that horse intimately after the past months. 'I know that horse well enough. He threw Dick Handley last year at the two-year-old races in Newmarket and a slew of other riders too. But I've seen him this year. Lady Phaedra has the touch. He's a different horse but just as fast.'

'I don't know, Basingstoke. I've already got a couple of races lined up that day.' Matt began to prevaricate, that was a bad sign.

'She'll pay well and you can be the one everyone remembers. You'll be the jockey who mastered Warbourne.'

Matt chuckled. 'He's just a horse, Basingstoke. There's a hundred more like him. No one will remember.'

'Everyone remembers Derby winners.' Bram dangled the proverbial carrot. 'Lady Phaedra means to establish a stud afterwards. You can come along for the ride, quite literally in this case.' Bram paused, letting his offer sink in. 'It's been a while since you've had a spotlighter, hasn't it? What was it, two? No, three years ago you had that filly at the Oaks.' Bram let his voice trail off with a sigh. 'I need this, Matt. I need this favour, but we'd be kidding ourselves if we didn't admit you needed it too. Warbourne can be your chance to show everyone you're back.'

Matt put his booted foot on the fence rail and looked down at the ground. 'You're right about that. Since the accident, offers have been scarce and the mounts I have been getting have been mediocre.'

Bram nodded. He could smell victory. 'I'll see you at six tomorrow for the morning rides and we'll see what we've got. If you need me, I'll be at the Waterloo on the high street.'

It was nearly dark when Bram returned to the inn. Phaedra was still in the parlour. Her face fell when she saw him. 'I thought I told you to go.'

'Only if I couldn't contribute.' Bram pulled up a chair and turned it backwards before sitting down. 'I found you a rider. I would say that definitely counts as a contribution.'

'Really? You found me a rider?' The joy spreading across her face made the risk worthwhile. In that moment, Bram didn't care if he was penniless if he could just see her smile and know he was the cause of it.

Suddenly, Phaedra's smile stopped and she became wary again. 'One good deed doesn't make up for what happened. I'm still mad at you.'

Bram gave a throaty laugh. 'But you almost forgot. You had to remind yourself.'

Phaedra picked up a tiny decorative pillow from the sofa and threw it at him. 'I didn't forget how insufferable you were.'

Bram caught it with quick hands and rose to go. He wouldn't push his luck. 'I missed you too.' He'd take her temper as good sign. Anything was better than the frigidly polite indifference she'd shown him that afternoon. He'd count this as progress.

Chapter Twenty

'Tell me again he wasn't the only jockey left in town. Tell me you didn't pull him out of a pub and bribe him to ride.' Phaedra worried out loud the next morning while she and Bram waited for Matt Somerset to arrive at the stables. She'd fought between elation and anxiety all last night after Bram's news, thrilled Bram had found a rider and worried beyond words that the rider was not nearly good enough to handle Warbourne.

'He's better than that, Phaedra,' Bram told her, but she could see he was anxious too. His eyes kept darting to the entrance where Matt Somerset was expected. 'Don't worry, he'll be here.'

She was sure he said that as much for himself as for her. Warbourne was saddled with Bevins walking him outside. The colt was ready to work. She'd been exercising him herself since their arrival and he knew the schedule. Mornings were for workouts.

Bram stiffened and Phaedra followed his gaze. A wiry fellow with a tanned face entered the stables. 'Is that him?'

Bram grinned, full of his usual confidence. 'I knew he'd come.' Bram waved the man over and made the introductions. 'This is Lady Phaedra and Warbourne is outside.'

Matt Somerset whistled in appreciation at the sight of Warbourne. 'He looks better than he looked last year, I'll say that much,' he complimented, running an experienced hand down the colt's front leg. 'Good legs. His bones are strong, his coat is glossy. You've been feeding him well. What are his training times?'

'A minute fifty.' Phaedra was unable to keep the pride out of her voice. She knew it was a good time for a mile and a half. 'Faster than Nectar last year.'

'Faster than Nectar *with* a trained rider on board in Bill Arnull,' Somerset corrected. 'Who has been riding him in exercise? The boy?' He gave a nod in Bevins's direction.

'I've been riding him,' Phaedra said swiftly. Why couldn't anyone accept that a woman could ride a horse and get decent times? Was it that impossible to believe?

Somerset raised his eyebrow at this. 'Have you now? Has he thrown you?'

'No. But I'm his only rider.' She held Somerset's gaze, a private message passing between them. The real test today wouldn't be about Warbourne's speed. It would be about getting on his back. Most of Warbourne's problems had come from the starting line.

'I'm impressed you've stayed on.' Somerset rubbed Warbourne's muzzle and spoke soft encouraging words. 'What's the secret?'

'It's the knees. He'll bolt if you clench your thighs too tightly.'

Matt nodded. 'It's natural to do that at the starting line. It explains why better riders than you, no insult intended, were thrown. However, it's a prime communication point. We'll have to find another way. Basingstoke, how about a leg up? Let's see what this horse can do.'

Bram tossed him up. Phaedra held Warbourne's bridle and her breath, the phrase *let him stay on* running like a litany through her mind. Bram stepped away from the horse and gave the signal. She let go and crossed her fingers.

Warbourne snorted and tossed his glossy mane, prancing under the weight of the new rider. Matt kept the reins tight, fighting for control, and at last he had it. Warbourne settled beneath him and Phaedra breathed again.

Bram clipped on a lead rope and together the little group headed to the practise lines. They were not alone. With the race nearing, everyone with a possible entrant had the same idea. Phaedra knew they were cutting it close. Today would be the last real workout day. Tomorrow, the Derby races would begin, leading off with the Oaks Stakes for fillies only.

They garnered their share of stares as they passed. Fine, Phaedra thought, her head held high. Let them look. Let them see what the competition is going to do to them. But she couldn't ignore the whispers that followed in their wake—speculation about the horse, about the rider, about her, all of them outsiders in their own way.

Beside her, Bram whispered, 'Don't listen to them. Come race day, they'll be the sorry ones.'

Just then, a horse nipped at Warbourne. Warbourne leapt towards it, ready to retaliate. It took all of Bram's strength and Matt's skill to hold him. But the rumblings had already started—the colt was still wild, unpredictable. A couple of people recognised Matt in the saddle and called out jokes. 'You gonna stay in the saddle this time?'

Bram stared them all down and Phaedra tried to

do the same. They found an open spot and Bram flipped open his pocket watch. Phaedra flipped open an old watch that had been Edward's and exchanged a look with Bram. 'Ready?'

'Set.' Matt's heels went down in the stirrups.

The second hand hit the twelve. 'Go!'

Warbourne leapt at a secret signal from Matt and they were off, flying over the turf, Matt bent low over Warbourne's neck. Envy and pride warred inside her at the sight of it. That was *her* horse. She knew precisely what Matt was feeling, the bite of the wind in his face, the strength of muscle bunching beneath his legs. She'd not *seen* Warbourne run before and the sight was glorious. She would not have missed it for the world.

Warbourne reached the finish line and she glanced at her watch. One minute forty. If all went well, that would be a winning time. She looked up to confer with Bram but Warbourne chose that moment to swerve.

He headed towards a group of horses and riders bunched together on the downs doing short sprints. He was going to go right through them. 'No, no,' Phaedra spoke her thoughts out loud. 'Leave them alone.'

Warbourne broke through the pack, scattering

horses to the right and left as he passed them. 'What is Mr Somerset doing?'

Bram chuckled. 'Giving them something to re-member. They'll be sure to give him plenty of space on the track if they can help it next time.' The next time would be race day. Somerset would need the space too. At last count, twenty horses were registered. It would be a crowded field.

'What do you think?' Bram asked while they waited for Somerset to bring Warbourne over.

'He'll do,' Phaedra conceded, and gladly. She was out of time to be right. She was happy in this case to be wrong, her worries misplaced. 'A min-ute forty is nothing to ignore.'

Nor was the man beside her. Bram Basingstoke had done the impossible for her. He'd found a rider, and a good one at that. Matt Somerset was not some over-the-hill, dried-up jockey. It shouldn't make a difference. Bram had refused to marry her. He didn't want her for more than a casual affair and yet she was melting. Again. Veering towards foolishness with him. Again. This morning at the stables, with the horse to act as a buffer, it had been too easy to fall back into the usual patterns, to feel at home with Bram as if the disastrous night of the ball had never happened. Everything seemed nearly as it had been before, before he was an earl's son and she a duke's ruined daughter. She had to be strong. She couldn't forget what was real and what was fantasy.

By mid-morning their work at the stables was done. Warbourne was in good hands between Bevins and Somerset, and Phaedra was feeling distinctly positive.

'I'll walk you home and we'll see what kind of trouble we can get into on the way.' Bram leaned close to her ear with the old familiarity. 'Since you managed to wear a riding habit today instead of breeches, I'd hate to let the opportunity go to waste.'

Phaedra held her resolve. 'This doesn't change anything. Don't think for a moment that it does.'

Bram's face turned grim and he pulled her roughly aside into an empty tack room. 'Then tell me, princess, what will?'

'Take your hands off me,' Phaedra warned.

'Not until you listen to me,' Bram growled.

Phaedra shook free to make her point. 'I *have* listened to you. I listened to you tell my brother you wouldn't marry me. I am nothing more than a dalliance. What we did meant nothing to you.'

'You did not hear me say *that* to your brother,' Bram interrupted. 'You're wrong. It meant every-thing to me.' His voice rose and he looked about to make sure they hadn't drawn any attention before lowering it again.

'What do you think I'm doing here, Phaedra? Do you think I travelled the length of England on a whim?'

She would not be melted so easily. 'No, I have no idea why you're here.'

'Giles sent me. He was worried sick about you. He had no idea where you'd gone. I offered to come.'

'You've been sent to drag me back home before I can tarnish the family name any further.' Phaedra's chin went up in her defiant tilt.

'Not exactly. I wouldn't give up the details of your location and I made him promise you could race the colt.' The selfless kindness of the bargain stymied her momentarily.

'However did you make him concede that?'

'I wrestled him for it.'

'And won?'

Bram laughed. 'Yes, I won. Giles Montague isn't entirely invincible even if he is your brother.'

He'd done this for her even though their last interaction at Castonbury had been full of anger. He'd found her a rider. It left her more confused than ever. 'I'm afraid I don't understand, Bram.' She couldn't afford to understand. If she did, she might also start to hope. 'You told my brother you wouldn't marry me.' She clung to that one last defense. He'd rejected her. She could not forget that.

'Eavesdropping, Phaedra? You couldn't have been in the room for that.' Bram frowned in disappointment. 'I told your brother I would not marry you under these circumstances. I would not have you forced to the altar. You and I did not start this with marriage in mind. We shouldn't have to end it that way unless that's a conclusion we come to ourselves.' Bram sighed. 'I knew how you felt about the suitors being pushed on you at the party. I didn't want to be another one of those.'

Phaedra studied him. She was smart enough not to ask the obvious question: did that mean he *wanted* to marry her? She wished she knew if she could believe him, if she could trust him. 'All right.'

'All right what?'

'All right. You said you'd walk me back to the inn.' Phaedra smiled. Maybe she didn't have to. Maybe it was enough that he was here. They would have the Derby and then they'd see.

She slipped her hand through the crook of his arm as they set out, walking up the high street, halting every so often to peer into shop windows. Even window-shopping was fun with Bram. They stopped to laugh at a ridiculously garish hat on display at the milliners and to watch a juggler on the street corner. With the big race looming the town was bustling with visitors and entertainment. It was like one gigantic village fair.

Phaedra's stomach growled. She put a hand over her belly as if to stop it but it was too late. 'Hungry?' Bram cocked a suspecting eyebrow.

'I didn't eat breakfast this morning. I was too nervous,' Phaedra confessed. It was all she had to say. Bram had them seated at a tea house with a pot of tea and a plate of scones in record time. Phaedra thought it had something to do with the way he'd smiled at the woman running the place.

'You're shameless.' Phaedra bit into a delicious lemon scone.

'Doesn't seem to affect your appetite,' Bram teased.

He was devastating like this, playing the gentleman with his display of manners, and yet so very easy to be with. 'You're staring, Phaedra,' Bram said in low tones, clearly not minding the attention. 'Should I be worried? Are you still mad and planning to skewer me with your butter knife?'

Phaedra shook her head with a smile. 'No. I imagine women don't stay mad at you for long.'

Bram laughed and reached for a scone. 'That might be true.'

He was irresistible. He couldn't help it. She knew the kind of man he was, a heartbreaker and a rogue by all accounts, and yet she couldn't help but crave him. Maybe it was the mystery of him, the challenge of him. He was a man who didn't stay in one place for long. But she had him now. Presumably she had him until the Derby was over, three short days from now. She'd have to decide what she wanted from those three days, what she could afford.

He wasn't a groom to be dallied with any longer. The stakes were higher. If she wasn't careful she'd end up married. Earls' sons and dukes' daughters couldn't dally with each other without consequences. Those consequences might be worth the risk. The thought warmed her cheeks.

'Phaedra? You're wool-gathering. I was unaware my conversation was so lacking in entertainment.'

'I am sorry, what were you saying?'

Bram smiled. 'Care to share? Whatever they were, the thoughts must be good ones—you're blushing.'

Phaedra leaned close across the table. 'I was thinking of you, to tell the truth.' It was more fun to be like this with him than tense and aloof.

'What about me?' Bram pressed with dancing eyes, draining the last of the tea.

He'd found her a rider, he'd travelled to Epsom for her with no obvious reward for himself. No man she knew did such things. 'I was thinking, you might be in danger of becoming a good man.'

The door to the tea shop opened, the little bell over the door frame jingling. A fashionably dressed man and woman entered. Both Phaedra and Bram glanced their way but Bram turned back towards her and rose. He extended his hand, his wicked smile playing on those sinful lips. 'Then we'd better go rectify that immediately.'

The words shot heat to her veins. If Bram seemed a bit hasty in his departure from the tea shop, Phaedra took pleasure in being the reason for it. Outside, they'd gone no further than a block when Bram pulled her into a little-used side street, more like an alley than any type of thoroughfare, and kissed her soundly.

Bram kissed her hard. It felt good to do that. She'd been driving him mad with lust in that riding habit since early this morning. Her hair pinned up beneath a little hat placed at a jaunty angle made her look every inch the regal woman. Made him want to take that hat off and pull her hair down pin by pin until she looked appropriately tousled.

His hands were at her waist, drawing her firmly against him, wanting her to feel how much he desired her, wanting her to know that, in spite of his ulterior motives for leaving the tea shop in a rush, he'd wanted her nonetheless. It had been a near-run thing in there, a reminder of how close to the edge he was living by coming to Epsom.

He'd known the couple that had walked in. George Rupert, the Earl of Elsford's son, and his sister, Gwendolyn, a former pupil at Nannerings. He'd been to their home for an entertainment or two over the years. There was no reason for them not to acknowledge Lord Bram and within moments they would have. He wasn't ready to be discovered yet. He had too much discovering of his own to do before the game was up.

Phaedra moved against him, her hips seductive in their motion. 'We should probably stop before this goes much further,' Bram murmured.

'When, then?' Phaedra's eyes were serious as they held his, her arms still about his neck. 'I want to be with you again, Bram. From the feel of things, you want to be with me too.' Her voice was quiet, her proposition more honest than bold, and it touched him quite unexpectedly.

He should refuse. He tried. 'I promised your brother—'

Phaedra cut him off. 'We have three days, Bram, a gift.' Her hand dropped between them, cupping him through his trousers, and he knew he was in trouble. The student had become the master in such a very short time. 'We should spend them as we wish.' She kissed him on the mouth, on the column of his neck, at the base of his neck where his pulse beat hard beneath his shirt.

'Then what?' He had to try one more time to make her see reason. Things had ended badly at Castonbury.

'Then we'll see what happens next.' Phaedra kissed his mouth once more. 'Say yes, Bram. I want three days, not a lifetime.'

'A good man would refuse on moral grounds.' Good heavens, he did not want to be that man right now. He wanted to say yes.

Phaedra reached up on tiptoes and blew gently against his ear, the apple-cinnamon scent of her teasing his nostrils. 'I don't want a good man, Bram. I want you.'

'Then you shall have me.' *For however long it lasts.*

'I'll save the having for tonight, if you don't mind,' Phaedra whispered impishly.

What had he gotten himself into? Epsom would be a challenge. For now, he had his hands full, or rather Phaedra did, and he intended to enjoy every moment of it.

Chapter Twenty-One

Phaedra raised her knuckles to knock on Bram's door. How he'd managed a room at the crowded inn she didn't know, but she wasn't going to quibble. Tonight, *she* was going to seduce *him*. She was going to show him she'd meant what she'd said about their three days.

Bram answered, dressed in shirt and breeches. She stepped inside and shut the door behind her. She said nothing, just reached for the pins holding her hair.

Once the Derby was over, the future between them was once again uncertain. She'd go back to Castonbury and establish her stud. Bram would go to who knew where and do who knew what.

His mouth found hers; his hands rested possessively at her waist, her arms about his neck, her body pressed to his. She'd asked for this and it wasn't enough, it was nowhere near enough. She was supposed to be doing the seducing.

Bram's hand at her breast, palming and stroking through the fabric of her bodice, was building a whole other heat that raged low in her stomach. The fabric that had seemed so thin when she'd bought the gown now seemed too heavy, too confining.

'Take it off,' she breathed, her own hands pushing at the small sleeves. But Bram stilled her impatient movements.

'Easy, you'll rip this and not have anything to wear.'

'And if *you* rip it?' Her voice was hoarse with excitement and need. These were heady paths she travelled on tonight.

'You still won't have anything to wear.' Bram laughed. 'But I'll be careful, I promise. I like undressing you.' Bram trailed a line of kisses down her neck, his own hands taking over, pushing the delicate sage-coloured silk-and-lace confection over her shoulders. Phaedra shivered decadently at the feel of nearly naked skin.

'Ah, no silk smalls tonight. I've been missing them,' Bram murmured. His hands deftly worked the lacing of the short stays over the thin linen chemise. The corset was not tight, it was only meant as support, yet Phaedra felt she'd been freed as her breasts fell into Bram's hands.

He pressed the fabric of her chemise taut against her breasts and knelt in front of her, taking first one and then the other in his mouth, the wet heat of his mouth and the friction of the cloth a delightful torment to her senses. Her hands clenched in his hair as the sensations he evoked threatened to swamp her.

His hands moved to her waist, gathering up the chemise in his fingers until she was bare to him. He looked up at her from his intimate crouch, his eyes burning, his smile wicked. 'Sit down, Phaedra, I'm going to put my mouth on you.' She trembled at the decadent words. This was definitely no longer her seduction, and she no longer cared. Her thoughts had become nothing more than a kaleidoscope of sensation, her body searching for the satisfaction that lay beyond these pleasure-laden shores.

Her hands found the bed behind her and she sat down hard. Bram breathed against her mound, doing those wicked things she loved so much with his tongue, his mouth, until she thought she'd scream, her mind holding on to one slim thought: release would come. When it did, she was more than ready for it, her hands anchored in the bed sheets, letting it take her in a rush of gratification.

Phaedra fell back on the bed, a sigh of repletion escaping her lips. 'Heavens, Bram, you'll be the death of me.'

The narrow bed took his weight and he stretched out beside her, his dark head propped on his hand. His other hand was warm on her midriff, an entirely possessive touch, and her body revelled in it. Phaedra covered his hand with her own where it lay on her stomach. She interlaced her fingers with his.

'I'm not worried, you feel very much alive to me.' Indeed, she felt as if she'd not been alive before Bram, that her life had been a shadow of its present self, waiting for him to release her from the chains of her upbringing.

Phaedra rolled to her side and reached for him. 'It's like that for you too, isn't it?' It wasn't really a question. She remembered the way he'd looked on the island when she'd taken him in her hand, the way he felt when he clenched inside of her. His release had been as great as hers.

She stroked him through his trousers, then stopped suddenly. 'No.' She gave him a gentle push, enough to send him over the bed's edge if he hadn't put his leg down for balance. 'Take them off.' She would reclaim part of this seduction.

Bram grinned. 'I beg your pardon, my lady?'

She grinned back. 'You heard me. I said take them off.'

'As you wish.'

Bram rose off the bed. He pulled his shirt over his head in an enviously fluid motion, his hands resting provocatively at his waistband. He was going to make her pay for her sauciness.

He undid the fall of his breeches, strong tanned hands against the paler buckskin and brass buttons. Phaedra's mouth went dry. She was supremely conscious that his eyes never left hers while his hands worked the fall. He was watching her watching him. Encouraging her voyeurism even with that searing gaze of his.

He pushed his trousers down over slim hips and lean muscled legs, baring himself unabashedly before her. Phaedra wet her lips at the sight of him. She'd never get tired of seeing him naked. Her blatant perusal pleased him. A dot of moisture beaded at his tip and wicked inspiration struck Phaedra. She'd taken him in her hand before, but never this. 'Come here, I want to taste it.'

Her actions didn't surprise her as much as her words. She was entirely wanton with him where she'd scarcely noticed other men before. Yet everything about Bram was captivating, addicting.

'You're a veritable hussy,' Bram scolded, but she noticed he happily obliged, edging closer to the bed to let her tongue do its work.

She teased him with her tongue in the manner in which he'd teased her, pleasured her. She knew full well no decently bred girl engaged in such an act—an uncivilised act, some would call it. Neither would any decent girl throw her sacred virtue away on a mad romp with a man who could give her nothing, a man who couldn't or wouldn't marry her. But when she looked at Bram, she didn't see that. She saw a man who shocked her, challenged her, encouraged her passions and so much more.

'Enough, or I'll spend too soon.'

Phaedra obeyed. This was her turn to grin. She borrowed his line. 'You liked that.'

'Damn right I liked it.' Bram's voice was hoarse. 'I liked it enough to forget to play the gentleman for a moment.' He came up over her, bracing himself above her. 'I won't be able to ask this again, Phaedra. Do you want me to stop all this before it goes any farther?'

'Are you crazy? Whatever gave you that idea?' Stop? With the intimate parts of his body grazing her? With the power of him rising above her? Who in her right mind would want him to stop now?

Bram gave a slight shake of his head, his dark hair falling forward, shadowing the planes of his face. 'You know what I mean, Phaedra.' But she recognised he was hedging his bets. They'd not stopped before the consequences had been disastrous. If they kept this up, they might be travelling down the same road to the same unfortunate conclusion. Then again, this time it might be different. They wouldn't know until they got there.

He pressed a fluttering kiss against her neck. She recognised he no more wanted to stop than she did. Phaedra put her arms around his neck, drawing him into the circle of her embrace so that their bodies met, skin to skin. 'No, Bram, I don't want you to stop.'

She opened to him, taking him perfectly, intimately, in the cradle between her legs. Phaedra arched against him, feeling her body stretch and be stretched to accommodate him.

He kissed her full on the mouth and they were off again, their bodies synchronised not unlike a horse and rider.

A smile flitted across her face at the idea but she had little time to let her thoughts wander that path. There was no time to think, only to feel, only to follow Bram where he led down this new path of pleasure. She felt herself flow into him, unable to discern where one began and the other ended. Bram gave a final thrust and quickly withdrew with a rough, ragged sigh, casting her adrift on a sea of sensations. She had shattered and was sailing on the shards of her release, boneless and supple.

Bram lay next to her, his head propped in his hand, his free hand tracing little patterns on her bare skin. 'So now you're ruined, again.'

Phaedra gave a drowsy sigh. How could this be bad? She felt *glorious*. She felt absolutely *alive*.

Epsom mirrored the vibrancy she felt. When Bram escorted her to the stables to check on Warbourne, she was amazed by the racing crowds that swelled the streets to bursting. 'Look at all these people!' Phaedra exclaimed, keeping a close hold on Bram's arm in an attempt not to be swept away by the sheer mass of people. Visitors came in all varieties: the wealthy gentleman come to bet on the horses, the London lady looking for diversion, the clerk and the banker, the farmer. All classes of people thronged the streets.

'I'd watch your reticule, if I were you,' Bram

warned. 'Race days draw an unruly element as well.'

Phaedra nodded, tightening her grip on the small beaded bag she carried. She'd heard up on the Epsom Hill a pit had been set up for cockfighting and vendors had put up booths to take advantage of the crowds that would flock there for the races that afternoon. The crowds were beyond her expectations. She had some small amount of interest in seeing the displays on the hill, but they were outweighed by her gratitude for Bram's foresight. He'd managed to get them reserved seats in the grandstand.

At the stables, they checked on Warbourne. Matt and Bevins had so far been vigilant in their duty to watch Warbourne night and day. They'd taken turns sleeping in front of his stall, as had the other trainers with their own horses, to prevent any trickery or injury. Phaedra had not believed in such a necessity at first, but after seeing the crowds, she was glad she'd been talked into taking the precaution. With so many people swarming the streets and racetrack, it would be easy to slip into a horse's stall.

Warbourne was fine. Matt gave her a full report before going to weigh in for the Oaks. The horse had eaten and exercised early. Matt would be riding that afternoon in the Oaks so the day shift fell to Bevins. Phaedra nodded and listened intently to Matt's report. Part of her wanted the Derby to be over. The suspense was deadly. But part of her recognised that other things would be over too, things she was in no hurry to rush.

She'd awakened in Bram's room that morning, his arm draped about her waist, her bottom nestled against his groin in a most intimate fashion. It had not taken long for things to progress from there to a most pleasurable conclusion. She could get used to waking that way every morning. The problem was, she didn't have *every* morning. She had two mornings. She knew already two mornings was not going to be nearly enough. Two weeks hadn't been enough so why ever would two days suffice? And yet it would have to do.

Chapter Twenty-Two

Bram shook Matt's hand and wished him luck. He'd be riding in the races that afternoon as well as tomorrow's. It was time to go and claim their seats for the races. Bram was turned out to perfection today in a coat of bottle green that matched his eyes, immaculate tan breeches and boots that would have done any London gentleman proud. She was proud to be seen with him.

'Are you sure we're sitting here?' Phaedra asked, scanning about, surprised. This was an elite location, set aside for the likes of Lord Grafton and Sir Charles Bunbury.

Bram grinned. 'I am sure, Phaedra. Have a little faith in my connections.' They slid into their seats with prime viewing of the finish line and the second half-mile. 'Would you like me to place a wager on your behalf?' Bram enquired close to her ear as the first race neared. There'd be several undercard matches before the stakes.

'I wouldn't know who to bet on. It's ironic, isn't it? The odds mean nothing to me. If I could see the horses up close that would be a different story,' Phaedra confessed with a laugh. 'By the time I was old enough to go to the races in Doncaster, we weren't going any more.' The boys had been off to war and Father had lost interest in going very far from home.

Bram smiled, banishing the dark memories that threatened to steal the joy from the day. 'Good, then I'll have something to teach you.' He settled back in his seat and began to explain the odds system.

Bram was a good teacher. By the second race, she'd placed a modest 'practise' bet on a middling horse to finish first, second or third and had won her money back. By the fifth race, she'd picked a horse to place in the top two. She'd wanted to pick him to win but Bram had argued against it. Bram had been right. The horse finished second.

'Why didn't he win? He had the best odds?' Phaedra protested afterwards. She tossed Bram a coy look from under her wide-brimmed hat. 'More important, how did you know he wouldn't win?'

'He was too much of a favourite. Heavy favourites don't win as often as you think.' Bram laughed and then lowered his voice. 'It will be the same with the Derby tomorrow, you know.'

She'd heard that piece of wisdom before. Rumour, legend, myth, truth, whatever one wanted to call it, held that favourites seldom won the Derby. 'That should serve us well, then,' she said confidently. 'I doubt Warbourne will be the Derby favourite.'

Betting with Bram had done the trick. Her nerves were settling and she'd been able to enjoy the day. The sun was out, the weather fine; her dream of watching her colt run in a classic thoroughbred race under her command was only a day away from coming true.

If she could accomplish this, she could accomplish the next step: setting up a breeding operation at Castonbury to rival Lord Darlington's at Raby Castle in Yorkshire or Lord Egremont's stud at Petworth. Both those fine gentlemen were here today, sitting a few rows to their left. Darlington's bay colt, Brother to Christopher, would run in the Derby tomorrow. Current odds picked the bay to be a mid-pack finisher at twelve to one. Maybe that was good news, if the legend could be believed.

Darlington looked in their direction and tipped

his hat. Bram nodded back. Phaedra smiled. There would be an assembly at the Waterloo tonight, a bit of a ball, really, to celebrate the Oaks. Darlington and others would be in attendance. It would be a prime opportunity to make advantageous connections and let others know of her plans to establish a stud. People might look down their noses at women in the horse-breeding business but no one who loved racing could ignore a winner. If Warbourne won, people wouldn't care who owned him. They'd only care if they could get breeding rights.

The afternoon progressed well. Matt Somerset rode two horses to third-place finishes and stayed safe doing it. She and Bram took one more trip to the stables to look in on Warbourne and young Bevins and then it was time to get ready for the celebratory assembly.

Phaedra dressed carefully in a dark blue ball gown trimmed in startling white ribbon. The gown had a quiet loveliness to it while maintaining an understated elegance that said she hadn't forgotten who she was—a duke's daughter and a young woman somewhat newly come out of mourning.

People might not want to admit a woman could train a champion, but their spirits would be high tonight, and tomorrow, they would not be able to dispute the incontrovertible proof right in front of them. Her horse, a horse that the racing world had discounted as too mercurial to win, would race to victory in front of their very eyes. Warbourne's day was tomorrow, but tonight was hers to shine and lay the groundwork. She'd have to make a good impression. Phaedra smoothed her skirts and took a final look in the small mirror on the wall of her room. She was ready.

In the corridor, Bram waited for her, dressed in dark evening clothes of a calibre one would find only in London. Nothing of the Castonbury groom remained about him tonight and she wondered how she could have missed such refinement before. Even that first day when she'd looked at his boots she'd had a twinge of insight. She should have paid attention to it. Aunt Wilhelmina had been right. A gentleman could be judged by his boots.

Bram was on display tonight as well. They were a couple and there would be no escaping the fact that people would start to ask questions. What was a duke's daughter doing travelling to Epsom to race a horse? Was she really travelling alone with only Mr Basingstoke for company?

'You're worried about something,' Bram divined.

Phaedra shrugged. 'No, just thinking.'

Bram's hand was warm at her back as they made their way to the infamous Waterloo staircase with its carved balustrade leading to the Assembly Room. 'While I am flattered, you'd better keep those thoughts to yourself,' he whispered.

'What thoughts?' Phaedra felt her cheeks heat.

'The ones that have us in bed for the duration, my sweet.' Bram's voice was seductive and low. Heat curled in her belly as he gave words to her mental images. 'Don't worry, love, the night is young. We won't be at the ball for ever.'

Chapter Twenty-Three

Phaedra was doing splendidly. From the sidelines, Bram watched her dancing a country set with the Duke of Grafton's heir. She'd already danced with Darlington and Mr Payne, both of whom had horses entered tomorrow. She'd charmed them all. People were intrigued by her. Specifically, *men* were intrigued by her. Lovely and knowledgeable, she was in her element tonight, surrounded by people who were just as enthralled with horses as she.

Grafton's heir said something that made her laugh and Bram felt the vice of envy tighten in his stomach. He should be happy for her. If she could win acceptance among the right people fast enough, perhaps scandal wouldn't have a chance to take root.

Winning over Grafton's heir would be a step in that direction. Aligning herself with him, Bram

Basingstoke, a man of scandal, would not protect her. Just the opposite, in fact. Such an alliance would court ruin. He was the rumour-ridden second son of the Earl of Hartvale. Association with him meant there would be no escaping scandal's brush.

But that didn't stop the wanting. Phaedra was fresh, and dazzling, beautiful, intelligent, and most of all forthright in her opinions and her passion. She'd put to shame his usual strategy of 'once is enough.' Once had only whet his appetite for more and now he wasn't sure what to do about it.

He had told Giles to trust him, to trust them. Now he had Phaedra in his bed, promising him nights together at Epsom without consequence. That was naivety talking. There would be consequences. Maybe not a pregnancy or a forced wedding, but there would be consequences. There already were, the biggest one being he didn't want to let her go after the Derby. He knew what it meant. He'd probably known it for a while. There was only one way to keep a woman like Phaedra and that was to marry her, the one thing he couldn't do.

How could he propose with any credibility? He'd already looked that gift horse in the mouth and refused when Giles had put the question to him.

If Warbourne actually won, she'd think he was caught up in the moment. Even without a victory queering his pitch, she'd think he felt motivated by honour. He'd deflowered a virgin and he knew his duty. Worse, she'd think he was proposing because of some threat from Giles.

The set ended and Phaedra's escort returned her to his side. Grafton's heir bowed to Phaedra and thanked her for the dance. 'I will be in touch,' he said with a warm look in his eyes Bram didn't care one iota for. 'I would be delighted to count you among my correspondents, Lady Phaedra.'

Phaedra smiled graciously and effused her own delight over the sentiment. Bram felt the vice tighten once more. 'What was that all about?' he growled once the young man was out of earshot.

Phaedra shot him a quizzical look that said he was overreacting. 'I feel the need for some air, why don't you take me outside?'

Later, he would find some humour in the way she all but dragged him from the ballroom. *He* had not taken *her* from the ballroom. They found an empty room down a dark hallway and Phaedra turned up the lamp. 'You've been glowering from the sidelines nearly the whole night. What is going on?'

How the hell did a man answer that question? Bram pushed a hand through his hair. 'I thought the duke's son was ogling your bosom too much.'

Phaedra raised her eyebrow. 'And Mr Harris?'

'He danced like a clod. I thought you might turn an ankle.' Bram began to pace the room.

'I see.' Phaedra crossed her arms over her breasts, a knowing smile on her lips. 'You're jealous. I suspect there was something wrong with each of my dance partners.'

'Damn right there was something wrong with them. They weren't *me*.' She was *his*, damn it. The realization was fierce and visceral as was the solution. If he wanted her, he should claim her. 'You are mine, Phaedra, and no one else's.'

Phaedra swallowed hard against the desire rising, hot and fast, invoked by his words. The gentleman's clothing could not hide the primitive man prowling inside them. She backed up, letting him stalk her until her back met the hard surface of the wall. She was not afraid, she welcomed this, welcomed Bram and the mad release he'd bring. This is what their nights in Epsom were meant to be about, storing up memories against farewell.

He bracketed her with his hands, his mouth claiming hers in a hard kiss, making sure of his welcome. Then his hands were at her skirts, rucking up the delicate material. This would not be about seduction and its subtle nuances. This would be about claiming and it would be rough.

'Wrap your legs around me, Phaedra.' Bram didn't wait for compliance. He lifted her and she clung to him, braced between the wall and his strength, her legs finding their natural way about his waist.

Bram moved a hand to the flap of his trousers, freeing himself to press against her bare skin. There was to be no foreplay, no readying games, and she was glad for it. At the feel of him, her body had begun to cry out. Bram positioned himself at once and entered. She squeezed hard, clutching him to her in the most intimate of manners, her head thrown back, her neck arched, as she savoured the presence of him. How could anything match this?

Then Bram began to move and not only matched it but exceeded it, the strength of his legs flexing with the rhythm of their mating. She held on to him, letting the power of their release wash over them both, leaving them panting and sated. This was decadence at its finest.

Bram moved them carefully to the long divan, his shaft still seated deep within her. 'It doesn't feel like a sin,' Phaedra murmured, relaxing her grip on his waist as he laid her down. It didn't occur to her until he moved out of her that he hadn't withdrawn this time. How could he have? They'd been lost in their pleasure, overwhelmed with it, beyond thought.

Bram laughed at her comment. 'Good things never do.' His voice shook though, a testament to how thoroughly the experience had overcome them. 'Phaedra, I'm sorry. I couldn't—'

Phaedra placed a finger on his lips. She didn't want reality to intrude quite so immediately. 'Let's not borrow trouble without cause, Bram.' She'd been around horses all her life. She knew well the risks of what they'd done. But for now they were risks only. She smiled up at him, trying to dispel the resigned worry that lingered in his eyes. 'What now, Mr Basingstoke?'

A ghost of a smile took Bram's mouth. 'We go back to the ballroom and dance. Then, we go and win the Derby.'

Phaedra kissed him one last time. 'I like the sound of that.' It was the 'we' part she liked most. She said nothing to correct him.

Bram claimed the next dance, a waltz. He'd just

swept her into the turn when there was a clamour at the Assembly Room entrance. Bram brought her to a stumbling halt, his grip on her waist tight as he craned his neck to see the commotion. 'Oh, my God, Phaedra. It's Bevins.' On the strength of Bram's shoulders, they pushed their way to the front. Bevins stood there, pale and shaking.

'Lady Phaedra, Mr Basingstoke, you've got to come quick. It's Warbourne. He's taken powerfully ill.'

Phaedra sank to her knees beside Warbourne, heedless of the rough straw raking against the delicate silk of her gown. The colt was on his side, his breathing ragged and his eyes rolling. She laid a soothing hand along his neck to check his pulse. It was fast, probably from anxiety over being sick and panic at not being able to help himself.

Behind her, she was vaguely aware of Bram talking with Bevins and others. There was a sense of relief in knowing Bram would handle everything. He would gather information, he would learn what he could and he would be her gate-keeper. He would provide a buffer between her and any prying eyes.

Phaedra reached for a handful of hay and sniffed, searching for signs of cyanide or arsenic.

There was no telltale scent of almond. That was a blessing. Little could be done about cyanide poisoning other than letting it run its course and hope the horse was strong enough to survive.

She rose and went to the water bucket, dismayed to find it still half full. 'Bevins,' she called out. 'Have you refilled this bucket today?' Horses needed ten gallons of water daily to stay hydrated. If the bucket hadn't been refilled, Warbourne had only drunk half of his daily ration.

Bevins hurried over, his cap in his hand. He was clearly worried he'd done something wrong. 'No, Lady Phaedra.'

Dehyradration, then, Phaedra thought. What would cause Warbourne to stop drinking? She scooped up a handful of water, the droplets staining the skirt of her dress. She sniffed. Detecting nothing, she cupped her hands to her mouth and took a cautious sip. Salt!

Bram hurried over. 'What is it? Have we determined a cause?'

'He's dehydrated. Someone put salt in his water.' Salt water created a double bind for Warbourne. Either he kept drinking to appease his growing thirst or he stopped because he sensed something was wrong with the water.

Phaedra drew a deep breath. 'The good news is

we can remedy this. I can take care of Warbourne if you can figure out how this happened. Bevins, you stay with me. I'll need help.'

Bram reached for her hand and squeezed. From the look in his eyes, he wanted to do more but didn't dare with the little crowd standing at the entrance to Warbourne's stall. 'I'm glad he'll be all right.' Warbourne would be fine. The bigger question was whether or not he'd be well enough to race in fourteen hours.

'Come on,' She motioned to Bevins, 'We've got work to do.' Now that things had settled, she wondered where Matt Somerset was.

When asked, Bevins merely shrugged. 'I haven't seen him since suppertime.'

Phaedra nodded. 'Tell Mr Basingstoke. Maybe he knows. Then you and I need to get Warbourne up and on his feet.'

Getting a horse on his feet was the single most important thing for curing most horse ailments and wasn't easy. She and Bevins tugged, pushed and cajoled a thousand pounds of thoroughbred to his feet. Phaedra walked him up and down the aisle, crooning soft words to him while Bevins washed out the water bucket and refilled it.

Now it was time to drink. Clean water was the best medicine she could offer Warbourne. The cure was alarmingly simple but getting him to take it was not. Back in his stall, Warbourne showed only the most sceptical of interests in the water bucket. It confirmed for her what she'd suspected. He'd stopped drinking after finding the water a bit off.

'Good boy.' She patted his big shoulder. To Bevins, she said, 'Our boy was smart. He sensed something was wrong and he stopped drinking. That means there's less salt water in his system to contend with.' Her hopes started to rise. Warbourne only needed to start drinking. He didn't have to flush anything out of his system. Recovery in time for the race was possible.

Phaedra tugged the lead rope, urging Warbourne towards his bucket but he was far too skittish. Just because she'd solved the mystery didn't mean his symptoms had faded. His pulse was still fast and he was weak on his legs. The danger had not passed yet.

'Bevins, in the tack trunk there's a small vial marked peppermint.' Peppermint extract in the water often enticed dehydrated horses to drink. But Bevins just stood there.

'Well, go on, fetch it,' Phaedra urged crossly. 'Every minute counts tonight.'

Bevins looked down at his hands. 'I can't read, Lady Phaedra.'

She regretted her impatient tone immediately. 'I'll get it if you can hold Warbourne.'

Out in the aisle she ran into Bram holding up a sagging Matt Somerset. 'I found him, Phaedra,' Bram said grimly. 'Whoever went after Warbourne did a number on Matt too. He was in the back of the tack room.'

Matt favoured her with a smile through cracked lips. 'Don't worry, I can still ride. They didn't break my ribs, just bruised me up a bit. How's the colt?'

'He will be fine. I'm off to get some peppermint from the tack trunk.'

'I'll get it,' Bram said tersely, helping Matt to sit on the wooden crate outside the stall. 'I don't want you down there alone, Phaedra, in case the culprits are hanging around to savor their handiwork.'

'He likes you,' Matt said, watching Bram head down the aisle. 'In the three years I've known him, he's never shown this kind of interest in a woman. They're always one-night stands.' He paused. 'Sorry, that's not polite talk.'

Phaedra glanced down at her hands. 'I don't mind, truly.'

'Most of it is his father's doing, if you ask me. His father is a stickler for honour and duty. Bram's a bit more about living, about the adventure of life. It's not a good fit.'

'We're an awful a lot like them,' Phaedra offered softly. 'I have a good family, but lately I just haven't fit in. I can't be what they want.' She missed Giles, missed Castonbury. She'd been gone from home long enough to know that she wasn't ready to leave it. Her life to date had been there and she wanted her future to be there too. But Giles would have to accept that her future would be different from the one he had planned for her.

Bram came back with the vial. 'You two look cosy.'

'I've been telling tales on you, Bram old boy.' Matt gave a hoarse laugh.

Bram grinned. 'Then you must be feeling better.'

The peppermint worked. Lured by its scent, Warbourne took a tentative drink. Convinced the water was safe, he began to drink in earnest, although Phaedra was careful to moderate his sips. She didn't want to risk him bloating.

Bram came up behind her and wrapped his arms about her, drawing her close against him. He was warm and smelled of the barns. 'It's going to be a long night. Why don't you go and get some sleep and I'll keep watch? I've got Matt on a cot in the

tack room and Bevins will keep me company.'
Bevins was currently out running an errand to
the inn.

Phaedra shook her head. 'Warbourne needs me.
I wouldn't be able to sleep anyway.' The colt's
pulse was calming but Phaedra thought a lavender
massage would help that process along.

'Then we'll keep watch together,' Bram murmured against her ear.

Together. She thought of Matt's brief words and
her hopes soared. Maybe there was a chance, after
all. She'd tamed enough horses, though, to know
she couldn't *make* Bram stay any more than she
could make a colt do anything he didn't want to
do. A green colt had to want to be trained. Perhaps
Bram would decide for himself that he wanted to
stay. Perhaps she should let him. After all, there
had to be a great deal of good in a man who loved
horses so well.

Phaedra turned in his arms. He had to know
she'd welcome him staying. 'Win or lose, Bram,
I don't want it to be over tomorrow.' She looked
up into his face, trying to read it for signs of acceptance.

Bram reached for her hair, smoothing back an
errant tendril. 'Honey, I have nothing to offer you.
I'll never be anything but trouble to any woman.

I think we both know I'm better off as a fond re-
membrance. You can look back in your dotage and
say, "At least we had Epsom."' He gave a sensual
laugh. 'I know that's what I'll tell myself.'

He wasn't saying no. He was trying to save
her from making a mistake. Phaedra smiled and
moved against him lightly. 'We could have so
much more than Epsom, Bram. We could have
the Castonbury Stud and a lifetime of Epsoms,
and Newmarkets and St Legers. This is only the
beginning.' And she wanted him there for the rest
of it. If she'd doubted her feelings or his, tonight
had confirmed it. He'd stood beside her in a time
of near-tragedy. He'd been a complete partner. And
it hadn't only been tonight.

He kissed the tip of her nose. 'We'll talk tomorrow. Sometimes the things we say in the night
sound different in the light of day.' Bram shrugged
out of his evening jacket. Like her dress, it would
be ruined by dawn. Already it was showing signs
of barn wear. 'Take my coat.' He draped it about
her shoulders. 'Since I've known you, you've never
brought a coat to the stables.'

Phaedra protested. He'd be cold without it.
'No worries, my love.' Bram winked and settled
against the stall wall. 'I sent Bevins for coffee and

sandwiches and a blanket or two. We shall survive the night quite nicely.'

They did survive it. During the long hours of the night, Bram told her what he'd learned of the potential culprits. One was tall, the other stocky. Both with Derbyshire accents. 'We might have better luck catching them at home than finding them here,' Bram said, but he was only half joking.

'You think Sir Nathan arranged for them?' Phaedra said with a shudder. The idea that she'd been tracked sat poorly with her.

'It's possible. Nobbling is a criminal offense. Sir Nathan wouldn't dare try it directly. If these men point their fingers his direction, he can use his rank and deny it. There's little chance of pinning this on him directly.'

Just as there was little chance of finding two men in the race crowds. Sixty thousand were expected for the Derby. It would literally be a needle in a haystack search.

'I still don't understand how they got the salt into the water.' Phaedra yawned. Warbourne was sleeping. She was envious but not willing to give in.

'I do,' Bevins said quietly. 'Early in the afternoon, I stepped out to use the loo. Matt was gone and I was on my own nearly all day. It was just a few minutes. There were two fellows hanging about the barn that meet the description. I don't know them. I didn't recognise them from home but that's not saying much. I haven't been in the area long and most of my time is at the estate. They must have done it while I was outside. I am sorry.' He looked on the verge of tears.

'It's all right.' Phaedra wanted to do more than offer the boy words of comfort but, with Bram there, it would probably embarrass Bevins to be hugged in front of his hero. 'Everything's ended well. We didn't lose the colt.'

By the time the barn began to bustle with race-day activity, Warbourne seemed outwardly restored and the colour had returned to Somerset's face. The real tests would be internal, however. There was no way to know what kind of toll the ordeal had taken on Warbourne's reserves. Would he have the stamina to race the mile-and-a-half course? Would Somerset have the strength to help him?

Word of Warbourne's close call had spread. Pheadra was grateful for Bram's efforts. He spent most of the morning shooing away people who'd come to look at the colt, most of them odds makers. Convinced Warbourne wouldn't be able to race capably, the odds on the colt had soared.

'Sixty to one against,' Bram said after his latest foray through the barn for news. 'That's more than the odds on Azor and Young Wizard.' He plopped down on a bale of hay, his attire completely dishevelled. 'By the way, Payne and Wilson are livid over their odds.' They owned Azor and Young Wizard, respectively. 'Payne feels he should be the favourite.'

'Against Manfred?' Phaedra warmed to the conversation. 'Manfred just won the Two Thousand Guineas at Newmarket. People are looking to him to win.'

'He's got good odds at four-to-one,' Bram affirmed. 'He's the favourite actually. No one's got better.'

'But favourites don't win, is that what you're thinking?' Phaedra chided.

Bram winked. 'That's exactly what I'm thinking. I'm also thinking, this isn't a flat race like Newmarket. A horse has to do more than just run a straight line as fast as it can from start to finish.'

Bram didn't have to complete his thought. Phaedra nodded. Manfred was a bay colt with a redoubtable sire in Election but small. The Derby course would take a more powerful horse and perhaps a better rider. Azor on the other hand was a chestnut colt with the reputable Jem Robinson on board. It would come down to what mattered most: the rider or the horse. Jem Robinson had captained plenty of mounts to victory and it wouldn't be his first Derby.

'Sixty-to-one?' Phaedra eyed her colt. 'And the favourite never wins?'

'Never.' Bram grinned, his eyes lighting up with laughter.

'Sounds like perfect odds to me.'

Chapter Twenty-Four

Phaedra had left the stables long enough to change and look presentable for the Derby. The worst was over. When she returned, Bevins had groomed the horse to gleaming perfection and Matt Somerset had the situation well in hand, which was saying something. Warbourne was in high spirits as if he knew exactly what was going on today. And well he might. This was not his first time to race. But it would be his first successful completion, of that she had no doubts.

Phaedra ran her hands over Warbourne's legs, checking for heat, the standard sign of lameness or strain from his bout with dehydration the night before. She'd found none.

'Phaedra, we have to go,' Bram said quietly at her side. He, too, had found time to change. In fresh clothes, the night hadn't left a mark on him.

'Just a moment.' Phaedra took off her hat, a wide-brimmed confection with ribbon to match her violet-sprigged dress. She pressed her head to the colt's. She closed her eyes, her hand resting along the length of his neck, and she listened, listened to the steady throb of his pulse, the strong beat of his heart, listened to the life force coursing through him, and was reassured.

She murmured a few words to the horse and stepped back, returning her hat to her head. 'I'm ready now.' The sleepless night was taking its toll on her. She wanted to cry but that was utter silliness. 'I wish Edward was here,' she said softly.

'Come on, Phaedra, let's find our seats.' Bram gently urged her out into the aisle way. 'Matt will take things from here.' Matt had just come from the pre-race weigh-in with the clerk of scales, weighing in at precisely eight stone including his saddle. He was smiling and looking well, all things considered.

'He's ready for you, Matt,' Phaedra said with a smile. 'He told me so himself.' She wished she felt as ready. A minute and forty seconds would decide her future.

They had the same seats as yesterday. Only today, people recognised them and stopped by to enquire about Warbourne. The Duke of Rutland sent his condolences over the incident via a bottle of champagne. 'Maybe we should send it back with our condolences when Warbourne beats Sylvanus,' Bram whispered naughtily at her ear, making her laugh in spite of her nerves.

'You do know what this means?' Bram gestured towards the champagne. 'It means you've already won. Even if Warbourne doesn't win, you already have. You charmed them last night at the ball and shown them you're worth taking seriously. The mere fact that Warbourne is here cannot be discounted. His breeding lines are impeccable. He might not be a race-winner but, chances are, he'll beget winners. You just had to remind people of that.' But Phaedra knew she hadn't won alone. Rogue or not, people liked Bram and he'd paved the way with a little of his charm. It was one more thing he'd done for her without her asking.

The bugler sounded the call to post, the traditional cavalry tune—'Boots and Saddles'—as the horses stepped onto the track. The horses would parade by the grandstand and then disappear for the start, which was behind them.

'There he is!' Phaedra cried in a loud whisper. Warbourne stood out brilliantly, the only black horse in a race populated by four chestnuts, and

four browns with five bays. Matt's silks showing the Rothermere colours of red and gold sent a
surge of pride through her.

There were fourteen horses in all. A large field
to be sure, but not as large as years past. It wouldn't
have been unusual to have twenty horses racing.
Still, fourteen would be a challenge. Matt would
have to navigate with skill in order to avoid being
trapped in the middle.

Matt looked up into the crowd and saluted with
his crop before the horses dropped out of sight.
Phaedra's stomach was a tight ball of nerves.
Warbourne looked ready and Phaedra felt her chest
tighten with pride. Her eyes threatened to mist.
This had been her dream, and Edward's dream, for
as long as she could remember. It was her dream
alone now. She had no illusions that she was doing
this for Edward and the past. This was for her and
for the future. It all begins here, she thought.

'There's still time to place a bet,' Bram offered,
rising in his seat.

'Are you going to bet?' Phaedra looked up quiz-
zically. She was confident but she didn't want
Bram losing money on Warbourne. She wasn't
sure he had funds to lose.

'Absolutely.' Bram was grinning. 'I'm going to

bet it all on the biggest long shot there is.' With that wicked grin, she couldn't tell if he was joking.

Bram came back still grinning. Phaedra wished she could be so sanguine. She could see the course in her mind. She'd walked it thoroughly with Matt Somerset, talking through each turn, each rise and fall. The course was a horseshoe full of tricks for the unsuspecting horse and rider. Not only that, it was a left-hand course, making it what some called 'the supreme test' for a racehorse. Most courses were right-handed.

'Here.' Bram passed her a set of binoculars. 'Now you don't have to guess where your horse is at.' He chuckled. 'Handy little inventions, don't you think?' Around them, others raised their binoculars to their faces. It must be nearly time. Phaedra followed suit.

She could just make out the start. 'The flag is up, Bram. I see him. Matt's holding him well. He's prancing a little. Now he's still.' The out-riders that had escorted the horses to the starting line were drawing back. But Phaedra knew they'd remain until the race had started. It was their job to pick up any horses that became riderless, like Warbourne had been last year.

The starter flipped the flag in a figure-eight gesture and they were off. Phaedra bit her lip. Matt surged with the rest of the pack. Warbourne had passed the first test: his rider had stayed on. The next test began right away. There was a right-hand bend and a slow uphill climb that would tax a horse's stamina for the first half of the race.

Nearly up the hill, the pack began to separate, Manfred the favourite with Student, Azor and Young Wizard starting to surge away from the pack with Warbourne moving with them. A few rows behind them, Phaedra heard the Duke of Rutland curse as Sylvanus remained with the pack.

The five started the downhill slope, Matt using the descent to propel Warbourne forward. The downhill swept towards Tattenham Corner and another thirty-four-foot drop in elevation. Warbourne was pushing Student now, forcing the horse to give way while Warbourne ate up ground. Manfred faltered, unable to keep up with the longer-legged horses. The pack was nothing now. They were running steadily behind but there would be no catching the leaders.

Phaedra held her breath. Coming out of Tattenham Corner, it was Azor and Warbourne vying for position against Young Wizard. The crowd in the stands rose in anticipation of a close finish.

Phaedra's hands were white on the binoculars where she gripped them. *Do something, Matt,* she thought. A tie would mean a run-off. After his illness, Warbourne wouldn't win a second race. Foam flecked Warbourne's dark coat. Matt Somerset was whipping away in encouragement on the horse's right side.

The last three furlongs were a straight away. Matt crouched low over Warbourne's neck, keeping his weight out of the saddle, giving Warbourne every freedom. Warbourne would need it. The last one hundred feet was a final rise before the finish. Student fell off, vying with Manfred who made a last but futile surge. Azor and Young Wizard began to show signs of tiring, the last one hundred becoming a challenge for which they had little energy left.

It was Warbourne by half a head, then Young Wizard with Azor not giving in. In front of them, Mr Payne was nearly standing on his seat in excitement. *Faster*, Phaedra wished in her head. Just a little faster, just a little farther. She looked desperately through the lenses. In a sudden move, Matt Somerset switched his crop to his left hand, whipping away on Warbourne's other side. Warbourne surged! 'Bram, do you see it?' Phaedra yelled to be heard.

'I see it, he's got it, Phaedra, he's got it!' Bram's excitement was as genuine as hers.

Warbourne crossed the finish a half-length ahead of Azor with Young Wizard following close behind. They had won. There was still the stewards' official announcement but the race had been clean and the finish, while close, had been obvious.

She was in Bram's arms, and he was kissing her, uncaring who saw. Amid the excitement, no one would mind about the propriety of such a display. There was no better feeling than this. Exclamations erupted all around her, disbelief, excitement, disappointment. Warbourne had been a long shot, after all. Those who had won had made extraordinarily good money but they'd won at the expense of others who'd made safer, statistically wiser bets. It shouldn't have happened. But it did. Her horse had won the Derby.

She smiled at Bram, tears glistening on her cheeks, emotions swamping her. After two years of deaths and disappointments, she'd found the light. She had emerged.

'You did it,' Bram was whispering against her ear. 'You believed that colt could be saved and you saved him.' Bram swung her about in a tight circle, her body pressed close to his. 'Let's head down to the winner's circle and see how old Matt is doing with his new-found success.'

It was all noise and light, a blur of sensations and emotions in the winner's circle. People were shaking her hand, and asking questions. Phaedra could hardly follow most of what was being said. She just kept repeating herself, conscious of Bram's bulk quietly behind her, supporting her. 'Yes, this is Warbourne by Noble Bourne and Warrioress.' And 'Yes, I trained him at the Castonbury stables. Yes, I plan to begin a stud in earnest come next spring.'

The crowd eventually ebbed away, lured by the prospect of the other races that afternoon—the Durdan Stakes and the Denbies would follow. There would be parties that night and she would need to attend to solidify her new-found fame. The Duke of Rutland had already invited them out to his home in the Epsom countryside, the Durdans, the stakes' namesake, for supper and dancing that evening. But there was a moment's peace for now.

They needed to go and check on Matt and Warbourne back at the stables but there was something she needed to say to Bram first. She drew him aside in a rare quiet corner. 'Thank you.'

'For what?' Bram smiled, trying to tease but she wanted to be serious.

'Don't shrug this off, Bram. Thank you for everything. For helping, for coming after me, for finding me Matt Somerset. I know I didn't do this alone.' *For being my family when I had none, for making sure I didn't have to celebrate alone.*

He rewarded her with solemnity of his own. 'You're welcome, Phaedra. I wouldn't have missed this for the world.'

'I know.' Phaedra furrowed her brow. 'I mean, I know it cost you everything. I don't suppose your father *won't* hear about this.'

Bram shook his head, his hands resting lightly on her waist. 'No, I'm sure by this time tomorrow he'll know, if he doesn't already.'

'What will you do?'

'For starters, I'm going to collect my winnings and then I'm going to take the victorious Lady Phaedra to the Durdans and bask in her success.' Bram laughed as if nothing else mattered. What had Matt said? That Bram liked the adventure of living?

'Our success,' Phaedra corrected.

'That's very generous of you. But tonight, I'd rather it be *your* success.'

Bram pocketed his winnings. They were substantial. He hadn't been joking when he'd told Phaedra he'd bet every cent and pound he'd had on the long shot. His winnings wouldn't support him for ever, but he didn't want that. He wanted enough to buy a ring at the discreet jewellers on South Street. Tonight, he was going to bet on something far more important than a race.

He knocked on Phaedra's door shortly before eight o'clock and escorted her to the curricle he'd rented for the short drive to the Durdans. The evening was clear, stars twinkled overhead and the weather was mild, a perfect night for a drive, a perfect night for deciding his future.

Phaedra sat beside him, stunningly beautiful in a gown of deep red crêpe over a satin slip of palest gold. 'Rothermere colours?' He noted wryly.

She tossed him a smug little smile. 'Rothermere colours indeed.'

The Durdans was located on the North Downs and the drive was short. The stately house with its Palladian columns glowed with lights, carriages lining the drive. This would be a dinner party extraordinaire featuring the crème of the racing world.

Bram bided his time and waited for his moment. If Phaedra had been nervous for the Derby, he was having his share of nerves now. He waited through the seven-course dinner and countless glasses of wine. He waited through dances until it was time to claim his own. Everything preceding it was an especial kind of torture designed to heighten his wanting.

She'd been dazzling at dinner, beautiful and refined, and knowledgeable. She hadn't hesitated to speak her mind. It set his teeth on edge to know every man in the room wanted her. Who wouldn't?

Finally they could dance, although Bram thought it hardly should qualify as one of the two dances he was limited to. It was a country dance that required he rotate through different partners. It barely counted as a dance 'with' Phaedra. But it was afterwards he was looking forward to.

The set ended and he escorted Phaedra out onto the terrace. The house was beautifully set, making the most of the serene countryside. He had no qualms about doing it here. Others might quail at the propriety of proposing at a ball, but he didn't. No matter where he did it, it would be between him and Phaedra regardless of who was around. And he had to do it tonight, before their proverbial clock struck midnight, before their Epsom escape came to an end.

'Phaedra,' he began, slowly, feeling his way towards the conversation he wanted to have. He should have rehearsed this, practised this. He was feeling decidedly unprepared now. 'I've been thinking about what you said earlier.' She nodded, encouraging him but perplexed. She'd probably said a million things 'earlier' and was wondering which one he was referring to.

Enough with the small talk and careful preludes. Bram reached inside his inner coat pocket and pulled out the small box. He flipped it open with a thankfully steady thumb. He let the diamond band catch the moonlight for a poignant moment. 'I want a lifetime of Epsoms with you, Phaedra. I want you to marry me, not for Giles, or to squelch rumours or for any other reason than that I love you and probably have for some weeks now, although I was too obtuse to realise it.'

His hand holding the box trembled a little when she said nothing. She just stared. Bram rushed onwards. 'I know I'm not a great catch.'

'Shh.' Phaedra put a gloved finger to his lips. 'You're not a great catch, you're *my* catch.' She pulled the glove off with maddening slowness and took the ring from the box, sliding it onto her finger. She held it up to the moonlight. 'Yes. I say yes.'

'Are you sure? I have a ridiculous father who's all but disowned me and that's a mere technicality.'

'I'm sure, Bram,' Phaedra said quietly, pulling her glove on over the ring. It would be their private secret tonight. 'Everyone's family is a little nuts. My father lives in the past.' She gave him an ornery grin that warmed him to his toes. 'And I'm thinking your parents will get along famously with Aunt Wilhelmina.'

They laughed together in the warm darkness. 'I'm not good odds, Phaedra. I don't know what kind of husband I'll make.'

'Most people don't know. Having not been married before, I'm not sure what kind of wife *I'll* make. We'll figure it out, Bram. Besides, long shots are our specialty.'

He kissed her then, long and lingering, drinking in all her confidence, all her spirit. She thought she needed him, but in truth, he knew the reality: he needed her. She filled the empty places in him.

Chapter Twenty-Five

'He was magnificent! The little chapel at Castonbury was filled with wedding guests but Phaedra had eyes only for Bram waiting for her at the end of the flower-bedecked aisle. He was dressed in a dove-grey morning coat and trousers, his dark hair brushed to a raven-hued sheen, but it hardly mattered what he wore. She would think he was magnificent anyway.

'Are you ready, Phae?' Giles squeezed her arm, his eyes mysteriously misty. 'I had no idea I'd be giving away both my sisters within a year.' He kissed her cheek. 'Father's down front. I'm sorry, he's too frail to make the journey down the aisle.'

'I'd rather have you, Giles,' Phaedra said softly. 'It will be your turn next. It hardly seems fair you were the first engaged but the last to marry.'

Giles chuckled. 'Don't worry about me. I'll have

my moment soon enough. Today is for you. You look lovely. Mother would have been so proud.'

Phaedra nodded, too moved to speak. Despite Aunt Wilhelmina's cool greeting when they had returned, Aunt Willy, as Bram liked to call her in private, had managed to unearth her mother's wedding dress, a pale cream confection of chiffon over satin. 'It had never really fit Kate right' was all she'd said, and she'd been correct. The gown had fit Phaedra much better and Phaedra was proud to wear it.

Reverend Seagrove gave Giles a little nod of his head and they began the walk. The four weeks since Epsom had been heady. They'd journeyed home to Castonbury, Warbourne in tow. Phaedra had written ahead to Giles with their news so banns could be posted. Instead of detouring through London for a special licence, Bram had insisted they marry after the traditional calling of the banns. Phaedra had been touched by the gesture. Such tradition would go a long way to remove any speculation of scandal.

Phaedra had been unsure of their reception but Giles had welcomed her with open arms and he'd shaken Bram's hand with sincere congratulations. Aunt Wilhelmina had met them with a noncommittal 'humph' and the begrudging concession that at least he was an earl's son. But she'd seen to the decorating of the chapel with spring flowers and to the arranging of the wedding breakfast that would follow.

They arrived at the front without mishap. Giles relinquished her to Bram and, at Reverend Seagrove's instruction, Bram pushed back the thin veil. The ceremony was a blur of words and responses. It was neither long nor short. She lost all track of time. She would have stood there all day just to look into Bram's eyes.

It was her turn to slip the ring on Bram's finger. 'I think you're very brave to marry into the Montagues,' she whispered, acutely aware that Bram stood before her today alone. His family had not come. But in a few minutes he'd have a new family.

Bram smiled. 'No braver than you are to marry me.'

It was time to kiss the bride. Bram swept her into his arms and kissed her hard on the mouth, hard enough to make Aunt Wilhelmina gasp disapprovingly in the front row and her father to be heard to remark, 'By Jove, that's the way to kiss a woman.' Phaedra blushed. What possessed him to say such a thing? Had he lost his mind? Oh, right, he had.

* * *

'We're married. For the rest of our lives.' Bram chuckled as they lay in the dark of their marriage suite.

'For better or for worse,' Phaedra teased, shifting in the crook of his arm. The 'breakfast' had finally broken up by late afternoon and the family had politely left them to themselves in the newly prepared wing she and Bram would call home.

'I have a gift for you, Phaedra.' Bram stretched for something on the side table. 'I wanted to give it to you this morning but Aunt Willy…'

'Say no more.' Phaedra sat up, shaking her hair over her shoulders. Aunt Willy had been a termagant about the groom not seeing the bride before the wedding.

'Actually, I have two things. Open this first. It's a letter from my father. He sends his regrets.'

Phaedra opened the letter, written on heavy white paper. 'I thought you were supposed to send felicitations.'

'No, regrets about not being able to attend, not the marriage,' Bram corrected. 'Apparently marriage has made me respectable.'

A bank draft fluttered out between the folds. Phaedra read the amount with wide eyes. 'Apparently so.' She passed the bank draft to Bram but he turned it away. 'It's yours. For the stud.'

Phaedra smiled. 'Then it's ours. The stud is *ours*. We're married now, there is no more yours and mine. You didn't listen to Reverend Seagrove very well.'

'I was a little distracted.' He handed her a long slim box. 'This is what I really wanted to give you.'

Phaedra protested. She didn't need anything more than him. She had all she needed to make her happy, but when she opened the box, her eyes misted. Inside the box lay her mother's pearls, the ones she'd sold for Warbourne.

'How?' was the only word she could articulate.

Bram leaned over and kissed her tears. 'Love always finds a way, my dear.' He kissed the column of her throat as he fastened the strand around her neck. 'You were wearing them the first day I saw you. I thought you were magnificent, and I was right.'

* * * * *

**Read on to find out more about
Bronwyn Scott
and the**

**CASTONBURY
PARK**
A Regency Upstairs Downstairs

series…

Bronwyn Scott is a communications instructor at Pierce College in the United States and is the proud mother of three wonderful children (one boy and two girls). When she's not teaching or writing, she enjoys playing the piano, travelling—especially to Florence, Italy—and studying history and foreign languages.

Readers can stay in touch on Bronwyn's website, www.bronwynn scott.com or at her blog, www.bronwynswriting.blogspot.com—she loves to hear from readers.

Previous novels from Bronwyn Scott:

PICKPOCKET COUNTESS
NOTORIOUS RAKE, INNOCENT LADY
THE VISCOUNT CLAIMS HIS BRIDE
THE EARL'S FORBIDDEN WARD
UNTAMED ROGUE, SCANDALOUS MISTRESS
A THOROUGHLY COMPROMISED LADY
SECRET LIFE OF A SCANDALOUS DEBUTANTE
UNBEFITTING A LADY +
HOW TO DISGRACE A LADY*

* Rakes Beyond Redemption trilogy
+ Castonbury Park Regency mini-series

And in Mills & Boon® Historical eBooks:

LIBERTINE LORD, PICKPOCKET MISS
PLEASURED BY THE ENGLISH SPY
WICKED EARL, WANTON WIDOW
ARABIAN NIGHTS WITH A RAKE
AN ILLICIT INDISCRETION
PRINCE CHARMING IN DISGUISE

AUTHOR Q&A

Apart from your own, which other heroine did you empathise with the most? And which hero did you find the most intriguing?

I really liked Claire in Ann Lethbridge's story, because it's so hard for her to 'go home again' and she knows she made a terrible mistake. Now all she can do is try to pick up the pieces and put her life back together.

As for heroes—all the Rothermere boys are pretty hot guys. It's hard to decide, but I'd have to go with Giles simply because we get to spend the whole series with him and as writers we got to know him very well. I think readers will get to know him too and look forward to his appearances in the books. We all kept sending Carole e-mails asking if Giles could come out to play—I am sure the weirdest e-mail she got was mine. Since we were all writing our stories at the same time, I wasn't sure how intimate Giles was going to be with Lily, since his wedding was going to have a long traditional engagement before it and was to be put off until the following year, so I wrote: *Dear Carole, Is Giles having sex with Lily? How much sex? Is he going to be celibate the whole year or what?* But I made it up to Giles by getting him a horse the next day. That e-mail went something like: *Dear Carole, I got Giles a big black horse today. What does Giles want to name it?* To which Carole replied: *Name it Genghis and say he rescued it in the war.*

What is your heroine's favourite childhood memory of Castonbury Park?

She has two. The first is riding ponies and horses across the Castonbury lands with her brother Edward, the one who was killed at Waterloo. They were the two youngest by several years, so they hung out together. Edward was slightly older than Phaedra and he encouraged her to do all sorts of wild things. The wildness stuck. Even after Edward is killed, Phaedra continues to pursue their mutual dream of raising racehorses and winning the Derby—something they fantasised about in their childhood. Her second favourite memory is from the summers when all the Montague kids would swim or row out to the little island on the lake—this little island is also the scene of her first big intimate encounter with sexy Bram Basingstoke.

Which Montague do you think Mrs Stratton the housekeeper let get away with the most?

Edward. He was the youngest male and he and Phaedra looked more like their mother than the other Montague children. Edward is described at a couple of different points as having 'an angel's good looks but the wild waywardness of a devil'. He'd have charmed his way out of everything.

Which stately home inspired Castonbury Park and why?

Kedleston. It's been featured in films like *The Duchess*. The house is located up in Derbyshire as well, which helped us get a feel for what kind of natural features would be on the land—rivers, lakes, that sort of thing—and what kind of flora and fauna and weather conditions too. I was thrilled to find really good descriptions of the Kedleston stables for Phaedra's book, which helped immensely. We had fun posting photos of the interior and exterior on our website to help each other with set pieces for the stories.

Where did you get the inspiration for Phaedra and Bram?

I wanted to do a horse story, but I didn't want to do a steeplechase for several reasons. 1) I'd done a steeplechase story in *Untamed Rogue, Scandalous Mistress* and steeplechasing wasn't officially all that popular in 1817. It didn't gain momentum as an officially recognised format until the 1830s, so it was also too early. 2) My husband had just got back from touring the big Kentucky breeding farms and was going on about the huge stables. 3) My daughter Catie rides English hunt seat and we'd just bought her first jumper. 4) Flat racing was/is such a big part of English tradition.

As for Phaedra, my Catie is a lot like her. She can talk to horses and we haven't met a horse yet Catie can't ride. As for Bram, it was easy to decide on creating a groom for the continuity. We wanted to have some upstairs-downstairs-style storylines between the family and the servants and I thought a groom was the perfect choice—lots of good reasons to be taking his shirt off and for being outdoors. As for how Bram looks—can I just say I find the Ralph Lauren Polo model highly inspirational?

What are you researching for your forthcoming novel?

I am just finishing the final handful of chapters for the last book in my autumn 2012 series Rakes Beyond Redemption and then I will kick off a duet about ladies behaving badly—only they're not ladies in the *ton*nish sense. Readers will get to meet Mercedes, daughter of a billiards champion, who is also an incredible billiards player in her own right, and the dashing half pay officer Grier Barrington in a *Color of Money*-style story. I've been spending time researching the state of billiards in 1835. Readers will also get to meet Eloise, daughter of a yacht designer, and the sexy rogue Dorian in a story based around the annual regatta—I'd like to call the story *Sex with Pirates*, but we'll see (smiles). Then, after that, I have a big surprise planned for *my* next series. I can hardly wait. It's already researched and sitting on my shelf, waiting to go.

What would you most like to have been doing in Regency times?

Dancing with handsome men! Shopping, buying horses and more dancing with handsome men!

AUTHOR NOTE

I hope you're enjoying the Montagues! I was thrilled to be part of this continuity series and even more thrilled to be working on another horse story. One element we wanted to emphasise in the series was the upstairs-downstairs-style interaction between the family and the servants. What better relationship to explore than a groom and a headstrong youngest daughter? Grooms are notoriously sexy and they have lots of reasons to take their shirts off while they're working the horses. What more could I ask for?

On a more serious note, I love a heroine with a dream and Phaedra has one: to race a colt she's trained at the prestigious Epsom Derby. It was great fun to research Epsom and accounts of the Derby. I've tried to be as true to fact as possible in my fictionalised account of the race. The comments about the difficulty and layout of the course are accurate. The names of the horses that raced that year and their riders or owners are also accurate, as is the description of the Waterloo Inn, where Phaedra stays, although it was not clear that the Waterloo had changed its name at that point. Buxton is also accurately represented as a home of many popular and well-attended horse fairs during that time period.

I want to give many thanks to the Epsom Historical Society, who helped unearth some key data.

I hope you enjoy Phaedra's story and the evolution of the Montague mystery as more is revealed about Jamie Montague's demise, Alicia's identity and Giles's attempts to keep the Rothermere dynasty together against impossible odds.

Keep reading and I'll see you out there.

Drop by the blog and leave your thoughts at: www.Bronwynswriting.blogspot.com

Don't miss the next instalment of Castonbury Park—
REDEMPTION OF A FALLEN WOMAN
by Joanna Fulford

'Time is running out and only you can save our family…'

Harry Montague *must* discover the truth about his family's missing heir—for better or worse. But his thoughts are side-tracked from the moment he first sees Elena Ruiz, beautiful and fierce in her bright red dress.

She's innocent, yet Spanish society has condemned her. Harry can help this woman in need with the security of a marriage made on paper—*but nothing more*. For his heart is armoured by pain and regret from the past. And yet soon he finds himself fighting an unexpected longing for his new wife that grows each day…

REDEMPTION OF A FALLEN WOMAN

Joanna Fulford

'You've run away?'

'Yes. I'm sorry to spring this on you, my lord, but I had no choice.'

The grey eyes were steely. 'To spring what on me, exactly?'

Her heart pounded. 'Concha and I want to travel with you.' Seeing his expression, she hurried on. 'We are both accomplished riders, we both know how to take care of ourselves, and we're used to rough living.'

'I dare say. All the same…'

'We won't slow you down and we won't be a nuisance.'

'You cannot seriously imagine…'

'All we ask is the protection of your company until we reach England.'

'England! Now, look…'

'I have a married sister who lives in Hertford-shire. She will help us. Only first we have to get there.'

'I'm not going to England, Elena. Not for months yet.'

'Of course not. First we will help you to discover the truth about your brother. Then we will go.'

'Elena, you must see that it isn't possible.'

There it was again, the familiar use of her name, yet it didn't seem in any way disrespectful on his lips. Rather it afforded her a glimmer of hope.

'I will not go back, my lord.'

'I wasn't suggesting that you should, but nor is it fitting that you attempt such a journey.'

'If you do not help us then we shall go on alone and face what comes.'

'It's too dangerous. Quite apart from the vagaries of the weather, and the numerous natural obstacles you are likely to encounter, the mountains are full of brigands.'

'It would be less dangerous with four,' she replied. 'Concha and I both shoot well.'

Harry felt winded, as though he had fallen from a great height and then landed between a rock and a hard place. Desperately he tried to marshal his thoughts. Elena wouldn't go back, and he didn't blame her for it, but neither could he let her go on alone. Every masculine instinct forbade it.

Yet the implications of their going on together were fraught with difficulty too. No matter what she said to the contrary, he would be responsible for the two women. It was a burden of care he could do without. Besides, his track record in that area was abysmal. Had he not already failed the woman who had trusted him most? Had he not also failed the man who had been his best friend? Their trust in him had been misplaced and both were dead. His jaw tightened. If he abandoned Elena and Concha now he would be adding two more to that score, because they would likely perish before they ever saw Seville, never mind England. Conscience dictated that he couldn't let that happen.

'All right. You travel with us, but it will be on the condition that you take orders from me.'

'Of course.'

'I mean it, Elena. All our lives may depend on it.'

She nodded. 'Very well.'

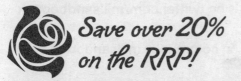

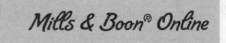

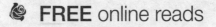

& Have Your Say

You've just finished your book.
So what did you think?

We'd love to hear your thoughts on our
'Have your say' online panel
www.millsandboon.co.uk/haveyoursay

- Easy to use
- Short questionnaire
- Chance to win Mills & Boon® goodies

The World of Mills & Boon®

There's a Mills & Boon® series that's perfect for you. We publish ten series and, with new titles every month, you never have to wait long for your favourite to come along.

Blaze®

Scorching hot, sexy reads
4 new stories every month

By Request

Relive the romance with the best of the best
9 new stories every month

Cherish™

Romance to melt the heart every time
12 new stories every month

Desire™

Passionate and dramatic love stories
8 new stories every month